Death

in the

Margins

Also available by Victoria Gilbert

Death

in the

Margins

A BLUE RIDGE LIBRARY MYSTERY

Victoria Gilbert

CROOKED LANE

NEW YORK

Copyright © 2022 by Vicki Lemp Weavil

Published in the United States by Crooked Lane Books, an imprint of The Quick Brown Fox & Company LLC.

Crooked Lane Books and its logo are trademarks of The Quick Brown Fox & Company LLC.

Library of Congress Catalog-in-Publication data available upon request.

ISBN (hardcover): 978-1-63910-130-6
ISBN (ebook): 978-1-63910-131-3

Cover illustration by Griesbach/Martucci

Printed in the United States.

www.crookedlanebooks.com

Crooked Lane Books
34 West 27th St., 10th Floor
New York, NY 10001

First Edition: December 2022

10 9 8 7 6 5 4 3 2 1

For Fran—
Thanks for helping me to get this far,
and for always encouraging me
to climb higher.

Chapter One

There's no such thing as sleeping late on a Saturday when you have pets.

Awakening after a particularly loud howl, I stared into a fierce pair of emerald eyes. A cat muzzle banged into the hand I immediately lifted to shield my face from any paw swipes.

"All right, all right," I muttered, sitting up in the bed. Glancing at the rumpled sheets and pillow beside me, I realized that my husband must've ducked into the adjacent bathroom without bothering to feed the cats. "Thanks a lot, Richard," I called out, even though I knew from the rushing sound of the shower he couldn't hear me.

The sleek tortoiseshell cat, who'd retreated to the foot of the bed to sit next to a large ginger tabby, continued to eye me with her unblinking gaze until I scooted to the edge and stood up. At that signal, both cats leapt to the floor and dashed out the open bedroom door.

"Okay, guys, I'll feed you. Just don't trip me on the stairs."

While Loie, the tortoiseshell, heeded this command, the tabby, appropriately named Fosse after the famous dancer and choreographer, decided that it would be more fun to leap through the stair railing so he could mount a sneak attack at the bottom step. I grabbed the newel post to steady myself before attempting to make my way down the hall and into the kitchen.

After filling both food bowls, I shuffled over to one of our soapstone kitchen counters to set up and turn on the coffeemaker. "Necessities first," I told the cats, who ignored me as they happily munched their kibble.

I wandered back upstairs to our bedroom just as Richard stepped out of the bathroom.

"Good morning," he said cheerily. He was wearing a pair of boxer shorts as he rubbed his damp, dark brown hair and bare torso with a towel. "Thought you were going to sleep in today."

I eyed him, distracted as always by his lean, well-toned physique. A respected contemporary dancer and choreographer, Richard's career required him to stay in shape. At thirty-eight, he had the body of a much younger man.

Being a library director fortunately doesn't require the same level of fitness, I thought with a wry smile. I was two years younger than Richard, but since I'd never been particularly athletic, I had a harder time fighting the tendency to put on weight. I tried to walk as much as possible to keep fit, but despite being perfectly healthy, I was still plump. While Richard insisted that I was beautiful, I often wished to be slimmer. Not to please anyone else, but to make it easier to buy clothes. My short, curvaceous figure often made finding a good fit difficult.

"I would've slept later if I could have. However, someone—not saying who, but his initials are Richard Muir—forgot to feed the cats," I said, crossing to the walk-in closet.

"Oops." Richard draped the towel around his neck. "In my defense, a solution to a choreographic problem occurred to me right as I woke up, and I had to jot that down. The cats slipped my mind."

"Sadly, their need for breakfast did not escape their ravenous little brains," I replied, pausing beside Richard before I headed into the closet. "But they're fed now, so no harm done, I guess." I stepped up on tiptoe to kiss his cheek. "Besides, I might as well get an early start on the day. I want to do some gardening this morning. It gets too hot in the afternoons to do much then."

Richard pulled me into his arms. "You're still planning to stop by the theater today?"

"Yes, around five. I'll bring dinner for you and Karla, since I know you won't have much time between the afternoon and evening rehearsals." I looked up into his gray eyes. Fringed with black lashes any female would envy, they always made my heart flutter. "It's probably the only way we can have dinner together this weekend."

"I'm afraid so." Richard examined my face intently. "Thanks for being so understanding about all these extra rehearsals, Amy. If we were just working with the professionals, it wouldn't be so intense, but with children involved . . ."

"I know. It takes a lot more time." I patted his arm. "Don't worry. I'll stick around, no matter how many days you leave the house early and come home late. Even if I barely see you, I promise not to forget I'm married to you."

"I'll make sure you don't," Richard said, drawing me closer and giving me a passionate kiss.

I enjoyed this distraction as long as possible before slipping out of his arms. "I need to change. And you should eat something before you rush off to your morning meeting with Karla."

After I dressed in a pair of cotton shorts and a tattered concert T-shirt, I headed downstairs to find Richard at the kitchen table, checking his cell phone as he ate breakfast.

"I cut up some fruit. It's in the fridge if you want it along with these muffins Lydia dropped off yesterday," he said.

"First, coffee. Then I'll think about food." I filled my mug at the counter, stepping over Loie, who'd decided the middle of the kitchen rug was the perfect place to take a nap. When I reached the round oak table that filled one sunny corner of our kitchen, I had to chase Fosse off the chair before I sat down. "Cats," I said. "Love them, but they sure complicate things."

"Good practice for kids," Richard said without looking up from his phone.

I stared at him for a moment, then took a long swallow of my coffee. I knew Richard wanted children, and though I agreed with this desire, I still hadn't wrapped my mind around how we would manage to juggle a family with our hectic lives. As director of the Taylorsford Public Library, I not only worked full-time but also had to be on call when my two part-time assistants or our volunteers couldn't cover their scheduled shifts.

Then there was Richard, who taught dance at Clarion University during the academic year, traveled for frequent choreographic or dance gigs, and also participated in projects like a summer dance institute sponsored by the local school system. He did have help from his long-time dance partner, Karla

Tansen, who'd agreed to be in charge of the summer institute. But Richard's involvement in that program, and the upcoming premiere of their new choreographic suite, still meant he spent many hours away from home.

Reaching across the table, I grabbed one of the whole-grain muffins my aunt, Lydia Talbot, had brought over the day before. Aunt Lydia, who lived next door, often gifted us delicious baked goods, especially when she was trying out recipes for future county fair competitions.

"So how are things going now that the guest artists have arrived? Any problems?"

"Not with Tamara or Dav, but Meredith"—Richard wiped his mouth with a napkin—"well, she's being Meredith."

"I'm still surprised you hired her, knowing how difficult she can be," I said, swirling the remaining coffee in my mug. Meredith Fox had once been engaged to my husband, and while I knew Richard didn't harbor any lingering feelings for her, I still felt awkward every time we met.

Richard shrugged. "She's the perfect dancer for the part, and she was free, so I thought it would be okay. Even though Karla finds her insufferable." He grinned. "I sometimes have to run interference between those two."

"I bet." I set down my empty mug to peel the paper baking cup away from my muffin. "I can't imagine Meredith having much patience with the younger dancers, and I know Karla's bound to be protective of the students in her studio."

"That's definitely part of the conflict. The other problem is Meredith's jealousy of Karla's dancing."

I nibbled on my muffin as I considered this information.

Loie, who'd slipped under the table while we were talking, leapt up onto one of our wide 1920s farmhouse windowsills. Richard stared out the window as Loie hunched down, her tail thrashing. "Ah, that's what's got you so riled up, girl—that annoying rodent again." He looked back at me with a smile. "Might as well call them squirrel feeders at this point."

"The birds do get some of the seed, I guess." I finished off the muffin and dabbed at my lips with my napkin. "Why would Meredith be jealous of Karla? She's had the more celebrated career."

"Yes, but for all her faults, Meredith is a good judge of talent. And she's definitely aware that Karla's inherently more gifted than she is." Richard pushed back his chair and rose to his feet. "Meredith has the body and look dance companies preferred when they both started out, but she knows as well as I do that Karla is the better dancer. Even if no company would give Karla a chance back then."

"I guess it's too late for Karla, but I hope there are a few more diverse companies now," I said, picturing Richard's friend and frequent dance partner, who'd always been too tall to find a place in a company.

Richard strolled over to my chair. "A few. There's still a long way to go. Which is why Karla's so determined to open her studio to a wide range of young dancers." Richard leaned in to kiss my temple. "Gotta run. Karla and I need to work through some changes this morning, before our younger dancers show up for rehearsals."

"See you later," I said as Richard dodged Fosse, who'd decided to dash across the kitchen to join his sister at the window. "I'd say, 'Break a leg,' but it looks like Fosse already tried to make that happen."

Richard flashed a smile over his shoulder as he left the room. "Good thing I have excellent reflexes."

* * *

After weeding our raised vegetable beds all morning, I took a shower and changed into a simple peacock-blue sundress before running to the grocery store for some ingredients for the healthy picnic-style dinner I planned to take to the theater.

Richard and Karla's new choreographic work, the *Folklore Suite*, was to be the inaugural show opening an old Art Deco movie theater that had recently been renovated to serve as a venue for live performances as well as films. Located in the neighboring small town of Smithsburg, it was about a thirty-minute drive from Taylorsford.

I left home a little early, concerned about congestion on the two-lane road that connected the towns. But traffic was light enough that I reached Smithsburg around four thirty. Parking in the newly paved lot behind the old cinema, I pulled a small cooler from the trunk, walked around the building, and entered through the lobby.

Just inside the doors, I stopped dead. Two people faced off on the brilliantly hued tile mosaic that mimicked the floor medallions of ancient Rome. Above them, a multitiered chandelier dripping with crystals cast rainbows of light, streaking their pale faces with color.

Like warriors painted for combat, I thought, struck by the resemblance to the start of an ancient hand-to-hand battle.

Although these women didn't look like gladiators. Both were petite—one wiry and sharp-featured, with short, coffee-brown hair; and the other lean and toned, with a lovely heart-shaped face, perfect posture, and auburn hair spilling over her shoulders.

I didn't know the dark-haired woman, but the other was Meredith Fox. Tightening my grip on the cooler, I stood frozen in place as the women shouted at one another.

"How dare you insult my daughter like that." The dark-haired woman's hands clenched into fists. "You've no right to say such things. You made her cry, you harpy."

As Meredith tossed her head, light shimmered off her wavy mane of hair. "If we're going to talk about who has the right to do what, let's discuss the fact that your daughter doesn't have any business being on a stage with real dancers. She almost tripped me with all her flailing about. And I warn you—any injury I incur is worth thousands in a civil judgment. So why don't you take your extremely annoying child and go home. And stay there."

I swallowed back a swear word as the other woman lunged forward, fists raised. "I don't care how great a dancer you are, you're a horrible person!" she shouted.

Meredith's green eyes flashed. "I'm trying to make a point about safety, if nothing else."

"Nonsense. You're just prejudiced against kids like my daughter." The dark-haired woman judiciously stopped short of smacking Meredith. "I heard you tell Quinn that she had no business dancing and needed to take her weird behavior else-where. That really hurt. She was practically hysterical."

"Looks like you're the one who's reduced to hysterics," Meredith said with a lift of her sharp chin. "Like mother, like daughter, I guess."

The dark-haired woman, her mouth falling open, stared at Meredith for only a second before taking a swing at her.

Chapter Two

Fortunately, Meredith stepped back in time to avoid the other woman's slap.

Excellent reflexes, I thought as a low voice said, "Uh-oh, looks like they're at it again."

I turned to the woman at my side. "Hi there," I whispered. "What's going on? I don't know the dark-haired lady."

Samantha Green, one of the part-time assistants at my library, raised her black eyebrows. "That's Janelle DeFranzo. She's the mother of Quinn, who's in the same dance studio as Shay. They've become friends, so I've gotten to know Jan pretty well."

"What's the issue between her and Meredith Fox?" I asked, as the auburn-haired dancer executed a perfect pirouette and flounced off. She hurled a rude statement over her shoulder before taking the stairs to the lower level of the building, which housed several dressing rooms and two rehearsal studios.

Janelle DeFranzo threw up her hands and exited the lobby, shoving open one of the marble-column-flanked doors that led into the auditorium.

Samantha waited until both women disappeared, before she spoke again. "Quinn's autistic and easily overwhelmed by new experiences. Apparently Meredith Fox finds her presence distracting."

I widened my eyes, realizing the ramifications of this issue. Karla, who ran a local dance studio, often worked with students with physical or mental differences. In fact, part of her mission was to normalize using dancers of all types in productions. "Karla told me she was going to include a few of her disabled students as part of the corps, which I think is great."

"Glad you think so," Samantha said, her tone darkening. "Obviously, not everyone does."

I made a dismissive sound. "Meredith always finds something to complain about. But she does appear to be overstepping the boundaries in this case." I shifted the cooler to my other hand. "I'll have a word with Richard and Karla. I'm sure they'll order Meredith to behave. Since you're friends, maybe you should tell Ms. DeFranzo to simply avoid her in the future."

Samantha nodded. "I'll do that." Looking me over, her dark-eyed gaze rested on the cooler. "I should let you go. It appears you have food to deliver."

"It's dinner for Richard and Karla," I said. "They only have a short break between rehearsals today, so I said I'd bring them something to eat."

"I'll let you get to that, then. I need to go and round up Shay anyway. Her scheduled rehearsals are over. For today, at any rate. See you soon," Samantha said, heading for a door that led to a side hall.

I decided to take a shortcut through the auditorium to reach the backstage area and adjacent green room. As I made my way down the center aisle, I admired the newly renovated stage, which had been expanded from its original size to cover a small orchestra pit. It could now accommodate the demands of live theater and dance performances, especially since the original movie screen had been replaced by a retractable version that could disappear into the fly space when not in use. New midnight-blue velvet drapes flanked the deeper stage, but the elaborate pseudo-Roman frieze had been restored rather than removed. Its plaster decorations gleamed with a new coat of paint and touches of gilt.

Passing by Janelle DeFranzo, who was slumped in one of the reupholstered sapphire velvet theater seats, I debated saying something to her about ignoring Meredith. But one glance at her face kept me walking. The anger tightening her lips told me my advice would probably not be welcomed, especially since we'd never officially met.

Pushing my way through the exit door, I made a quick left to access the steps leading backstage. Reaching the edge of the black curtains hung to shield the audience's view of the wings, I waited while Richard conferred with someone seated at an upright piano. The man, who had a slight build, was dressed in the customary theater "blacks"—a dark, long-sleeved T-shirt and black slacks. Despite his receding hairline, he looked to be no older than thirty-five. He adjusted his wire-rimmed glasses before playing a short passage from the musical score propped open on the piano.

In the center of the stage, a slender older teen with a shock of wheat-colored hair continued to practice a complicated move that involved a turn into a leap. Richard looked up at the sound of footfalls.

"Conner," Richard called out as he stepped around the piano. "Hold up. You need to center yourself or you're going to fall."

As Richard strode over to give the young man individual instruction, I moved closer to the accompanist. "Hi," I said, extending my free hand. "I'm Amy Muir, Richard's wife."

"Riley Irwin. Nice to finally meet you. Here, set that cooler on the piano bench." After I followed this advice, Riley clasped my hand briefly, his light-brown eyes searching my face. "You're the library director in Taylorsford, right?"

"Yes. Have you visited? I don't remember seeing you, but I don't work at the library every day."

"Not yet. I actually live close enough to the university to use the library there." Riley shoved his drooping glasses up to the bridge of his nose. "I teach piano and do some accompanying for the dance and theater departments at Clarion."

"That's right. Richard told me he'd hired an accompanist he'd worked with at school." Looking into Riley's pleasant but rather undistinguished face, I noted a shyness that made me offer him a warm smile. "Are you enjoying the experience so far?"

"Pretty much. Working with your husband and Karla is great, and I actually enjoy the younger dancers too."

"But not all of the professionals? I know that can be problematic in some cases," said a male voice behind me.

I turned, coming face-to-face with a tall, well-built man in his late twenties. With his head shaved to display his gleaming dark scalp and the chiseled features of a runway model, he was unequivocally striking.

"Hey there, Dav," Riley said, scooting back the piano bench and rising to his feet. "Are you and Tamara ready to run through that pas de deux?"

"Yeah, but I should introduce myself first." The younger man bobbed his head at me. "I'm Davonte Julian. You must be Richard's wife."

I offered him a smile. "Yes, I'm Amy. How did you guess?"

Davonte grinned. "Oh, Richard has a photo of you as the screensaver on his phone. I got nosy one day when we working on *Return* at Jacob's Pillow and asked him who it was." Davonte's grin broadened. "Which turned into him positively gushing about you. How amazing you are in every way, among other things."

"Really? That's nice, although I think he's a little biased," I said as heat rose in my cheeks. "I mean, he's the real talent in the family."

"Not according to him," said the elegant young woman who stepped out from behind Davonte. Also tall, she was equally lean and well-toned, although her black hair was braided into tiny, bead-decorated, plaits that hugged her scalp. "I'm Tamara Hardy. One of those professional dancers Dav mentioned."

"Nice to meet you both," I said, focusing on Davonte's handsome face. "I suppose the problem person you referred to is Meredith?"

"Correct." Davonte shared a cryptic look with Tamara.

"We've all had a few run-ins with her in the past," Tamara said. "But trust me, that's not something we'd allow to affect our dancing."

"That's because you *are* professionals." Riley moved closer to the two dancers. "Shall we?" he asked, gesturing toward the steps leading offstage. "Richard and Karla said they won't need me at the start of the next rehearsal since they're doing some specialized work with the university dancers. So if you don't mind, I'd like to go ahead and run your pas de deux. That way I'll have time to grab something to eat before I'm needed again."

"Sure thing," Davonte said, giving me a nod. "Nice to meet you, Amy."

"Yes, it was good to finally put a face to the name." Tamara smiled. "Richard does talk about you a lot."

"I guess that's better than pretending I don't exist," I said with an answering smile. "I'm glad I got a chance to meet you all. We'll have to arrange a dinner at the house sometime."

"As long as you leave Meredith Fox off the guest list, I'm in," Davonte said as the three headed off the stage.

"Ditto," Tamara said with a wave over her shoulder.

Riley's expression remained pleasant, although I noticed a definite tautness to his lips. He wished me a good day, then followed the two dancers.

I stared at their retreating backs, wondering what Meredith had done to elicit such dislike from Davonte and Tamara. As I mused over this question, the object of their disdain appeared in the wings on the other side of the stage, with Karla right behind her.

"Do you think you can stay for the later rehearsals?" Richard asked Conner.

The young man nodded. "Sure. I'll just have to call my mom and ask her to pick me up at a different time." He swept the fall of cornsilk hair away from his broad forehead. "Do I have time to run out and grab something to eat?"

"That'll be fine. We have a break now, and then Ms. Tansen and I are going to be working on another scene before we'd need you." Richard laid a hand on the boy's shoulder. "Just be back by seven, okay?"

At these words, Meredith stormed onto the stage. "Are you seriously thinking about bringing this boy in to dance the *Will o' the Wisp* variation with me, Richard? You said you'd be dancing that part."

Karla strode up beside Meredith. Tall, big-boned, and gorgeous, Karla always reminded me of a Greek goddess come to life. She towered over Meredith, glowering with displeasure. "Richard wants to use younger dancers whenever possible. The performances are meant to benefit youth dance programs, after all."

"Maybe so, but I'm not going to entrust my safety to someone so inexperienced." Meredith jabbed a finger toward Conner. "I was one of the judges at that competition where you dropped your partner."

"I know. You were the one who marked me down, even though it was clear that my partner was the one who made the error." As Conner stepped back, fury reddened his face. He shot a quick glance at Richard. "Even Brittany said it was her fault, but one of the judges gave me such a low score, I lost out on a scholarship that would've really helped jumpstart my career." Shifting his gaze back onto Meredith, with his eyes narrowed into slits, he added, "I always assumed that was you."

Meredith squared her shoulders and met Conner's stare with a sneer. "It was. And I'd do it again in a heartbeat. You weren't ready to properly partner anyone then, and you aren't now. If I'm honest, I suspect you may never be."

Conner, appearing stricken, swallowed back some retort and fled the stage, almost running into me. He stepped to the side and cast me a questioning look.

"I'm Richard's wife, Amy," I whispered, hoping to put him at ease. It seemed to work. He stayed close to me, watching the rest of the scene play out.

Karla placed her hands on her hips and looked Meredith up and down. "You're not in charge here, whatever you may think," she said with a toss of her sienna-brown bob. "Richard and I will make the decisions as to who dances what, and you'll either like it or leave."

"Hah!" Meredith spat out. "As if you have the professional experience to back that up. Everyone knows you're just a local dance instructor who's never performed with any major companies. You don't have the clout to talk to me like an equal."

Richard took two strides forward. Although he was only slightly above average height, when he stood toe-to-toe with Meredith, he appeared to loom over her. "What you need to understand," he said, his voice vibrating with anger, "is that this is Karla's project as much as it is mine. Which also means her word is as good as mine." He snapped his fingers in Meredith's face. "Don't forget—I hired you. I can fire you."

As Meredith raised her chin to look him in the eyes, I had to admire the picture they made. With their finely honed bodies, perfect postures, and Richard's dark hair contrasting beautifully with Meredith's copper-penny locks, they made a striking couple. *They're the perfect dance partners. On the surface anyway.*

But looks can be deceiving. I knew my husband, and although he wasn't easily roused to anger, he also wasn't one to put up with any nonsense.

"Oh, for heaven's sake." Meredith took a step back, sweeping one hand gracefully through the air. "A lot of sound and fury over nothing. And let's be honest, Richard—you're bluffing. You'd never find anyone who could learn and perform my role on such short notice. Now, excuse me. I need to head downstairs to rehearse my solo." She blew him a kiss, then strolled toward my side of the stage.

As she sauntered past, she flicked her hand through the air again. "Sorry, Amy. Guess it's up to you to calm him down. Good luck with that." She cast Conner a dismissive look as she brushed by him.

I made a face. "Someone's going to slap that woman silly someday. Maybe even me."

"Get in line," Conner said.

Chapter Three

After Meredith disappeared, I grabbed the cooler off the piano bench and followed Richard and Karla to the green room, which was located behind the stage, near the back entrance to the theater. It included a kitchenette and a couple of small round tables as well as two sofas and stackable chairs. Fitted with an intercom system so the stage manager could call performers to the stage, it was the one place in the theater where food and drink were officially permitted.

"Unbelievable. And then she doubles down by being rude to Conner Vogler," Karla said after I shared my encounter with Janelle DeFranzo and Meredith in the lobby. She stabbed the air with an apple slice. "I'll ask it again, Rich—why'd you hire her in the first place?"

Richard leaned back in his chair. "Because, for all her faults, she's a great dancer. A quick study too. It doesn't take hours in the studio to teach her a part."

"But she's just so . . . unpleasant." Karla made a face.

"She wasn't always like that," Richard said. Realizing his main motivation in defending Meredith was to keep the peace on the production, I just shrugged. "She got a lot worse after her disastrous marriage to Nate Broyhill," he added, with a frown.

"The guy she dumped you for," Karla said, before popping the apple slice in her mouth.

"Well, yes. Although I've no hard feelings about that these days." Richard cast me a look—one that made warmth rise up the back of my neck. "Anyway, Meredith was always a bit of a diva, but she could be charming and amusing too. She had a playful spirit, at least before her marriage. After that relationship imploded, she was different—bitter and mean-spirited rather than simply high-maintenance."

Karla's tea-brown eyes narrowed as she studied Richard for a moment. "You feel sorry for her."

"A little." Richard rolled his shoulders.

"Which is another reason you cast her in this production, isn't it?" I asked, confirming this suspicion from the expression on Richard's face. "I bet she doesn't get a lot of offers with her current attitude."

"It might have had something to do with it," Richard said. "Although I wouldn't have hired her if she couldn't dance the role."

"I know. Still, there are others who could perform it equally well." Karla frowned. "I admire your loyalty and generosity, Rich, but I won't stand for anyone abusing young dancers. If it were up to me, I'd fire her right now. Of course, we'd have to immediately find someone who could take over her role."

Richard leveled his beautiful, gray-eyed gaze on Karla. "You could."

"Not this again. I've told you why I don't want to do that." Karla slid back in her chair. "I need to be available backstage to manage the younger dancers," she added, with a glance in my direction.

"If that's the only stumbling block, I could help," I said. "I mean, I don't know much about dance, but I've worked with plenty of children and teens in my library career. I think I could keep things running smoothly backstage."

Karla shook her head. "Thanks, but it just feels weird for me to perform too much when we're supposed to be featuring the students."

"You're dancing the pas de deux with me. And we have other professionals performing throughout the piece. I don't think anyone would find it strange if you did more dancing." Richard stretched his arms over his head. "And we could tell Meredith to take a hike."

"Tempting," Karla said as she balled up her napkin and the plastic wrap from her sandwich. She tossed the bundle across the room, making a perfect dunk into the open trash can. "But for now, let's leave things as they are. I'll try to keep a closer eye on Meredith, particularly when she's around Quinn or any of the other dancers from my studio."

Richard stood up, shaking out his hands. "All right, we'll give her one more chance. But any more bad behavior, and she's out. Even if I have to take over her part," he said with a grin.

"Now that would be something to see." Karla rose gracefully to her feet. "Especially when you'd have to partner yourself."

Richard arched his dark brows. "You don't think I could do that?" He did a quick lunge, then a spin, before holding up his arms as if catching someone in mid-air.

"I'm sure you could," Karla said in an indulgent tone. "But maybe your choreography would be better presented with a partner." She cast me an amused look. "Don't you agree, Amy?"

I lifted my hands. "I'm staying out of it."

"Smart girl." Richard strolled close enough to kiss me on the forehead.

"That's why you married me, isn't it? For my intelligence?" I asked, looking up at him with a sly smile.

"That and . . . a few other things," Richard said, before kissing me again, this time on the mouth.

Karla pointed toward the wall clock. "We'd better get a move on, Romeo. And not the kind you probably want. Rehearsals are about to resume, and we don't want to keep the students waiting."

"Are you going to stay for a bit?" Richard asked me as he stepped back.

"Sure, if you want. But I think I'll lug this cooler out to the car first. And maybe grab my sweater." I rubbed my bare arms. "It's a little chilly in here, despite the heat outside."

"Sorry, we have to keep it cooler for the dancers," Karla said.

"I know. It's the same way at home when Richard is rehearsing in his studio." I gave a fake shiver. "I've learned to layer."

Richard quirked his lips. "The things you have to put up with. It's a wonder you stick around."

"Oh, there are a few compensations," I said, rising on tiptoe to kiss his cheek.

"All right, go collect your sweater. I'd better get back to work." Richard patted my shoulder before following Karla out of the room.

I gathered up the rest of the trash from our simple meal and deposited it in the can, then grabbed the cooler and headed for the back entrance to the theater, which included a loading dock. Following a trick I'd learned from Richard, I stuck a small block of wood in the door so it wouldn't close and lock me out.

As I made my way down the cement stairs and crossed the parking lot to reach my car, the air outside wrapped around me like a warm blanket. It seemed foolish to need a sweater on such a hot June day, but I knew from prior experience how chilly the auditorium could be.

Once I'd dropped off the cooler and retrieved my cotton sweater, I hurried back to the loading dock. I'd only reached the bottom step when I stopped, my attention captured by the sight of two vehicles loitering at the far side of the parking lot. They had to have shown up recently, since I was sure I'd have noticed such a flashy SUV and the older model metallic-blue sedan if they'd been parked in the lot when I'd arrived. I slid behind the arching limbs of a large forsythia shrub to get a better look at the two vehicles without the drivers seeing me. The parking lot was clearly marked at all entrances, forbidding its use by anyone except theater patrons, performers, or staff, but I was aware that might not deter everyone.

Especially if this is a drug deal or something equally illegal, I thought as the owner of the SUV left his vehicle. I squinted but was unable to see how many people were seated in the sedan. I certainly couldn't tell what the driver or passengers, if any, looked like.

However, I could take mental notes on the man who owned the maroon SUV. *Just in case the Sheriff's Department needs a description later, if there really is some illegal activity going on,* I told myself, while admitting that part of my motivation was simple curiosity. The tall, slender stranger had pale blond hair cut long enough to flip up at the collar of his charcoal-gray polo shirt. I squinted, wondering if my first suspicions had been wrong. He didn't look like some street thug—his elegant posture and tailored black slacks, along with the expensive vehicle, spoke of money. *Although a drug dealer could have plenty,* I reminded myself as he flung out one hand in response to something the driver of the sedan must've said.

That's interesting. He's definitely anxious, I thought, pressing my back against the brick wall of the theater. The man's voice rose, allowing me to catch the end of his last statement.

". . . it shouldn't be that difficult," he said. "Follow my instructions, and it'll be fine."

As the blue sedan drove off, heading, I assumed, for the lot's back exit, the man turned his head, allowing me to catch a glimpse of his profile. Despite his trim but muscular physique, he was not a teenager—I judged him to be in his mid-forties, at a minimum. But he was quite handsome, in a fine-boned, aristocratic sort of way.

Like one of those landed gentry fellows on a British period drama, I thought, waiting to move from my hiding spot until the man climbed back into his SUV. Unfortunately, he didn't start the engine immediately, and while I'd hoped to watch him drive off, I decided it was smarter for me to simply duck inside. For all I knew, the man intended to sit in his vehicle for quite some time. *Which is not really a crime,* I reminded myself.

Slipping through the loading dock door, I removed the block so the door would lock behind me and made my way backstage. Before heading for the stairs that led to the vestibule and adjacent auditorium, I draped my sweater over my arm and paused to watch the action onstage.

I must've stood there for at least twenty minutes, admiring the dancers from Richard's university studio as they ran through a sequence of steps. Feet striking the wooden stage floor resounded into the rafters as they performed without music, simply following the sound of Richard calling out the beats. At the end of one run-through, Richard told the dancers to take a short break and watch as he and Karla demonstrated the complicated combination.

It's magic every time, I thought, as I observed my husband and his favorite dance partner. Always in tune with one another, they were mesmerizing when they performed together. I examined the dancers Richard had brought in from his college studio. Admiration lit up their faces. *They know true artistry when they see it, and are just as impressed as I am.*

Knowing I'd have a better view from the auditorium, I decided to take a seat out front. But as I turned to go, Richard called out my name.

"Hold up a minute," he said, jogging over to join me in the wings while Karla stayed onstage, leading the other dancers in a new sequence.

"What's up?" I asked, when Richard reached me.

"We need a favor," he said. "Karla can't find the tablet with some of her choreographic notes. She thinks she might have left it in one of the rehearsal rooms. Would you mind running downstairs and seeing if you can locate it?"

"Sure." I wrinkled my nose at him. "I might not run, though, if that's okay."

"I guess walking is fine, Miss Wordsmith." Richard tapped my lips with one finger. "Anyway, the professional dancers may still be rehearsing with Riley in one of the rooms, but don't let that deter you. They'll understand."

"Even Meredith?" I rolled my eyes. "Okay, I'll go look. But if she yells at me, all bets are off."

"If she yells at you, she'll be history," Richard said, giving me a wink before turning and striding back to join Karla.

Knowing he'd follow through on that threat, I smiled and took off at a fast pace, heading to the exit vestibule, which included access to the lower level of the building. Clattering down the stairs, I resolved to avoid losing my temper if there was a confrontation with Meredith. If she opened her mouth to complain about me barging into a rehearsal, I'd calmly tell her that Richard had sent me to retrieve something essential to the production and dare her to say anything more. *She has to know she's on pretty shaky ground with Richard and Karla already,* I thought as I stepped into the main basement hallway.

I decided to check the rehearsal studios before the dressing rooms. Although the lights had been left on, the first studio was empty. I swept my gaze over the room, which was simply a large rectangle with floor-to-ceiling mirrors covering one wall. Moveable dance barres were stacked against the opposite wall, and a lone upright piano sat at the far end of the room. Searching the barren space for any sign of Karla's tablet, I found nothing except some rehearsal call sheets stacked on the piano and an empty Styrofoam coffee cup that I tossed in the trash. I flicked off the lights and left.

Lights also blazed through the window in the door to the other rehearsal room. Pausing with my hand on the latch, I took a deep breath, preparing to face Meredith's ire. But this studio, a mirror image of the first, was just as empty. Relieved I didn't have to disturb a rehearsal, I stepped inside. A quick glance revealed no sign of Karla's tablet, although I did spy something white in one corner of the room. Checking it out, I found a folded notecard, slightly bent, as if someone had crumpled it in their hand before tossing it aside. I shoved the card into the pocket of my sweater, which was still draped over my arm. I'd look at the note later and return it, if possible, to its rightful recipient.

Once again turning off the lights, I exited the second studio. *No use wasting electricity,* I thought, as I looked up and down the hallway. Although I couldn't imagine why Karla would've left her tablet in a dressing room, I decided to check those spaces as well, just so I could reassure her that I had looked everywhere.

Except for the two rehearsal studios, the dressing rooms were the only other public spaces on this floor. There were two larger rooms, built to accommodate extras, the chorus, or the corps de ballet, as well five smaller ones for any principal performers. The rest of the basement was given over to the various pieces of equipment needed to raise and lower the orchestra pit, or to allow for the use of turntables or trapdoors on the stage. But those spaces and the mechanical rooms that supported the building's plumbing, heating, and cooling systems were always kept locked.

Determined to scour every possible space for Karla's tablet before I headed upstairs, I strolled down the hall, pushing open each unlocked dressing room door and peering inside. It was a slightly unnerving task. Devoid of the bustle of performers or technicians, the empty rooms gave off a spooky air. Mysterious thumps and wheezes from the mechanical systems occasionally made me jump, and the fluorescent overhead fixtures I flicked on and off to examine each dressing room cast illumination as harsh as the lights in an interrogation cell.

The hair rose on my arms. The theater was an old building, no matter how recently it had been renovated. History still lingered in its shadowed corners. Perhaps there were even ghosts . . .

Come on, Amy, you don't believe in such things. Not really, I told myself, even though some experiences I'd had in the past had shaken my skepticism. *It's just an empty floor, and not only are there plenty of people upstairs, Riley and the dancers may return any minute. They probably finished their run-throughs and decided to go and grab food or coffee or something before tonight's rehearsal. There's a café just down the block, after all.*

Reassuring myself that nothing dangerous lurked in the remaining dressing rooms, I cracked open another door. It was as empty as the rest, but as I stepped away, I noticed light seeping out from under a door across the hall. Not wanting to walk in on someone who might be changing into rehearsal clothes, I called out a loud *hello* before I swung open the door.

A scene from a Shakespearean tragedy met my eyes. A young man, his golden hair gleaming in the harsh light, his hand clutching a knife, stood over the prone body of a woman. *It's Conner Vogler,* I realized, as his wild eyes connected with my astonished gaze.

"Tried to help," he sputtered through trembling lips. "Wanted to stop it, but it kept gushing out."

My focus slid down his tensed arm to the fist gripping the knife. Blood slowly dripped from the tip of the blade, spattering the beige linoleum tiles.

Finally tearing my gaze off Conner, I stared at the woman sprawled on the floor. Auburn hair fanned out like a halo around her bone-pale face. Across the chest of her white leotard, blood bloomed like crimson poppies.

Tossing my sweater in the hall, I stumbled into the dressing room, falling to my knees beside the body. "Call 911," I barked out, as I pressed my hands against the wounds.

"Too late." As the knife dropped from Conner's hand and clattered to the floor, I realized it was a folding knife with a relatively long blade, the kind a workman or hunter might carry. "Wanted it to stop, but it was too late," he said.

I spared one glace up at his stricken face. "We need to call anyway," I said, in a gentler tone. Sliding one hand up to the victim's throat, I confirmed what I'd already suspected from the stillness of her chest. As I feared, there was no pulse.

Meredith Fox was dead.

Chapter Four

I pulled my cell phone from my pocket as I rose to my feet. "I'm calling now," I said.

Conner slumped into the dressing table chair and dropped his head into his hands.

"It'll be okay," I told him, although my words sounded hollow even to me. I reached the dispatcher and relayed our location and the nature of the emergency.

The scream of sirens sounded not long thereafter. Leaning against the doorframe of the dressing room, I kept my gaze locked on Conner, whose broad shoulders rose and fell with his quiet sobs. Crimson threads of blood from his hands streaked his pale hair.

When the sheriff's deputies arrived, they asked me to step out into the hallway while they examined the scene and questioned Conner. I huddled near the door to one of the rehearsal rooms, my blood-stained arms clutched over my chest. One of the officers asked me to detail my movements and what I'd seen when I'd first stepped into the dressing room. As I haltingly answered their queries, I caught sight of Richard. Trapped

"I suppose so, since it's not part of the murder scene. But I'll ask one of the deputies to grab it and take it upstairs to hand over to Richard." Brad looked me over. "You might want to clean up before you touch anything."

Glancing down at the bloodstains on my dress, I mutely nodded.

"Okay, I think that's enough for now." Brad stepped back just as two deputies led Conner out into the hall.

I sucked in a sharp breath. Conner was handcuffed. "Is that necessary?"

"I'm afraid so. He's our most likely suspect at this point." Brad turned away as the deputies led Conner toward the stairs. "Wait until they clear the stairwell," he called over his shoulder as he strode toward the murder scene. "Then you can go join Richard and the others."

Leaning against the wall to steady my wobbly legs, I stared after Conner and his escorts until the sound of footfalls on the stairs faded to silence. I looked over at the open dressing room door but made no effort to move closer. There was no point anyway, since Brad and several other deputies and investigators crowded the entrance, blocking my view.

They have work to do and you'd just be in the way, I reminded myself as I crossed to the steps.

Richard was waiting for me in the vestibule at the top of the stairs. "Thank goodness you're okay," he said, moving to take me in his arms.

I took a step back. "I'd better clean up before you hug me. Too much blood," I said with a grimace. I hesitated, then asked, "Did they tell you?"

"That it's Meredith? Yes," Richard said grimly. "I also saw them march Conner out under guard. What's that all about?"

"He was standing over the body when I found them." I bit my lower lip, then added, "Holding a knife."

"What?" Richard took a few step back. "You can't be serious."

I glanced around to make sure no one else was listening. "I'm afraid so. He told me he tried to help her, so I assume he found the body and foolishly pulled the knife out or something. A mistake," I said, shaking my head.

"But not surprising. He was probably in shock." Richard rubbed his jawline with his fist—a sure sign of his distress over this news. "Did they notify Conner's mother? He shouldn't be left on his own during questioning."

"I'm sure Brad would insist on that. He's one of the good guys, remember?" I bobbed my head to acknowledge the deputy who'd handed off my sweater to Richard.

Richard waited until the deputy strode off, before speaking again. "I know. It's just that Conner's not as tough as he looks. He was an up-and-coming sports star when he switched to focusing on dance. A lot of people have treated him pretty poorly since then."

"He was very shaken," I said. "The thing is, he was the only person I saw when I was downstairs, which makes it worse."

Richard frowned. "Dav and Tamara weren't rehearsing with Riley?"

"No, the rehearsal rooms were empty. I thought maybe they'd finished and gone out to grab something to eat." I made a face. "I didn't find Karla's tablet either."

"That's irrelevant at this point," Richard said, his expression growing thoughtful. "We should make sure the authorities question the other dancers and Riley, just to see if they noticed any strangers lurking about before they left the area."

I pressed my lips together. Davonte, Tamara, and Riley would have to account for their movements for other reasons as well, but I wasn't sure Richard was in any mood to consider that point. "Have you been questioned already?"

"Yes. Fortunately, both Karla and I have an entire corps of dancers who can testify to our whereabouts during the time Meredith was probably killed." Richard's lips twitched into a humorless smile. "So we and the university dancers are in the clear."

"I don't think anyone suspects me either," I said. "Even though I was wandering around the area near the murder scene."

Richard shot me a questioning look. "You didn't hear anything? If Conner actually stabbed Meredith, surely you would have."

"Not if it happened before I went downstairs. You told me this building was soundproofed to avoid noise from the dressing and rehearsal rooms reaching the stage and auditorium. And not to be gruesome, but we don't actually know how long he was in the room with her body before I found them, unless—" I broke off and curled my fingers into my palms. "When was the last time you saw Conner?"

"Before our dinner break," Richard said. "After that encounter he had with Meredith onstage."

"That was when he left to go and get something to eat," I said thoughtfully. "No one saw him return?"

"Not to my knowledge." Richard's jaw was visibly clenched. "I suppose the authorities will question everyone about whether they saw him or not, though."

"That's their job." I cleared my throat. "Why don't we allow them to deal with all that and see if we're permitted go home? I don't know about you, but I sure could use a rather large glass of wine right now."

"Good idea." Richard tossed my sweater over one shoulder and flashed a genuine smile. "First, let me check in with Karla and the other dancers and make sure the Sheriff's Department has plans to lock down the building. Then I'm with you—it's time to head home."

"I'll just go wash up and then wait here," I told his retreating back as he took off for the stage at a sprint.

* * *

It was dark by the time we got home, forcing Richard to be cautious in opening the front door. We always wanted to avoid our two cats springing onto the porch in their eagerness to greet us. Since our front yard was bordered by a road that saw a lot of turnaround traffic, and our backyard was flanked by woods that harbored a few wild creatures who might consider a cat a tasty snack, we never allowed Loie and Fosse to roam around outside. And then there was our concern over the cats killing the birds we lured to the yard with a variety of feeders. A few of our neighbors claimed our cats should be allowed outside to enjoy a more "natural lifestyle," but since Loie and Fosse had access to a screened back porch where they could get plenty of fresh air, we ignored such suggestions.

Besides, it was pretty obvious that the cats were happy with their living conditions. The only thing they seemed displeased about was the lack of constant snacks. They always demanded treats when either one of us returned home, so I wasn't surprised to discover Loie right inside the doorway when Richard turned on the light. Sitting primly upright, she was as elegant as an Egyptian statue. Her emerald eyes stared at us, unblinking, while her companion, Fosse, sprawled on his back, with his paws waving through the air. He widened his golden eyes as we stepped into our front room.

Part living room and part dance studio, the front section of our house was definitely not to everyone's taste. But I didn't mind the fact that half of the space was given over to a dance floor, a wall of mirrors and a barre, mainly because having a rehearsal space at home meant I got to see my husband once in a while.

Ignoring their implacable stares, I sidestepped the cats to stroll over to the stairs. "I'm going to change into something a little less reminiscent of that murder scene."

"I'll grab some wine." Richard hung my sweater on the coatrack and headed down the hall that led to our kitchen. The cats, still expectant, shot disdainful looks in my direction before following him.

After I cleaned up more thoroughly and changed into my favorite pajamas—a pair of short tap pants with a camisole top—I trotted back downstairs and into the living room to slump onto the sofa. Stretching my arms over my head to relieve the tension in my shoulders, I leaned forward and plucked the TV remote off the coffee table. Flicking on the monitor mounted on the opposite wall, I scrolled through several channels until I found a station offering local news coverage.

Meredith's lovely face greeted me. I winced as I read the caption to the photo and realized she was only thirty-four. *Far too young to die*, I thought. *Although, when it comes to murder, is there ever an acceptable age?*

"The beasts have been fed." Richard returned clutching two full glasses of white wine. "Not that they needed extra treats, especially Fosse, since he's getting a bit chubby. But I caved because I honestly didn't want to listen to any wailing this evening."

Richard handed me one of the wineglasses and took a seat next to me. Gazing up at the television, he grimaced and took a long swallow of wine as more photos of Meredith were plastered across the screen. "I bet they're going to mention the connection to me and my work," he said glumly.

Which they did, of course. The announcer talked about their former collaborations as well as Meredith's participation in the upcoming *Folklore Suite*. "Any press is good press?" I suggested, earning a side-eyed glance from my husband.

"Not sure a murder is going to generate ticket sales. But then again, you never know." Richard slipped his free arm around my shoulders. "Sorry you had to be the one to find her."

"Technically, that was Conner," I said. *If he's telling the truth.* Looking to change the subject, I studied Richard's stoic profile for a moment. "There is something I've been wanting to ask for some time now."

Richard turned his head and met my speculative gaze with a wry smile. "Why Meredith and I ever got engaged in the first place?"

"Yes." I slid closer to his side. "Having gotten to know her a little better over the last few years, I've found it an odd pairing. You don't seem to have much in common other than dance."

"To be honest, that was basically it." Richard took another swallow of wine before adding, "We were paired together in that one company, and it just felt . . ."

"Convenient?" I suggested as I swirled the remaining wine in my glass.

"Something like that." Richard looked down at me, his smile broadening. "We had chemistry onstage, which I mistook for a real connection. I mean, you know my parents. It's not like I had great models for a loving partnership."

I took a sip of my wine, nodding my head in agreement. "True. But you must've been in other relationships before you met Meredith."

Richard shrugged. "Nothing serious. Anyway, Meredith pursued me, if you want to know the truth. I guess I was flattered enough that I simply allowed myself to be caught." He tightened his grip on my shoulder. "Examining my motives after the fact, I've admitted that maybe I simply felt it was time to marry. To shut up my father, if nothing else. You know how he feels about men who dance."

"Hmm, I can see why that would add some pressure," I said, finishing off my wine.

"So I ignored all the red flags and our basic incompatibility and forged ahead with the engagement."

"I mean, I can understand it. Both of you were great dancers, dedicated to your art. And both in great physical shape and very attractive." I looked up at him from under my lowered lashes. "I guess it seemed like a good match at the time."

"But it really wasn't, which I was already beginning to realize before Meredith abruptly broke things off and ran off to marry someone else." Richard lifted his wineglass and pointed it toward the screen. "That guy, as a matter of fact."

I stared at the TV, where a reporter was offering in-depth coverage on Meredith's past. The photograph of a handsome blond male dancer, caught in mid-leap, filled the screen.

I sat up and placed my wineglass on the coffee table, then squinted at the image. While the photo captured the dancer's grace and elegant figure, it was difficult to see the man's face. "That's Meredith's ex-husband?"

"Yeah, Nathaniel Broyhill. Back when he was dancing, of course." Richard set down his own glass and swiveled to face me. "That was some years ago. I only met him a few times, at the end of his career. I didn't like him, personally, but I have to admit Nate was a great dancer. He was independently wealthy too, which didn't hurt, as far as Meredith was concerned."

"Ah, I remember. You said her husband was rich."

"Still is, as far as I know," Richard said. "But it was really his stepfather's money. Kyle Lance was some sort of computer guru and entrepreneur. Nate's mom, Glenda, married him when Nate was just a kid. Kyle died a while back and left a pile of money to Glenda as well as to Nate and his half brother." Richard leaned back into the sofa cushions. "Ironically, Glenda Lance owns a horse farm not far from here. Outside of Smithsburg, actually. She doesn't live there full-time, but her son Oliver does. I guess he manages the farm. I know he's a star of the equestrian world. Anyway, Kurt knows them and got Glenda and Oliver to donate to the *Folklore Suite* production. So there's a weird connection there." Richard grinned. "I never told Meredith about that, of course."

"I bet you didn't." I pressed my hand against Richard's chest. "It was smart to keep that close to the vest."

"Yep. Oh look—a more recent photo of Nate." Richard motioned toward the television screen. Good to see he's aged just like the rest of us. Although he still looks pretty good."

As I glanced up at the screen, a little squeak escaped my lips. "That's Nate Broyhill?"

"That's the guy. Why?" Richard fixed me with a searching gaze.

I stared at the TV, examining the photo of a forty-something man with aristocratic features. "Because I saw him today."

"What? Where the heck was that?"

I folded my hands in my lap before delivering my bombshell. "He was loitering in the parking lot outside the theater around the time Meredith was murdered."

Chapter Five

Aslant of light, falling from the deep-set windows that lined the reading room of the Taylorsford Public Library illuminated the faces of a group of young girls seated around one of the sturdy wooden tables. Their animated expressions and excited chatter made me smile. Working on shelving some books in the adjacent stacks, I'd picked up enough of their conversation to know that they were discussing the latest book in a popular young adult fantasy series.

They could be talking about their school friends. That's how real it is to them, I thought as I rolled my empty book cart back to the circulation desk. A piercing burst of laughter followed me down the aisle. The girls were a little loud, but I had no intention of telling them to be quiet. For one thing, there was no one else in the reading room. More importantly, they were reading and talking about books. I thought that was worth a little noise.

"Do you want me to go and tell Shay and her pals to pipe down?" Samantha asked as I maneuvered the cart behind the desk. Her deep brown eyes were narrowed with concern. "When they let out one of those shrieks, I can hear them from here."

I shook my head. "There's no one trying to read or study back there right now. Let them enjoy their book discussion."

Samantha frowned. "I told Shay if they were going to meet in the library, they needed to keep their voices down. But they get so excited—"

"Over a book," I said. "Which I think is awesome."

"Of course, I'm glad Shay's found some friends who like to read as much as she does. I just don't want them to disturb any other patrons." Samantha pressed one palm against the pitted surface of the oak desk. Installed when the main portion of the library was built in 1919, it was worn from many years of service.

But the desk would not be replaced as long as I was the library director. Like the tall, deep-silled windows, vaulted ceilings, and plaster walls, it exuded a timeless elegance that could never be replicated in a modern building.

"All the other patrons are in the Children's Room at the moment. I doubt they'll notice." I cast Samantha a grin. The Children's Room, located in an annex that had been added in the 1960s, was always noisier than the rest of the library. But that was also fine with me. Children enjoying books and reading was more important than maintaining silence in the building.

"Good point." Samantha ran her fingers through her short afro. "I'm actually surprised so few people are in here on a Monday afternoon. Of course, it's been pretty quiet all day."

"It's so nice outside, everyone's probably at the pool or park or something. And you know how it is once school lets out for the year—all the families with kids immediately take off on vacation."

"Except for me and Shay." Samantha made a face. "Thanks to your husband and Karla, we're stuck here for most of the summer."

"Don't blame me. I'm not participating in the summer dance festival, and I'm still not able to get out of town. Unless I want to go somewhere on my own, of course."

"Not true." My other library assistant, and my best friend, Sunshine "Sunny" Fields, poked her head around the door to the staff workroom. "I asked Amy to take a weekend trip with me, and she turned me down flat."

"Only because that would leave Samantha to cover all the library hours," I said.

"She could've handled it, couldn't you, Sam? I mean, the volunteers would help." Sunny stepped out of the workroom to join us behind the circulation desk.

Worry lines creased Samantha's brow. "Normally I'd say yes, but with having to chauffeur Shay to dance rehearsals, I'm not sure how well that would work."

"Well, shoot." Sunny tossed her long, silky blonde hair behind her slender shoulders. "Richard has a lot to answer for." She poked her finger at me. "You tell him he owes me big time."

"I think he knows that, and not just because of this situation," I replied with a smile.

Samantha grimaced as another shriek of laughter wafted over from the reading room. "I'm going to tell them to pipe down. Just a bit," she added, casting me an apologetic look over her shoulder as she circled around to the front of the desk.

"Were we as giggly and noisy at that age?" Sunny asked as Samantha strode toward the reading room. "When we were involved in the summer library program here, I mean."

"Probably." Sunny and I had met as young teens when I'd spent several summers in Taylorsford, my mother's hometown. I'd stayed with my Aunt Lydia who still lived in the beautiful Queen Anne revival home next door to the more modest farm-house that Richard and I owned.

"To be fair, it's nice of Richard and Karla to allow young dancers like Shay to participate in their new choreographic suite," Sunny said. "I know it means a lot more work in terms of special rehearsals and that sort of thing."

"Oh, they think the extra work is worth it. Both of them are thrilled to have the opportunity to encourage more young people to dance." I tucked a loose strand of my shoulder-length dark brown hair behind my ear. "I respect their dedication, even if it means I've been turned into a dance widow. These days Richard rarely gets home before ten."

"But you have me." Sunny slid one arm around my waist and gave me a quick hug. "Plus Lydia. It's not like you have to eat dinner alone every night."

"True." I surveyed Sunny's lovely profile. "Although you're almost as busy as Richard these days, with your classes and working here. Good thing you decided not to run for mayor again."

"Well, once I decided to get the degree, I knew I couldn't work at the library and be mayor. Not successfully, at any rate. Besides, I think our new mayor is pretty awesome."

I couldn't disagree with that. Sunny had stepped away from the mayoral race once she'd decided to pursue her master of library science degree. Even though her classes were primarily online, she still had a lot of schoolwork to occupy her time.

Lacking the mayor's part-time salary, she'd also increased her hours working at the library.

In her absence, my aunt's childhood friend, Walt Adams, who was also the husband of her best friend, Zelda, had run for mayor, and won. I had to agree that Walt, a retired accountant, was an excellent leader. Following in Sunny's footsteps, he'd already made positive changes in Taylorsford.

"I guess it's just as well Walt is mayor now, so you can go to school, work here, and still find a minute or two to spend time with Fred," I said, studying Sunny's face for any reaction to this comment. "Is he out of town right now? I know Hugh's somewhere in Europe." Frederick Nash, a former police detective turned private investigator, often worked cases with my aunt's significant other, art expert Hugh Chen.

"Yeah, they're following a lead on a collection of stolen Elizabethan miniatures." Sunny shrugged. "Not sure when they'll get back. Which is one reason I thought you and I could take a weekend trip. Both of our guys being out of the picture right now."

"Richard does eventually come home each night. And I need to be around to occasionally take food to the theater so he and Karla can eat between afternoon and evening rehearsals."

Sunny shot me an inquisitive look. "Which is how you stumbled over the latest dead body, right?"

"Unfortunately, yes," I said as Samantha rejoined us.

"A tragedy," Samantha said. "Even if I didn't like Meredith Fox very much, I certainly didn't wish her any harm. It's totally disrupted the schedule for the dance production too, which is why Shay is here instead of in rehearsal."

"It's also terrible that Conner Vogler is the main suspect." I straightened the stack of flyers advertising summer community events. "Richard's upset about that as well as Meredith's death. He thinks Conner has a great future in dance. But this situation could derail everything."

"Not to mention send him to prison for the rest of his life," Sunny said, her expression darkening.

"Surely not." Samantha pulled some books out of the return bin under the desk. "I refuse to believe that Conner is a murderer. He's a quiet boy, always so polite to adults, and kind to the younger dancers, like Shay. He even defended Quinn DeFranzo when Meredith Fox insulted her the other day." As she stacked the books on the counter, a frown creased Samantha's brow. "Which I should probably share with the investigators, although I really wish I didn't have to."

"Yeah, that might create a definite pattern of him having conflicts with Meredith," Sunny said, shooting me a sidelong look. "Amy told me about Meredith verbally ripping Conner apart on stage right before she was killed."

I took a deep breath. "I admit it doesn't look good, but I think we have to be honest with the authorities. The truth is what's ultimately going to free Conner."

"If we can figure out what that is," Sunny said darkly. She elbowed me as she looked toward the front doors. "Speak of the devil, there's one of those authorities now."

Samantha and I shared a quick glance as Brad Tucker approached. "I think I'll go see if anyone needs help with anything," she said, stepping out from behind the desk.

"Didn't think I was that intimidating." Brad took off his hat as he watched Samantha head into the stacks.

"That's not the problem." Sunny looked Brad up and down. "I think she's trying to avoid you asking any more questions about the murder of Meredith Fox."

Brad rolled the brim of his hat between his fingers. "Because?"

"Because her daughter's involved in Richard and Karla's dance production, which makes the topic particularly upsetting." Sunny tossed back her long hair. "Are you here to ask questions?"

"Yes, but I only need to speak with Amy." Brad met Sunny's intense gaze with a crooked smile. "No need to go all protective mother bear on me. I promise not to use the thumbscrews."

I looked from the chief deputy to my friend and back again. Once upon a time, they'd dated. Fairly seriously too. But now Sunny was in a relationship with Fred, and Brad was married.

"How's Alison?" I asked, hoping to defuse the frisson of tension sparking between Sunny and Brad. Although Sunny felt no animosity toward the chief deputy, I knew she was wary of his law enforcement connection, especially when it came to her family or friends.

"She's doing great." Brad's smile broadened. "Finally got past the morning sickness, so that's a relief."

"I'm sure," I said. "When's the baby due again?"

"Early November." There was no mistaking the pride in Brad's voice.

I sneaked a look at Sunny. One reason her relationship with Brad had fallen apart was her reluctance to get married. She was also not interested in having children or, as far as I knew, had never wanted them in the past. Now that Brad and Alison were having a baby, I sometimes wondered if she ever had second thoughts.

Her expression and the lift of her chin reassured me that she hadn't. "I'm glad to hear she's doing so well. You both must be very excited."

"Pretty much over the moon." The sparkle in Brad's blue eyes confirmed this statement. "Ali's still working, you know. I couldn't convince her to quit."

Sunny arched her golden eyebrows. "You tried?"

Brad ran his fingers through his short hair. "Well, being a sheriff's deputy can be dangerous. And pretty physically demanding."

"I'm sure Alison can handle it," I said, remembering the times I'd encountered Brad's wife, who'd once worked in his department but now was employed by another county. "Anyway, you said you had some questions for me?" I gestured toward a door behind the circulation desk. "We can talk in the workroom, if you prefer."

"Thanks, that would probably be best." Brad acknowledged Sunny with a nod of his head as he grabbed his hat and stepped behind the desk. "Always good to see you, Sunny."

"Likewise," she replied, waiting until Brad's back was turned to roll her eyes.

I wrinkled my nose at her as I followed Brad into the workroom. Although I knew Sunny harbored no hard feelings over her breakup with Brad, these days she tended to find him, as she put it, a little "ridiculous." According to her, he was too obsessed with playing by the rules. Which was—again according to her—no fun at all.

I understood her feelings. Brad was a little too old-fashioned and chauvinistic for my taste as well. But I had to respect his devotion to duty, even if I did understand why my free-spirited friend would ultimately find him boring. "Does this have to do with the man I reported seeing in the parking lot around the time of Meredith Fox's death?" I asked as I closed the work-room door behind us.

"It does." Brad leaned back against one of the metal shelving units lining the walls of the room. "When you called me the other evening, you told me that he resembled a photo of Nathaniel Broyhill, Meredith Fox's ex-husband. Of course we had to check that out." He flashed a rather sheepish smile. "Exes tend to top our suspect lists."

Recalling one of my own ex-boyfriends, I nodded. "For good reason. So was I right? Was the guy in the SUV Nate Broyhill?"

"Yes, and he confirmed being in the parking lot of the theater around that time. But he actually had a good excuse. Or a convincing one, anyway." Brad tapped his hat against his hip.

"What was that? Seems awfully convenient," I said as a strange wave of dizziness swept over me. I grabbed the task chair from the computer desk in the corner and rolled it closer to the worktable.

Brad shrugged. "His younger brother lives just outside of Smithsburg on a big horse farm. Half brother, that is—Oliver Lance, who's apparently pretty well-known in the equestrian world."

I sat down. "Richard told me their mother actually owns the farm, but she doesn't live there full-time."

"Right. That's Glenda Lance. She's both Nate's and Oliver's mom." The lines bracketing Brad's mouth deepened.

"You've had dealings with her?" I asked, curious why his expression had soured.

"I was called out to the farm, a few years back, when some valuable paintings went missing." Brad's fingers tightened, crumpling the rim of his hat. "I was just offering a little extra help, since it wasn't really my jurisdiction, so I didn't get hit with the brunt of the family's anger, but they weren't too pleased with the efforts of their local sheriff's department."

"Was the thief ever caught?" I tried to remember if I'd ever heard anything on the news about the case, but it rang no bells. Which meant it must've happened before I'd moved to Taylorsford. *Or perhaps in your first year in town,* I thought, *when you were overwhelmed with learning all the ins and outs of your new job.*

"No, and the artworks weren't recovered either." Brad straightened to his full, impressive height. "The Lance family wasn't pleased, to say the least."

"I guess they didn't make any donations to the county Sheriff's Department after that," I said with a wry smile. "But getting back to the current crime—did you find out why Nate was at the theater?"

"According to Broyhill, he had arranged to meet with Meredith Fox. Just briefly," he added, obviously noticing my heightened interest. "Meredith had promised to return a valuable piece of family jewelry he'd given her while they were married."

"She agreed? That doesn't sound like Meredith."

"I found it a little strange as well. But my colleagues in the Smith County Sheriff's Department didn't think it raised that many red flags." Brad grimaced. "My department is collaborating with them since this is such a serious case, but they're taking the lead at this point. Which means they have the final say."

"The state hasn't sent in any special investigators?" I asked, remembering their involvement in a few past cases.

"Not yet. I expect they will once Smith County asks for additional assistance." Brad cast me a wry smile. "If they do."

"What about that other vehicle I saw—the blue sedan? Did you find out any more about who was driving that car?"

"No. Broyhill says they were just tourists looking for directions, and he didn't pay any attention to their plates. We're still checking into that, but it's a relatively common color for an older model sedan, and again, Broyhill didn't take any notice of the make or model of the vehicle."

"That's too bad. It could've offered another lead." I frowned, realizing how difficult it might be to track down such an ordinary car. "Is Conner still in custody?"

"For now, although I suspect he'll make bail because of his age and lack of priors, if nothing else." Brad cleared his throat. "He's still the main suspect, of course."

"I'm sorry to hear that. I know he was found over the body . . ."

"Gripping the murder weapon," Brad said.

"But he told me he tried to save her." I rolled back the chair and rose to my feet to face Brad across the workroom table. "He probably pulled out the knife, even though he shouldn't have touched anything. But if he thought he could help Meredith, he might've panicked and done that without thinking."

"And he might have stabbed her and then panicked." Brad examined me, his face solemn as a church statue's. "I know Richard's fond of the boy and thinks he has great potential as a dancer, but we can't allow such things to cloud our judgment. Conner Vogler did have a motive, or at least a few good reasons to be angry with the victim."

"There are other people who had equally valid reasons. I hope they're being questioned too."

"Of course." Brad tugged on the knot of his tie with two fingers. "To be honest, I'm going to look into Mr. Broyhill's story a little more closely. I don't know if I believe him about that blue car. I mean, that it was just a stranger asking for directions. It seems odd that someone would pull into that lot if they were lost. It isn't the most obvious choice."

"Thanks for that." I twirled a lock of hair around my finger. "If Conner is guilty, he needs to face justice. I just don't want to see a rush to judgment."

"There won't be." Brad flashed me a humorless smile. "Not on my part, anyway. I'm not sure I can vouch for all of my colleagues on that score."

I sighed. "I'm glad you're assisting the investigation, then."

"Not sure if I'm happy about that situation. It looks like it's going to be a messy one." Brad stared down at the floor for a moment before lifting his head to look me in the eyes. "You might be able to help,"

"How so?" I tried—and failed—to keep the excitement out of my voice.

"Well, the Smith County office doesn't seem to be too eager to pursue alternative options in terms of suspects. I thought since you have access to them, through Richard, maybe you could speak with a few people Smith County doesn't seem to want to focus on. Like those two dancers and the accompanist who were also in the basement for a while." Brad once again twisted the brim of his hat between his fingers. "I'm not saying they did anything wrong, and I wouldn't want you to imply that they did, but I would like to know more about where they went or what they might have seen not long before Meredith Fox was killed."

"Sure, I could do that." I met his steely gaze with a little bob of my head. "I assume you want to keep this confidential?"

"If you don't mind. I don't want to place you in any danger," he added, lifting his hand. "So I think it would be best if this was a very casual thing. With other people around, if possible. I'd just like to know what they'll say if they aren't being questioned by somebody in uniform."

"Okay." I looked him over, noting the tension lifting his broad shoulders. "You're afraid the other department is going to focus on Conner and not pursue anyone else?"

"I didn't say that," Brad said, although the look on his face told me I was correct in my assumption. "I just think it's worthwhile to leverage all our assets to get to the truth."

"I'll be happy to help. Mainly because I know you'll be determined to uncover the real facts, no matter where they lead."

"I'll do my best." Brad put his hat back on and strolled toward the staff door that led outside. "Thanks for agreeing to collect a little intel, Amy."

"If I can do anything else to help, like online research or anything . . ."

"I'll let you know." Brad paused in the open doorway and glanced back at me. "And in the meantime, if you do happen to hear anything interesting, please inform me immediately."

"Absolutely," I said, crossing my heart. "You know I always keep you in the loop."

Which just made him raise his eyebrows before wishing me a good day.

Chapter Six

With rehearsals at the theater suspended for a few days, Richard and I were happy to accept Aunt Lydia's dinner invitation Monday night. Hugh had just returned from his overseas work trip, and she'd made, as she put it, "far too much food for just the two of us."

After our meal, we gathered in the sunroom. Originally a porch which spanned the entire back of the house, it had been converted years before. Tall windows lined three sides of the space, while the fourth wall was the same stone as the exterior of the house.

Carrying our wineglasses out from the dining room, Richard and I crossed to a metal glider with cushions covered in a paisley slipcover. As we sat down, the glider swung back and clanged against the stone wall behind it. "Always love this view," Richard said, stretching out his legs to still the glider's motion.

"As do I." As Aunt Lydia settled into a wooden rocking chair, her gaze shifted, focusing on a vintage-style easel set up in one corner of the space. "Of course, that's the main reason we enclosed it years ago. It made the perfect art studio."

I stared at the man seated near her. His black hair offered a sharp contrast to the rose-patterned chintz cushions of his high-backed wicker chair. Fortunately, Hugh Chen, who my aunt had met decades after the death of her beloved husband, appeared unconcerned with this reminder of Aunt Lydia's romantic past.

"If I'm not mistaken, many of Andrew's paintings capture this scene," Hugh said, motioning toward the windows that offered a panoramic view of Aunt Lydia's backyard. A tall frieze of dark pines and emerald-leafed oaks and maples, topped with the azure scallop of the Blue Ridge Mountains, formed the backdrop to my aunt's lush and colorful garden.

"Yes, he loved depicting nature in his works." Aunt Lydia lowered her pale lashes over her bright blue eyes as she took a sip of her white wine.

Hugh's dark eyes focused on my aunt's elegant profile. "They aren't simply landscape studies, though, are they? I always feel as if he captured something deeper. They have a mysterious quality that sets them apart."

Meeting his gaze, Aunt Lydia offered him a gentle smile. "Exactly. Trust an art expert to see that."

"I believe anyone who studies Andrew Talbot's work will eventually come to that realization," Hugh said.

The love and affection in their shared glances were palpable. I elbowed Richard. "Maybe another wedding soon?" I whispered as he leaned in closer. "Now that Zelda and Walt have tied the knot . . ."

"What's that, dear?" Aunt Lydia asked, swiveling in the rocker to fix me with her sharp gaze.

"Oh, nothing," I said, keeping my tone light.

"Same old, same old." Richard raised his voice, despite my warning look. He set his wineglass on the small tile-topped table next to the glider and slid his arm around my shoulders. "Amy's just wondering when the two of you are going to follow Zelda and Walt's example and get married."

Color bloomed across my aunt's high cheekbones, tinting her pale skin pink. "I don't believe that's any of your business, Amy."

"Good thing you're a dancer, or I'd be stomping your foot right about now," I muttered to Richard, who just pulled me closer to his side. He knew, as well as I did, that I'd never actually do such a thing to anyone. Unless they were seeking to harm me or someone I loved, of course.

"It's all right, Amy." Hugh reached out and pressed his hand over Aunt Lydia's fingers, which were clutching the arm of her rocking chair. "I know everyone is asking that question these days. But the truth is"—he shared a swift glance with my aunt—"we rather like things as they are. At least for now. It's not a lack of love or commitment, you understand."

"Sorry," I said, warmth flushing my cheeks. "I didn't mean to pry."

Hugh swept his free hand through the air. "It's fine. I know your question comes from a good place."

"Shall we change the subject?" Aunt Lydia said, giving Hugh's fingers a squeeze before dropping his hand. "I'm actually interested in more details on this latest murder. Not that it's a pleasant topic, but since it does affect Richard's production, I'd like to keep up with what's going on with the case."

Richard pulled his arm away from my shoulders and slid to the edge of the glider seat. "We don't know much more than what you've probably heard on the news."

"I suppose the authorities have you shut out of the theater?" Hugh asked.

"For now." Richard leaned forward, gripping his knees with his hands. "They said we could return in a couple of days. In the meantime, we'll work with just the principal dancers, using Karla's studio space."

Hugh unfastened the top collar button of his robin-egg-blue dress shirt. "Such a tragedy. The victim was so young."

"Yeah, only thirty-four. And just as sad—the young man they arrested for the murder is only sixteen." As Richard sat back, the glider slammed into the stone wall again.

"You don't think he's guilty." Aunt Lydia didn't frame this as a question.

Richard ran a hand through his thick brown hair. "No, I don't. Conner is a sensitive, shy boy. I can't picture him stabbing someone to death, whatever the motivation."

"Zelda mentioned that several people heard Meredith Fox berating the young man right before the murder. Maybe he simply snapped," Aunt Lydia said.

I grimaced. Zelda Shoemaker, now Zelda Adams, was my aunt's closest friend. A warm-hearted, lovely woman, she was also unfortunately addicted to gossip. If she'd told Aunt Lydia about Meredith's conflict with Conner, you could bet that it was common knowledge throughout Taylorsford—and probably the surrounding counties. "We did hear them exchange a few heated words, but"—I shot Richard a speculative look—"I also witnessed another confrontation involving Meredith Fox that day, with the mother of one of Karla's dance students, Janelle DeFranzo." As I detailed the conflict between Quinn's mother and Meredith, Richard shifted his weight on the glider cushions.

"I don't know. Would someone knife someone just because they insulted their child?" Hugh asked, as he used two fingers to loosen his collar.

"Yes," said Aunt Lydia and I in unison.

"Maybe." Lines furrowed Richard's brow. "But if we're going to go out on that limb, you could add the other two professional dancers to the suspect list. I know there was bad blood between them and Meredith. Not exactly sure why, although Meredith and Tamara Hardy often competed for roles. As for Davonte, who knows? He and Meredith have danced together in the past, so it could've been over complaints about his partnering skills or something like that."

I opened my mouth but snapped it shut again. Brad had asked me to keep any questioning of Tamara and Davonte, or Riley Irwin, for that matter, confidential. Although I wouldn't remain silent if I discovered anything that might endanger Richard, Karla, or anyone else involved in the *Folklore Suite* production, I wanted to honor Brad's request to the best of my ability.

"But to kill someone over such a thing . . ." Hugh drummed his fingers against the wicker arm of his chair. "Still, if we accept the possibility that a teen would stab someone over insults or poor scores in a competition, I suppose we have to consider other rather weak motives as well. There are numerous leads to follow, at any rate. I'd definitely be looking into all of those people if it were my case."

"Agreed. Let's hope there isn't a rush to judgment," Aunt Lydia said. "I know Conner Vogler was standing over the body, holding the murder weapon, but his motive doesn't sound any more serious than others Amy and Richard have mentioned. He shouldn't be the sole suspect."

"Don't worry. I've spoken with Brad Tucker, and while he isn't the lead investigator on this case, he and his department are lending their support." I patted Richard's clenched hand. "You know Brad won't allow the investigative team to take everything at face value. As a matter of fact, I've already provided him with another viable suspect."

"Amy saw Nate Broyhill, Meredith's ex-husband, loitering outside the theater around the time of the murder," Richard said, loosening his fingers in order to entwine them with mine.

Aunt Lydia lifted her feathery eyebrows. "An ex? That's interesting."

"I saw him mentioned on the news. He's a former dancer. Did you know him, Richard?" Hugh asked.

"Not well. I knew of him, of course, as he was already famous when I started out. I saw him dance several times, and we occasionally crossed paths at fundraisers and things like that. I never liked him much, if that's what you're asking. And not because he stole Meredith away. That was really more of a favor." Richard rested our clasped hands on his upper thigh. "He had a rather . . . superior attitude, I guess you'd say."

I looked up at Richard from under my lashes. "Did you ever hear of him being abusive toward women or anything like that?"

"Not physically." Richard kept his gaze focused on Aunt Lydia and Hugh, but tightened his grip on my fingers. "There were rumors that he could be verbally abusive toward girl-friends, and I suppose Meredith wouldn't have been exempt from that sort of treatment. Which may be why she left him after only a year or so of marriage."

"Interesting," Aunt Lydia cast me a speculative look. "Per-haps Amy and I can learn a little more tomorrow. We're going to Zelda's to help construct some props for the *Folklore Suite*, remember, Amy?"

"Oh right," I said. "And along with you, me, and Zelda, some of the dance moms will be there. That could be interest-ing, especially if Janelle DeFranzo shows up."

"It will offer another opportunity to listen and learn, at any rate," my aunt said. Straightening in her chair, she rolled her shoulders, as if casting off a burden. "Now—what do you say we change the conversation once again? I'm sure we're all a little weary of discussing murder."

Richard exhaled a deep sigh. Of relief, I suspected. "That sounds like an excellent idea. Maybe you can tell us about your recent trip, Hugh? The parts you can share, of course."

Hugh launched into an amusing recollection of the expedi-tion he and Fred had made across Europe, tracking down the Elizabethan miniatures.

"Just like Indiana Jones," I said at one point.

"Only, without the hat or the whip," Hugh replied, his dark eyes sparkling with good humor.

Aunt Lydia side-eyed him, a smile quirking her lips. "Shame. Perhaps I should add those to my next Christmas list," she said, effectively diverting our conversation into laughter.

* * *

By the time we got home, I was exhausted.

"I realize it's not that late," I told Richard as we brushed our teeth side by side in our bathroom. "But I feel drained of all energy for some reason."

"Stress," he said after spitting out his mouthwash.

"You're probably right. Anyway, I'm just going to crawl into bed with a book. If you need to do some work in the office or whatever, go ahead. I know you prefer a later bedtime."

"Well, it depends," Richard flashed me a wicked smile before looking me up and down with a more concerned expression. "But since I can tell that you're truly dead on your feet, I think I will go downstairs and look over the changes the set designer sent Karla today. They're supposed to start loading in the backdrops soon, and I want to make sure it's all going to work with the current lighting plan."

"Such a workaholic," I said, leaning into him.

He tipped up my chin to give me a lingering kiss. "Mmm, minty fresh," he said.

I arched my eyebrows. "And that's what impresses you?"

"No, but I'd better not explore any of your other impressive attributes, not if you want to rest."

I wrinkled my nose at him. "Go on, you. Check over your plans or whatever."

"Not really as tempting as you, but okay." Richard kissed me again before following me out of the bathroom. "At least you'll still have company," he said, motioning toward the foot of the bed, where Fosse and Loie lay snuggled up close to each other.

After Richard left the room, I changed into my pajamas and grabbed a book from the pile teetering on my dresser. But as I slipped under the top sheet—disturbing the two cats, who expressed their indignation in no uncertain terms—I set the book on my nightstand and grabbed my cell phone instead.

"Let's see what we can find about Mr. Nathaniel Broyhill," I told Loie and Fosse, who simply yawned, both displaying sharp white teeth. Loie then curled up until her nose was touching the tip of her tail, while Fosse stretched out and rolled over, exposing his sleek, orange marmalade belly. "Fat lot of help you are," I said indulgently, as I searched the internet for mentions of Nate.

There were pages of hits, which meant refining my search to focus on reputable sources rather than some questionable sites that promised to reveal who Nate was dating, how tall he was, and how much he was worth. Not that those weren't interesting questions, but I knew from experience that I couldn't trust "facts" published from unverified sources.

I finally settled on his professional website, an entry on Wikipedia—whose information I could at least check against the linked news articles—and the biographical page from his most prestigious dance company residency. Of course, most of the information focused on Nate's dancing career, but comparing the various sources did give me a decent number of facts about his personal life as well.

"He certainly had a lot of high-profile relationships," I told Loie and Fosse, who didn't appear impressed by this fact. Bookmarking the list of Nate's romantic partners, I made a mental note to ask Richard if he knew any of the women. It was likely that he'd performed with a few of the dancers, at least.

Nate's connection to his stepfather was another interesting tidbit. Apparently, they hadn't gotten along particularly well, partially because Kyle Lance disapproved of Nate's choice of career.

"Shades of Jim Muir," I muttered, sympathizing with Nate for the first time. My husband's father had also opposed his son's dancing career, even when it had brought Richard a decent amount of money and prestige. But unlike my father-in-law, Kyle Lance had apparently provided Nate with more than adequate financial resources. "He didn't cut him out of the will either. I suppose that's something," I told Loie, who'd opened one emerald eye to stare at me.

Further investigation didn't offer much of interest other than a list of Nate's more popular roles and a few reviews of his performances. But just as I was about to give up, at least for the night, I spied a mention of Meredith's name, linked to Nate not simply through marriage but also because she was the principal dancer in a contemporary dance company he had apparently founded after retiring from performing.

Richard, standing in the bedroom doorway, tsked loudly as he turned off the overhead light. The room darkened, although the lamp on Richard's nightstand still cast a pool of light over the bed. "And here I thought you were going to get some sleep," he said, strolling over to join me. "But what do I find? You're researching again. That is what you're doing, isn't it?" he added, as he climbed into bed.

"Guilty as charged." I held up my phone. "You know how it is—I mean to just look up one little thing, and then get sucked down the research rabbit hole."

Richard plucked the phone from my hand. "Yes, I know all too well how it is. What's so fascinating?" He peered at the screen. "Habitus Dance Company? Wow, I'd forgotten about that debacle."

"Was it a disaster?" I asked, plumping the pillows behind me so I could sit up straighter.

"Pretty much." Richard handed back the phone. "From what I heard, Broyhill wanted to start a company primarily to showcase Meredith. When they were first married, of course."

"It didn't work out? The dance company, I mean. I know the marriage flopped."

"No. There were financial problems. Nate has money, but funding a company takes more than just individual wealth. You need ongoing support—a real base of donors or grants and things like that. Nate apparently couldn't keep Habitus going for more than a year, which incidentally is about how long he and Meredith stayed together."

"I guess she was supposed to be the star?" I asked, mulling over the implications of this failed partnership.

"That was the plan." Richard shrugged. "Maybe that was part of Nate's attraction, along with the fame and money. Meredith hadn't reached the level she thought she deserved in the dance world. If Nate promised her a company, that would've gone a long way to convince her to . . ."

"Fall in love with him?" I turned off the phone and set it on the nightstand.

"I was going to say marry him." Richard shot me a smile. "Not sure love really entered into it, honestly."

"Maybe on his part, though." I scooted close enough to lay my head on Richard's shoulder. "Perhaps Nate finally realized that she married him for his money, name, and the promise of a company. If he truly loved her, that might've created a deep well of resentment or even incited enough anger to make him want to harm her."

Richard slid his arm around my shoulders. "But this is after the fact. They've been divorced for several years. Why would he decide to murder her now?"

"Who knows? He said something to the Sheriff's Department about family jewelry. Maybe he wanted her to return more than the one piece he mentioned, and she refused?"

"Could be, although it still seems a little far-fetched to me. Now"—Richard leaned in and kissed my cheek—"hadn't you better shut down your investigation and get that sleep you were longing for earlier?"

I looked up at him from under my dark lashes. "Well, come to think of it, I don't feel quite as tired as I did. I think the research revitalized me."

"In that case, I promise not to complain about research ever again," Richard said as he turned off the lamp next to the bed and took me into his arms.

Chapter Seven

Aunt Lydia had arranged to pick me up after work on Tuesday so that we could attend the craft session at Zelda's house. As we drove the short distance from the library, she mentioned a memory she'd forgotten the day before.

"You were talking about Nate Broyhill and his family, and it totally escaped my mind that I met Glenda Lance once, at some fundraising event for the garden club," she said. "When we were introduced, she was quite interested, at least at first. Apparently, Kurt had sold her one of Andrew's paintings, and while she knew he'd been a local artist, she didn't realize that his wife was still living in the area. She became quite animated when she discovered I still owned numerous examples of Andrew's work."

I cleared my throat. "Was she looking to cut out the middleman and purchase another painting directly from you?"

Aunt Lydia cast me an amused glance. "How did you figure that out?"

"I don't know. Seems like something a wealthy person would do. They don't remain rich by wasting money," I said.

"I suppose you told her that you didn't intend to sell any of the paintings in your possession?"

"After which she immediately lost interest in me." Aunt Lydia parked on the street in front of Zelda and Walt's charming, one-story brick bungalow.

"What was your impression of Ms. Lance?" I asked as we strolled toward the covered front porch, which featured white-painted railings and trim. I paused on one of the concrete steps to admire the lush baskets hung above the balustrades and the wooden flower boxes overflowing with cascading purple petunias, silver dusty miller, and trailing ivy.

"She's a very attractive woman in her sixties. A Katherine Hepburn type—tall and lean and quite sporty. She was the typical image of an older equestrian, the kind that looks elegant in riding clothes." Aunt Lydia shrugged. "She seemed nice enough. Rather aloof, but perhaps that's the shell she's had to develop to keep people at bay. I'm sure she gets asked to fund every manner of thing in this region."

"No doubt," I said as I pressed the bell beside Zelda and Walt's wooden front door.

Zelda met us with a beaming smile. "Oh good—I was hoping you two would show up," she said as she ushered us into the house. The living room, a long, narrow space with a wall of windows opening onto the porch, looked somewhat different from the last time I'd visited. I attributed the changes to Walt. Citing his desire to allow Zelda to remain in the home where she'd cultivated an extensive garden, Walt had sold his townhouse and moved in with her after their marriage. *Although he insisted on replacing some of her furniture with his favorite pieces, I* thought, remembering the arguments this had initially caused. I'd heard all about the situation from Zelda, who was one of my most loyal library volunteers. Fortunately, these disagreements had blown over, as they always did where Zelda and Walt were concerned.

"Everyone's in the back," Zelda said as she led us through the living room, where I noted two leather recliners instead of the previous cream-colored armchairs. There were also photos of Walt's children and grandchildren decorating the moss-green walls, and in place of a seashell painting, Zelda and Walt's wedding photos hung over the white-painted brick fireplace.

Zelda trotted through her blue-and-white kitchen, her short, expertly dyed golden curls bouncing with each step. Like me, Zelda was shorter than average and curvaceous. Unlike me, she tended to wear extravagant, flowing clothes. Today it was a silky lounge dress in a bold tropical pattern that included vividly hued parrots peeking through palm tree leaves.

"Look who's here at last," she called out as she led Aunt Lydia and me into a newer addition to the house. An expansive, open rectangle, the room was painted a bland white and featured a row of windows across the back wall. It was set up as Zelda's crafting space, with two large worktables and storage cabinets. At one end of the room, metal shelving under grow lamps and a potting bench provided a space where Zelda could start seedlings for her garden.

"Sorry we're late," Aunt Lydia said. "Amy had to work until five."

Zelda turned to us, her light brown eyes sparkling with good humor. Although at sixty-eight, she was the same age as my aunt, the color in her full cheeks made her look younger. "No problem at all. The rest of the crew has been working diligently, so we've already knocked out quite a few things, although we can always use another pair of hands."

There were several people working at the two tables, mostly younger women, although I noticed a few men. *Probably dads of the dancers in Karla's studio,* I thought, also spying a couple of older women I assumed were grandmothers, and two of the university dancers.

My attention was piqued by the presence of Janelle DeFranzo, who had isolated herself at the end of the far table. Spotting Sunny working at the other end of that table, I crossed to join her. "I didn't know you were coming, especially since this is your day off."

Sunny looked up from the mask she was decorating. "I promised to help a while back, and you know I never renege on my promises." She adjusted one of the pins securing the crown of braids she'd wrapped around her head. "Besides, this is fun."

I looked over the supplies scattered across the table. Simple fabric masks that would only cover the upper portion of a face lay amid heaps of artificial feathers in shades of green and brown. "Oh, this must be for the ensemble in the *Owls Variation.*" I picked up one of the completed masks. "I didn't realize we were making costume pieces along with props."

"Originally that was true, but the costumer is swamped, as you can imagine," said the blonde woman standing beside Sunny. "She's had help from some of us with decorating leotards and things like that, but not everyone's a seamstress, so we agreed that the larger group could work on the masks."

"I see. Well, you'd better show me what to do. How many of these do we need, anyway?"

"A lot more than we have," Sunny said. "Anyhow, you just glue the short feathers on in layers, like this"—she pointed to the mask she was assembling—"based on the sketch on the table. It doesn't have to be perfect; just match it as close as you can."

"Okay, I'll give it try," I said, glancing across the room, where Zelda was showing Aunt Lydia how to decorate some polished tree branches that I assumed would be used in one of the forest scenes.

"You're artistic. You should be good at this," Sunny said, shooting me a grin.

"Excuse me, I studied art history. I can understand and appreciate art, not make it," I replied as I grabbed one of the blank masks and a tube of glue. I waved the glue at Sunny. "I think I'll head to the other end of the table. Looks like there's more space to work there."

Sunny widened her eyes. "I suspect you have an ulterior motive," she said under her breath.

"Bingo." I also kept my voice low before saying more loudly, "Let's see what I can do with this. Probably won't be as success-ful as you guys."

Marching to the end of the table, I found a spot right beside Janelle and set the mask and glue down in front of me, then reached over to grab a handful of feathers. "Sorry, I didn't mean to bump into you," I told her as I pulled back my arm. "I'm Amy Muir, by the way. Richard's wife."

The confusion clouding Janelle's brown eyes cleared. "Oh, okay—I knew I'd seen you at the theater, but wasn't sure why you were there. I didn't think you were one of the dance moms, because I've never seen you at Karla's studio."

"No mom of any kind," I said with a smile. "Not yet anyway."

"I have three kids," Janelle said. "Two of them are already in college. Quinn's the only one still at home. She was a late baby," she added, turning her attention back to gluing a row of feathers to her mask.

"She and Shay Green are friends, right?"

Janelle shot me a questioning look. "Yes. How did you know?"

"Samantha Green is a library assistant at the Taylorsford Public Library, where I'm the director, so I know both Shay and her mom." I picked up a feather and twirled it between my fingers. "Samantha mentioned Quinn being part of the corps when I was at the theater the other day."

"I see." Janelle bit her lip as she drew a fine bead of glue across her mask.

"Are the girls here?" I asked, looking around the room. A few of the younger dancers were working with Samantha at the other table, but I didn't see Shay or Quinn.

"Yes, but they went outside to play in the garden. They were helping earlier, but"—Janelle swept a straggling lock of hair out of her eyes with the back of one hand—"Quinn got a little over-excited, and I thought it best for them to burn off their excess energy outside."

"Makes sense." I side-eyed Janelle, observing her down-turned lips. She obviously didn't want to discuss Quin's autism, which I totally understood. I was a stranger, after all. "And Zelda does have the most magical garden."

That lessened the tension tightening Janelle's face. "Apparently. Quinn even ran back inside for a second just to tell me she thought it was like Narnia. Then she dashed back out again and I haven't seen her since." Janelle cast me a quick look. "Of course, she's with Shay, so I'm not worried about her being out there by herself."

"I doubt there's anything dangerous in the garden. No White Witch for sure," I added, with a smile.

"Quinn loves those books," Janelle said. "I don't know how many times she's read them. She's an excellent reader," she added, meeting my gaze with a look that dared me to challenge this statement.

So she does suspect I've heard about Quinn being on the autism spectrum, I thought. *I guess she encounters a lot of people who think that means her daughter is intellectually as well as socially challenged.* "She should come to some of our library programs, then. We have a monthly book club for our young adult readers. Shay's involved, so Quinn would know someone in the group."

Janelle stared into my eyes, as if looking for some sign that I was pranking her. Apparently convinced of my sincerity, she finally offered me a warm smile. "Thanks, I didn't know about that program. Quinn would probably enjoy talking about books. Maybe too much, sometimes."

"I don't think anyone can talk too much about books they love," I said, dropping the feather I was holding onto the table. "We aren't hosting sessions over the summer, but during the school year we meet every third Thursday at four o'clock. After school but before dinner."

Janelle sighed. "That's good timing. The only thing is, sometimes Quinn doesn't do so well in groups."

"I bet she'd be okay, especially with Shay there. And trust me, it's not like everyone in the club is perfectly well behaved. Anyway, she seems to be doing fine as part of the *Folklore Suite* ensemble."

"Some people didn't think so," Janelle said, her eyes darkening as suddenly as a summer storm. "Sorry, I know it's terrible that Meredith Fox was killed, but honestly . . . Well, let's just say maybe she had it coming."

"She wasn't the easiest person, that's for sure." I fought to keep my tone pleasant, not wanting to display my shock over Janelle's cavalier dismissal of Meredith's death. *Like she's truly happy the woman is dead,* I thought, forcing myself to maintain a neutral expression.

"She insulted my daughter. More than once." If looks could kill, Janelle's expression would've wielded the same damage as the knife that had stabbed Meredith. "We even had words about it."

"I guess that meant the detectives had to check you out? I'm sure that was a pain," I said.

"They definitely grilled me, even though that Vogler boy was found standing over the body, so you'd think that would be that." Janelle pushed her completed mask to the side and turned to face me. There was a defiant gleam in her eyes that made me take a tiny step back. "Thankfully, I'd left the theater long before that harpy was murdered. Plenty of people could vouch for that, so the detectives finally left me alone."

"That's right, the rehearsals for the younger dancers were over long before the dinner break," I said, speaking to myself as well as Janelle.

"Yes, I had to get Quinn home. She gets very upset if her meal times are changed." Janelle shrugged. "It can be a challenge, especially dealing with rehearsals, but I try to keep to her schedule as much as possible."

"Anyway, it's good you have a solid alibi," I said, mentally striking Janelle off my personal suspect list.

"Yes, thank goodness." Janelle spun around as a girl's voice called out "Mama!"

A slight preteen with dark hair pulled back into a tight bun bounded across the room, stopping right in front of Janelle. Quinn, I assumed.

"Can we go home now?" she asked in a plaintive tone. "I want to go home. It's almost dinnertime."

Janelle cast me a "see-what-I-mean?" look. "All right. I think I've done enough for today." She placed her hands on Quinn's shoulders and spun the girl around. "Let's go, my little rat."

The blonde woman working near Sunny turned her head sharply at hearing this, but since I'd learned that young dancers in the French ballet world were often called *les petit rats*, I simply smiled. It was clear that Janelle deeply loved her daughter. *Perhaps enough to kill for her. But she has an alibi,* I reminded myself as I wandered back to where Sunny was stacking up the masks she'd made.

Sunny stared at my empty hands. "You don't have one to contribute?"

"Not yet. But I promise to make a few before I go home," I said as I watched Janelle and Quinn leave the room. "I did accomplish something, though."

"By questioning one of your suspects, you mean?" Sunny shook her head. "You're incorrigible, Amy."

"As if you wouldn't do the same thing if you thought it would help an innocent person," I said.

"You mean Conner Vogler? But you don't know that he's innocent. Not for sure."

"It's true." I exhaled a gusty sigh. "And from what I just learned, Janelle is off the list of suspects, which doesn't help his cause at all."

As Samantha and her daughter strolled across the room, I heard Shay mention something about Quinn. Something about her friend being worried. "What's that?" I asked the girl when they reached Sunny and me. "Why was Quinn upset? I hope no one was being rude to her."

"Nothing like that." Shay, who was only an inch or two shorter than me, met my inquisitive gaze with a tilt of her chin. "It's just that she doesn't understand why her mom is lying about something."

"What do you mean?" Sunny looked from Samantha to me before focusing on Shay. "What would her mom lie about?"

"Maybe Quinn is just confused," Samantha said, laying a hand on Shay's shoulder.

The girl shook her head. "Nope. She says her mom didn't tell the police the truth." Shay looked up at her mother, her dark eyebrows drawn together. "Well, it wasn't the police, but you know what I mean. The day after Miss Fox was killed, Quinn overhead Mrs. DeFranzo tell the deputies that she drove Quinn home and stayed there the rest of the evening."

"But she didn't?" My hands clenched until my fingernails bit into my palms.

"Nuh-uh. Quinn says her mom went out somewhere right after she dropped her off at their house. Didn't say where she was going either. So now Quinn's really confused because she doesn't know why her mom would tell the deputies a lie like that." Shay squared her broad shoulders. "Quinn hates lies. They make her more upset than anything."

"Rightly so," Samantha said. "But I don't think Quinn, or you, should worry about this. I'm sure she just heard things wrong." Her fingers tightened on her daughter's shoulder. "Come on now—let's go. I need to get dinner started for the two of us."

As Samantha and Shay walked off, stopping to say goodbye to Zelda, I turned to Sunny.

"I know, I know," she said, lifting her hands. "Back on the list."

Chapter Eight

After I shared the information concerning Janelle DeFranzo with Brad, I told him I'd also try to talk to a few other people on the wider suspect list. He was grateful, if a little wary, warning me to watch my step.

"Don't forget that one of them might be a killer," he said.

"I know, but I think I can speak with them without raising any real suspicion. Which I know you can't do."

"I can't talk to them at all," he replied ruefully. "Or so I've been told by those in charge. We don't have enough reason to question them again at this point, according to the Smith County sheriff. I disagree, but I'm only assisting on this case."

"I know you have to follow their lead. Which is why I want to help."

"Just promise me to meet them in public places. And during the day," Brad said in a tone that brooked no opposition.

Keeping all this in mind, I arranged a meeting with Riley Irwin for late Wednesday afternoon—at Clarion University, where there were always plenty of people around.

I used the rather flimsy excuse that I wanted to talk about the day of the murder simply to ease my own trauma over finding the body. "I thought perhaps you could help me understand what happened before that discovery," I'd told him over the phone. "Right now everything is still such a blur."

If Riley found this request odd, he gave no indication and readily agreed to talk face-to-face. "It's great that you can meet me at Clarion," he said. "I'm playing for one of the voice teachers on Wednesday. It's summer school, so the parking shouldn't be quite so difficult."

I agreed to the time frame, assuring Riley that the trip wouldn't be a problem. "I need to double-check something in the library anyway," I told him. "Richard wants to use a quote in the program for the *Folklore Suite*, and although he remembers the book it came from, he needs the exact page number for the endnotes. This will give me a chance to grab that book for him as well as speak with you."

I left work early on Wednesday, leaving Sunny to oversee operations. Crossing to my car in the gravel lot behind the library, I noticed a small white vehicle, its engine idling. That wasn't so odd—sometimes parents sat in the back lot, waiting to pick up their children or teens. But when the white car followed me out of the lot and onto the side street without anyone exiting the library to enter the vehicle, I felt a tremor of unease. Before I drove on the main street, I paused and glanced in my rearview mirrors, but I couldn't make out the face of the driver.

The windows are tinted, I realized. I kept eyeing the road behind me as I drove to the university, unnerved when the white car continued to follow. As I drove onto the Clarion campus, I reached for my cell phone, resolved to call Brad or someone else at the Sheriff's Office. But when I turned onto the side road that led to the lot where Richard had a designated faculty parking spot, the white car veered off in the opposite direction.

Seeing danger where there is none, I chided myself. *Past experiences are making you paranoid.*

After parking, I checked my watch. It was still forty minutes before I was scheduled to meet with Riley, which gave me plenty of time to dash into the university library and track down the book Richard wanted. Since I'd once worked in the Clarion Library, I knew exactly which floor held the materials I needed and was able to head directly to the proper location.

I paused as I stepped off the elevator. Unfortunately, space limitations had recently forced the library to convert several sections of stacks into moveable shelving, which wasn't my favorite way to browse a collection. But I understood the necessity— most university libraries were short on funds as well as space.

The rolling stacks were mounted on tracks that allowed all but one or two aisles to be compressed together. It did provide a lot more shelving space in the same footprint, but when the library was busy, it also meant waiting for someone to clear an aisle so another could be opened. Fortunately, today was a slow day; or maybe it was simply the section. Folklore wasn't the hottest research topic.

Clarion had chosen to go with a mechanical system instead of a motorized one, which meant cranking a wheel on the end of the aisle to open it wide enough so you could browse. There was a lock that popped out when an aisle was open all the way—this was a safety feature meant to keep anyone farther down the row from inadvertently rolling the aisle closed. I always made sure the lock was engaged, although I knew many patrons didn't bother, especially if no one else was in the stacks.

But unfortunately, the lock on this row of shelving appeared to be jammed. I rolled the section back and forth a couple of times before giving up and stepping into the open aisle. I hadn't seen anyone on the floor and figured if anyone started moving another section, I could yell at them to stop in plenty of time to get out of the aisle.

Surveying the call numbers on the volumes lining the shelves on either side of me, I finally found the book I was seeking at the far end of the aisle, near a concrete block wall. Standing on tiptoe, I yanked the volume off the shelf, dislodging one of the thick tomes beside it, which clattered to the floor.

I swallowed back a swear word. As I bent down to pick up the book, the shelves to my left shuddered slightly and began to roll forward.

"Hey!" I yelled. "Stop—someone's in here!"

The shelves kept moving. I scurried toward the end of the aisle, continuing to shout at whoever was rolling the stacks. Afraid I wouldn't be able to get out of the way before the shelves closed in on me, I tossed the larger of the two books I was clutching onto the floor in front of me.

When the movable shelving slammed into the book and shuddered to a halt, several volumes rained down onto the floor. Although none hit my head, one heavy book struck my shoulder, causing me to swear again—out loud this time.

I leapt over the tome bracing open the shelving, to escape the aisle. Afraid that the patron would continue to try to turn their wheel, causing a catastrophic warping of the shelving unit, I strode down to the far end of the room.

There was no one there. I searched the entire area and saw no one except a young student who'd just exited the elevator. "Did you see anyone leaving this floor?" I asked her.

The girl shook her head. "No one got off the elevator when I got on," she said. "And it didn't stop anywhere when I called it up."

"Must've taken the stairs," I muttered. I advised her to avoid using the section of movable shelving I'd just left. "I'll get someone to come down and examine it," I told her before taking the elevator to the main floor.

I informed one of the library assistants at the circulation desk about the shelving issue while she checked out the book Richard had asked for. "You might need maintenance to take a look," I told her. "Someone kept cranking the shelving even though there was resistance. Who knows what damage they've done."

The assistant rolled her eyes. "Those shelving units can be such a pain. We're always finding jammed locks or books wedged under the rollers, or whatever." She looked me over as I picked up my book. "Don't tell me you were in the aisle when they tried to open another section."

"I'm afraid so. I wasn't hurt, though," I said, ignoring my bruised shoulder. "Not really. I'm just worried about anyone else trying to access that area. Several books tumbled to the floor, so I guess those need to be reshelved too."

The library assistant just sighed and thanked me. As I left the desk, she called one of the student library workers over, which reassured me that someone would look into the shelving situation so no one else would get hurt.

Since Richard's parking space was close to the building housing the music and dance departments, I decided to drop off the book at my car before meeting with Riley. As I crossed campus, I checked a couple of the visitor parking spaces, looking for the white car that had appeared to follow me earlier. Even if it had driven off when I turned, that didn't mean the driver hadn't parked somewhere close by and waited to see where I went. Someone could've easily left their vehicle and trailed me on foot right into the library—maybe to orchestrate a scare by squeezing me between a bank of shelves.

But why would someone do that unless they were somehow mixed up in Meredith's murder and also knew that I often helped the authorities with cases? As I walked to the music building, I reminded myself how unlikely it was that anyone would know about Brad's request for assistance on the current case. We'd talked primarily on the phone, and when we'd spoken at the murder scene, the hallway had been filled with other investigators and deputies. Surely no one in that crowd would be stalking me.

But Conner was there, perhaps close enough to overhear us. What if he told his family about my obviously friendly relationship with someone in law enforcement, and they decided to keep tabs on me?

I paused in the lobby of the music building to take a deep breath. Riley Irwin was waiting to meet me in a faculty lounge upstairs, and I wasn't about to turn around and leave without talking to him, even if someone *was* watching my every move.

I squared my shoulders and marched up the steps to the second floor. The faculty lounge, located at the end of a long hallway, was a high-ceilinged room filled with dark woodwork set off by creamy plaster walls. Tall windows lined three of the walls, flooding the room with light.

The lounge was empty. Wanting to sit down for a moment to relax after my experience in the library, I wandered over to a comfortable seating area to wait for Riley.

He appeared in the doorway as I contemplated whether to take a seat on an old leather sofa or a well-worn upholstered armchair. "Hi, Amy. So glad you could make it. Did you find that book Richard wanted?"

As he crossed the room, I noticed Riley seemed slightly out of breath, as if he'd just run from some other location. *Could he have tracked me to the library? But why? Does he have some hidden connection to Meredith Fox?*

I studied his pleasant face, finding no traces of guilt or guile. *So either he's innocent or an excellent actor,* I thought as Riley plopped down on the sofa. "I did. Just dropped it off at my car before I came to meet you."

"Good, good," Riley said, meeting my inquisitive stare with a smile. "I hope you didn't have trouble finding a place to park."

I narrowed my eyes as I settled into the armchair. "Richard has a reserved parking spot, which we pay dearly for, by the way. But since he has to be on campus at all hours during the academic year, it's a necessity. We purchased an extra sticker for my car," I added, crossing my ankles. The chair cushions were so soft that I'd sunk into them until my feet barely reached the floor.

"So, getting down to business—you wanted me to share what I saw and heard on Saturday, right?" Riley used his thumb to perch his glasses back on the bridge of his nose. "Just to see if what I experienced matches your recollections?"

"Something like that." I gripped the arms of my chair and pulled my body forward. "Sorry, it feels like this thing is going to swallow me whole."

"It's all a little beat up," Riley said, gesturing toward the rest of the furniture, "but beggars can't be choosers. We get the leftovers from the business school. Of course, their lounges are quite spiffy. Everything up to date."

"I know. Richard's office is filled with a similar collection of random stuff. There's a nice chair that came out of the chancellor's office during one of their many renovations, but the rest of it is older than he is. Although not in as good a shape," I said with a smile.

"Anyway, as to what I saw"—Riley crossed his arms over his chest—"really, it was nothing. I played for Meredith first. She insisted on that." Riley must've seen my reaction because he offered me a sarcastic smile. "No surprise there. Then she left the rehearsal studio. She told us she was going to pop into one of the dressing rooms to rest. I'd planned to go out and grab something to eat after the rehearsal, so I asked her if I could bring something back, but she didn't want anything. After Meredith left, I ran through Dav and Tamara's duet—sorry, pas de deux."

I leaned forward, gripping my knees. "Then all of you left the building?"

Riley nodded. "The three of us did—Tamara, Dav, and me. We assumed Meredith was still in one of the dressing rooms, but we didn't check on her."

"You didn't see anyone else downstairs before you left?"

"No. I did notice some guy in the parking lot, sitting inside an SUV, but that was it. I figured he might be a parent or friend of one of the university dancers, waiting to pick them up after rehearsal."

I almost confessed to seeing the man I now knew was Nate Broyhill but decided that wasn't a smart move. "Did you, Davonte, and Tamara eat dinner together?"

Riley's eyes, hidden behind the thick lenses of his glasses, were impossible to read. "Nope. We actually all went our separate ways. I took off first, heading for the café just down the street, and didn't see the others again until later, after the cops arrived." The worn leather crackled as he shifted his position on the sofa. "As a matter of fact, it looked to me like Tamara was loitering in the parking lot for some reason. Dav must've taken off already, but she was still hanging out near the theater building when I glanced over my shoulder."

Forgetting about the softness of my chair, I sat back, allowing the enveloping cushions to suck me in again. "You didn't see Conner downstairs at any point? Or even near the stairs? I just want to make sure I wasn't wrong when I told the authorities that there was no trace of him until I entered that dressing room."

"I never saw the kid. He must've gone down to the basement after we left." Riley fiddled with the earpiece on his glasses. "Such a shame, to have your life cut short like that. And I mean Conner as well as Meredith."

"I'm not convinced that Conner is guilty," I said as I struggled to pull myself back to the front edge of the chair. "He told me he simply found her and tried to help."

Riley tipped his head to one side and studied me for a moment before replying. "I know Richard had high hopes for the boy. As a sort of protégé, I suppose. But let's be honest—if Conner really wanted to help, he would've called 911 immediately, not simply pulled out the knife and stood over the body."

It was my turn to examine Riley's face, which displayed a certain tautness around the mouth and eyes. *As if he's holding back a wave of anger,* I thought. "I don't know. A young person confronted with that traumatic situation might not have been able to think logically. Heck, I'm not sure I could've done the right thing, especially at his age."

Riley lifted his hands in a mea culpa gesture. "I don't mean to throw the boy under a bus, but facts are facts. I heard he had an argument with Meredith not long before the murder."

"So did others," I said before I could stop myself.

"Really? I must've missed that." Riley took off his glasses and wiped the lenses on the hem of his white polo shirt. "Who else was fighting with her?"

"Oh, it wasn't a fight. A little disagreement between Meredith and one of the dance parents, that's all." I wasn't ashamed to use a white lie, especially since the intense gaze Riley had turned on me made me hesitant to disclose Janelle DeFranzo's name. His eyes, free from the glare of the glasses, shone unnaturally bright. *As if he's more upset over Meredith's death than he's letting on,* I thought. *Or perhaps desperately wants to cast suspicion on others to keep himself in the clear.*

Riley slipped his glasses back on. "Meredith did tend to accumulate enemies, as strong women often do."

I didn't quibble with his assessment of Meredith, although I knew that wasn't the only reason so many people had quarreled with her. "Well, I suppose I should run along. I don't want to keep you too long, since I imagine you need to get to the theater for this evening's rehearsals, now that the authorities have allowed them to resume."

Riley stood up and held out his hand. "Here, let me help. And yes, I should be heading out soon, especially if I want to grab something to eat first." He pulled me to my feet. "I just hope our conversation has helped clear up any confusion. I mean, not that I really saw anything of significance, but I guess it corroborates your statement that you didn't notice anyone wandering around when you went downstairs. Before finding the body, I mean."

"No, I didn't," I said, again refusing to mention that I'd also seen Nate Broyhill outside. "Anyway, thanks for taking the time to speak with me. It's nice to know that my recollections seem to have been correct." I slipped my purse strap over my shoulder. "I'd hate to have given the deputies incorrect information just because I was in shock or something."

"Glad to help." Riley pulled a chiming cell phone from his pocket and stared at the screen. "Sorry, I have to take this," he said, answering the phone.

I waved a goodbye and left the lounge. As I headed for the stairs, a woman with an elaborately wrapped scarf covering her hair called out a greeting.

"You're Richard Muir's wife, right?" she asked as I paused near the doorway to what was obviously her music studio. "I've seen you together at a few concerts and dance performances."

"That's right. Amy Muir," I said, extending my hand.

"I'm Deborah Holt, voice teacher," she said as she briefly clasped my fingers. "Were you the person Riley was planning to see?"

I met her inquisitive gaze with a wary smile, wondering why she was so interested in this information. "I guess so. We met briefly in the faculty lounge just now."

"That's funny." Ms. Holt widened her eyes. "He told me he had to leave my voice lesson early because he had another appointment. He was accompanying one of my students, you see. It was a bit inconvenient, but I thought he needed to run across campus or something. Not meet up with someone right down the hall."

I looked over my shoulder, making sure Riley hadn't stepped out of the lounge. "So he was here? In your studio?"

"Yes, so I don't know why he had to leave early." Deborah Holt shrugged. "Maybe he had to run an errand or something beforehand. It's really none of my business, I suppose. I just don't like my students to pay accompanists for a full session and have them skip out three-quarters of the way through. Unless they have a pressing reason, of course."

"I totally understand," I said. "But you'll have to ask him about it. He didn't tell me where he'd been, I'm afraid."

"No, no, of course not." Ms. Holt flashed a bright smile. "Anyway, it was nice to meet you, Amy. We all love your husband around here, you know."

"I'll be sure to tell him that," I said before wishing her a good day.

As I headed downstairs and out of the building, it was her other comment, about Riley leaving the voice lesson early to meet with me, that played in a loop through my mind. Given the time frame, Riley had to have gone somewhere else before joining me in the faculty lounge. The question was—was it enough time for him to find me in the library and try to frighten, or even injure, me?

Mulling over this distressing possibility, I pulled out my cell phone as soon as I reached my car, planning to call Brad. But as I stared at the darkened screen, I decided it could wait. All I had were vague feelings of unease, a car that was probably simply traveling in the same direction as I was, and an incident that could've easily been caused by anyone using the library stacks. I'd wait to call Brad until after I had a chance to speak with Tamara and Davonte. Then I could share any information or even personal impressions about the three people who'd been working in the basement around the time when Meredith was killed. What I had to offer now wasn't enough to give Brad any real leads.

But I did keep a close eye on the cars behind me as I drove home.

Chapter Nine

M y opportunity to speak with Tamara came along sooner than I expected—on Thursday, when I accompanied Richard to his evening rehearsals. I ostensibly tagged along in order to have Karla show me what I needed to do backstage to keep things running smoothly during performances. Since Meredith's death meant her various roles in the production had to be covered by others, Karla was making contingency plans.

Before we reached the theater, Karla texted and asked me to meet her in the costume shop set up in a former office space on an upper floor of the theater building. "Might need another pair of eyes," she messaged.

I was intrigued to see what was happening with the costumes. Always interested in furthering the talent of young people, Karla had hired Candace Jenson, an MFA student from Clarion's theatre department, to design the costumes for the *Folklore Suite*. Candace, who'd worked on some of Richard's university dance productions, had impressed him and Karla with her ability to design for dancers.

"It's a specialized type of costume construction, for sure," Karla said as she introduced me to Candace. "You have to allow for free and unfettered movement while still offering an appropriate design."

"I know all about that," I said, rolling my eyes. "Richard's complained about having to dance in certain outfits often enough." Noticing the concern clouding Candace's kohl-rimmed blue eyes, I hastily added, "Not your costumes, of course. These were actually from professional company productions."

"That's good. I mean, not for Mr. Muir, but I'm glad my designs have never caused a problem." As Candace ran her fingers through her short-cropped strawberry-blonde hair, I noticed the lattice of tattoos that decorated her right arm.

"Are those Celtic symbols?" I asked. "They remind me of the *Book of Kells*."

Candace beamed. "Exactly what I was going for. You have a good eye."

"Before I went back to school for my library science degree, I got an undergrad degree in art history," I said, offering her a warm smile.

"Which is one reason why I asked Amy to help me today," Karla said as she examined a rack of completed costumes. "She understands design better than most."

"That makes sense." Candace jumped off a work stool at the large cutting table and bounded over to join Karla. "See, this is one thing I wanted to run past you." She pulled an ice-blue leotard trimmed with diaphanous petals of white and silver silk off the rack. "This is for the lead in the *Will o' the Wisp* variation.

It was originally designed to flatter Ms. Fox, with her red hair and all. But now . . ."

Karla's sigh filled the crowded room. "You wonder who's dancing the part? So do I, honestly. And if it ends up being me, that won't fit."

"The color would still work, though," I said, circling around the cutting table to examine the garment. "Your hair has red highlights."

Candace held the decorated leotard up to Karla's chest. "It would suit you just as well. In a different size that works with your height, of course." She bit her lower lip, her face a study in concentration. "I guess the male partner is going to be someone different too? I mean, with Conner out of the picture and all."

"I'm afraid so. It looks like it will be Mr. Muir. Fortunately, you've built a few other costumes for him, so you already have all his measurements."

"Okay, I'll make those adjustments." Candace slipped the blue leotard back into the colorful explosion of costumes filling the rack. "I also wanted to check with you about the costumes for the corps in the final number. I know we wanted them to look like fairies or sprites that emerge out of the background, but now I'm worried they'll blend into the sets too much."

As Candace led Karla over to another rack of costumes, the bell attached to the door jangled.

"Hello there," Tamara said as she strolled into the room. "I had a little extra time before rehearsal, so I thought I'd pop in and try on the costume for my pas de deux."

Candace and Karla turned as one. "Oh hi, Tamara," Karla said. "Could you give us a minute? I wanted to finalize a few things with Candace before I have to meet Richard on stage."

"Sure, sure, no problem." Tamara strolled over to the cutting table and pulled out a stool. Straddling it with dynamic grace, she stretched out one of her long, limber legs. "Hi, Amy," she said, acknowledging me with a tilt of her head. "How are you doing? I'm sure it took a while to get over the shock of finding the body and all that."

I wasn't as shocked as you probably imagine, I thought, meeting her dark-eyed gaze. Of course, I doubted that Tamara was aware that this wasn't my first encounter with a murder victim. "I'm fine—thanks for asking."

"Such a disaster." Tamara shook her head. "And not just because of Meredith."

"It has created difficulties for the production," I said, studying her expression with interest. It was clear that Tamara wasn't broken-hearted over Meredith's death. "Of course, the murder is the real tragedy."

Tamara focused on something behind me. Perhaps she was watching Karla and Candace examine the costumes. *Or perhaps she's trying to dismiss any mention of Meredith, which is more intriguing.*

"Of course," she said.

"I'm sure you've probably danced together before, but did you know her well?" I asked.

"Not really." Tamara's gaze snapped back to me. "We were in competition for roles more often than not. Of course, she generally had the advantage, being more petite and having that lovely auburn hair."

And being white, I thought, deciding against voicing this aloud. Based on the scorn twisting Tamara's lips, I knew she was thinking the same thing. "I guess the height thing is still an issue, even today? I know it was a problem for Karla in the past."

Tamara shrugged. "There aren't that many tall male dancers, so it's hard to match up with a partner sometimes. That's why Dav and I end up dancing together a lot."

"Richard isn't super-tall—not like a basketball player or anything—but I guess he is on the upper end for dancers? I mean, he and Karla work well together."

"They're about the same height, at least when she's in flats. Which is fine. It's towering over your male partner that's a problem." Tamara straightened on the stool, squaring her shoulders. "I'm not as tall as Karla, but close. It has been a problem over the years, so I know what she's been up against."

Karla and Candace bustled forward, each clutching a bundle of costumes to their chests. "Would you excuse us for a moment?" Karla asked. "Candace and I want to check these on the stage. I mean, the lighting won't be the same, but we can get a sense of what they will look like."

"Do you need my help?" I asked, sliding off my stool.

"No, just wait here. We won't be long," Karla said as she and Candace exited the shop.

I didn't protest this request. This was my chance to speak to Tamara alone, and I didn't intend to waste it. "Speaking of the other day, I guess it was kind of a shock for you as well. I mean, you were rehearsing downstairs right before Meredith was killed."

Tamara leaned forward, resting her arms on the cutting table. "I didn't see anyone, if that's what you're asking," she said, lowering her lashes over her dark eyes. She scooped a scattering of straight pins into a tidy pile. "Like I told the deputies, Riley and Dav and I left the building right after our rehearsal. We didn't see anyone else enter or leave the basement. Or at least *I* didn't. I guess I can't really speak for the other two."

"That's what Riley told me when I . . . ran into him at Clarion yesterday," I said, deciding at the last second to avoid mentioning that we'd set up a meeting. "He said Meredith told you guys that she was going to rest in one of the dressing rooms, and you didn't bother to see if she was still downstairs before you left."

"He told you that?" Tamara stabbed one of the pins into the surface of the table. "Well, I suppose it's partially true."

"What do you mean?" I asked, opening my eyes in what I hoped looked like innocent surprise.

"Well, the part about not checking on Meredith is true. We just left, assuming she was fine. As far as seeing anyone around, I did spot that young man they arrested."

"Conner Vogler."

"Right. Anyway, before I left the area, I saw him lurking around the back entrance to the theater, near the loading dock. It looked like he was trying to get in, but of course that door is usually kept locked."

I swallowed an expression of dismay. "Riley didn't mention anything about that."

"Because he and Dav had already taken off at that point." Tamara's expression grew more guarded. "I was trying to decide what I wanted to do, you see. I'd brought something to eat, but I didn't know if I wanted to grab that from my car or go with the others. They were heading for some café nearby, or so they said."

"Really? That's funny, because Riley said he walked to the café by himself. He told me that Davonte must've gone somewhere else."

"Did he?" There was no mistaking the edge to Tamara's tone. "I don't remember it that way, but perhaps my memory got a little blurred after I heard what happened to Meredith."

"It's quite likely it did," I said, not believing this for a second. One of the two, Riley or Tamara, was lying. The question was—which one? "Anyway, you were saying something about noticing Conner outside the theater before you left?"

"Definitely saw him," Tamara said. "He couldn't get in the back door, of course, so he walked around the corner of the building. I didn't see where he went." She shrugged. "I assumed he entered through the lobby doors."

I hoped my smile didn't feel as forced as it felt. "And then you grabbed the food from your car or something?"

"No, actually I just . . . went for a walk. I wasn't terribly hungry and thought I could nibble on the energy bar I'd stuffed into my purse while I stretched my legs and got some fresh air." Tamara looked away, displaying her elegant profile while thwarting any hope I had of reading anything in her eyes. "I didn't return to the theater until the cops had already arrived," she added, turning her commanding dark-eyed gaze on me.

She certainly possessed enough self-confidence to persuade most people of her sincerity. But after hearing Riley's version of things, I wasn't convinced that she was telling the complete truth.

Of course, you weren't entirely sure that he was either, I reminded myself. "Oh, one more thing before I forget—did you happen to see an SUV parked at the far edge of the parking lot? I saw this guy sitting there when I ran out to grab my sweater before I headed downstairs. Just wondered if he was there earlier, when you guys left for your dinner break."

"What?" Before Tamara dropped her head to stare down at her clasped hands, I thought I caught a flash of concern in her eyes. But before I could press her for an answer, Karla and Candace hurried back into the room.

"Okay, we got that sorted out," Karla said, dropping her clutch of costumes on the cutting table. "Now I need to run or I'll be late for rehearsal." She cast Tamara a bright smile. "Thanks for waiting. I'm sure Candace can fit you now."

"Sure thing." Candace laid her pile of costumes on top of the others while Tamara stood and stepped away from the table. "I'll pull everything if you want to head into the changing room," she added, pointing toward a cubicle partitioned off by a heavy curtain.

Karla laid her hand on my shoulder. "Looks like I'll have to get your opinion on a few of the other costumes later, Amy. But we can still accomplish something. Why don't you come with me to the stage. Richard is leading the warm-up session, so I still have time to talk you through some of the backstage tasks I may need your help with, before I have to work with the university dancers."

"Sure thing," I said, slipping off the stool to follow Karla out of the room.

As I brushed past Tamara, she shot me a narrow-eyed look, making me wonder if my previous questions had aroused her suspicions.

Trotting to keep up with Karla's longer strides, I trailed her into the elevator. "How well do you know Tamara?" I asked as I punched the button for the auditorium level of the building.

Karla rolled her broad shoulders. "Not that well. As Meredith so succinctly said, I haven't danced with many professional companies. Not until Richard brought me in as a partner on some of his compositions, anyway." She looked down at me, her light-brown eyes bright with curiosity. "Why do you ask?"

"Oh, I just wondered if you knew of any instances of real animosity between her and Meredith, that's all."

"I don't, but that doesn't mean much." Karla stepped through the open elevator doors and into a hallway adjacent to the lobby. "I know they vied for roles in the past, but I really doubt that sort of competition would lead to murder."

I increased my pace to keep up with her as she strode toward the vestibule and the entrance to the stage. "You never know, but yeah it doesn't seem like that compelling a motive. Especially since they agreed to work together on this production. You'd think one or the other of them would've refused if there was a serious level of hatred raging between them."

Stopping short on the steps the led to the backstage area, Karla stared down at me, lines crinkling her brow. "You're helping the Sheriff's Department with the investigation again, aren't you?"

I lifted my hands. "Guilty."

"Does Rich know?" Karla's concerned tone reminded me that the sibling-style bond she shared with my husband would always drive her to consider his interests before anyone else's. Even mine.

"He's aware that I'm providing some research help."

Karla placed her hands on her hips. "I'm not sure questioning witnesses is exactly research."

"I'm not doing anything that will place me in danger," I said, automatically crossing my fingers. *Not knowingly, anyway,* I thought.

"Well, good. Because I know he worries about you when you start playing amateur sleuth." Karla dropped her hands to her sides. "As do I, if I'm honest. I suppose it's not really my business, but I'd hate to see you put yourself in a situation where you could get hurt. It *has* happened before."

"I know, and I swear I'm being cautious. Just chatting with a few people who might be more willing to talk to me than the authorities, that's all. And conducting a little research on the side. Nothing dangerous."

"Just be careful, okay?" Karla peered at her watch and sighed. "Do you mind waiting backstage for a minute? I need to check in with Rich before I can walk you through the tasks we may need your help with during performances."

"Sure, that's fine," I said, following her. While Karla marched out onto the stage, I absently pushed my way past a set of black drapes that partitioned the stage entrance from the working backstage area. Still mulling over the information I'd gleaned from Riley and Tamara, I bumped into the other person I'd been hoping to talk to, Davonte Julian.

"Well, hello," I said. "Sorry about not getting around to that dinner invite yet. Things have been a little . . ."

"Messed up? Yeah, I get that." He tugged down the short sleeves of his practice leotard The black material stretched tightly over his muscular upper arms. "At least you don't have to worry about whether or not to invite Meredith," he said, pressing his palms together. "Sorry, that was in bad taste."

"True, though." I stared up into his chiseled face. "You really didn't like her, did you?"

"Nope, and that was no secret. Like I told the deputies, she'd insulted me in several interviews she did when we were dancing together in a production of *Appalachian Spring*."

"The Martha Graham piece?"

"Right." Davonte rubbed his hand over his smooth scalp. "Meredith didn't mention me by name, but it was obvious from the context of her comments that she was referring to me. She openly praised the other principals in the cast while dismissing me with vague, but uninspired, words like 'adequate,' and 'workmanlike.' It didn't help my career any, I can tell you that."

"Why would she do that? I'm sure it wasn't actually anything to do with your dancing. I've seen you dance, and you're brilliant," I said.

"Thank you," Davonte said, looking slightly embarrassed. "It was probably because I corrected her a few times, during rehearsal, when she forgot a combination."

"That doesn't sound like Meredith. Messing up a routine, I mean. But I'll take your word for it."

"It wasn't typical for her, I admit. Which is why it took me by surprise and made me speak up without thinking things through." Davonte shrugged. "But that was right after she married Nate Broyhill. She seemed very distracted at the time. I think her head wasn't in the dancing, if you know what I mean."

"Was she happy with Broyhill?" Although I'd planned to ask Davonte about his movements after leaving rehearsal the day Meredith was murdered, this was too good a segue to pass up.

"Hard to say." Davonte rocked back on his heels. "She put on a good show—lots of PDA and all that. But I didn't entirely buy it."

"They certainly didn't last long," I said.

"Yeah, they folded about the same time as their dance company. I'm sure that was a factor. Had to be stressful. I think Broyhill had sunk a lot of his own money into the project, for one thing."

"You didn't happen to see him on Saturday, did you?" I asked, circling back to my original line of questioning.

"No—why would I?" Davonte appeared genuinely puzzled. "I know his mom has an estate or farm or something in this area, but I remember Nate once mentioning that he didn't visit often. Not much into the 'mud and manure,' I once heard him tell a reporter."

"It's just that . . . well, I saw someone who looked like him in an SUV parked in the lot behind the theater. And apparently, he admitted to the authorities that he was there. He was supposedly picking up a piece of family jewelry that Meredith had agreed to return."

"Really?" Davonte's eyes brightened, making me wonder if he was happy to hear that another person could be added to the suspect list.

Drawing suspicion away from him, I thought, my smile tightening. "That's what I've heard anyway. So I just wondered if you saw him or his vehicle when you left the theater after your rehearsal. I understand that you and Riley and Tamara all went outside at the same time."

Davonte frowned. "No, I didn't see Nate and didn't notice an SUV, although I admit I wasn't paying any attention to vehicles parked in the lot, so I might've missed that. And as for the three of us leaving together, that isn't exactly true. I was really hungry and took off before the other two. They were still loitering in the parking lot when I headed off to grab something for supper. Fast food, I'm afraid. Not the healthiest choice, but convenient, and I was starving."

"You didn't join Riley at the café, then? He mentioned eating there when I ran into him at Clarion the other day."

Davonte turned away, casting his face into shadow. "Never saw him again, or Tamara for that matter, until I returned to the theater. By that point, the cops had already arrived."

These last statements sounded both rushed and rehearsed, as if it was an answer Davonte had worked out in advance. *Something he'd carefully prepared before the authorities questioned him?* I wondered as I stared at his handsome profile. "Well, it looks like Karla's heading back this way, so I'd better join her. I'm planning to help out backstage, you see," I added with a brief smile.

"Okay. Good to talk with you again," Davonte said, striding onto the stage without looking at me.

I considered the differences in the stories I'd heard from Riley, Tamara, and Davonte. Each one had detailed a different sequence of events, especially in terms of who had left the area first and where they'd supposedly gone.

It could simply be faulty memory, I reminded myself as Karla joined me backstage.

Or it could be guilt.

Chapter Ten

O n Friday morning, I called Brad as soon as I got into work. Of course, I told him about the incident at the Clarion Library, prefacing that information with my doubts that it was anything aimed at me.

"Could've been just a thoughtless patron," I said before quickly switching the topic.

"It is interesting that the stories don't match," he said after I'd shared what I'd heard from Janelle, Riley, Tamara, and Davonte. "But it doesn't really provide anything that could clear Conner Vogler, I'm afraid."

"Maybe not, but I thought if you questioned those four again—separately, of course—it might be possible to find out which one of them is lying. Because one of them must be."

"It could be all of them, for that matter." Brad's thoughtful tone told me he intended to pursue this line of questioning. "Now I just have to convince the powers that be to allow me to talk to these particular witnesses."

"You don't have the authority to do that?"

"Like I've said, my department is simply supplying backup on this case. So no, I don't. But I'm sure if I offered to do a little follow-up, freeing some of the lead investigators' time, I'd be allowed to at least speak to the three people who were in the basement not long before Meredith Fox was killed. I can use the excuse that I've heard some chatter about them talking about the case, if nothing else."

"I hope you will. Even if they had nothing to do with Meredith's death, they may know something they aren't sharing, or aren't even aware of, for that matter. Like whether they actually noticed Nate Broyhill's SUV in the parking lot or saw him enter the building or anything like that." I stared across the room, into the shelving units that held interlibrary loan requests I still needed to process. "Well, I'd better get to work. I just wanted to let you know what I found out in case it can help the investigation in any way."

"And I appreciate your assistance," Brad said. "But I'll take it from here. That little incident in the Clarion Library has me concerned."

"I really think it was just some random patron. Anyway, I'm happy to do some online research on Nate Broyhill or any of the other people involved in the case," I told him, wanting to get his approval of this less dangerous method of investigation before we concluded our call.

I set to work processing the interlibrary loans as well as consulting my work computer for any additional requests. Samantha was covering the desk, which also allowed me time to compile some statistics for my monthly report to the town council.

Not glamorous, but necessary, I reminded myself. The town provided the bulk of the funding for the library. Although we did also have a few state and federal grants, and some money from the county, it was the town council that really held the purse strings. As director, it was imperative that I keep good records of all our receipts and expenditures to present to the council on a regular basis. I also liked to provide monthly statistics on library use. It was important to show how valuable the library and its services were to the community.

After lunch I took my place behind the desk. Since Samantha had completed her shift at one, and Sunny was scheduled to work on Saturday, I'd planned to cover the circulation desk as well as any reference requests until the library closed at five. But I hadn't anticipated how bored I'd be after an hour or so. It was an extremely slow day in the library, probably because of the nice weather, as well as many patrons starting their weekend trips early. Having completed all of my administrative tasks in the morning, and with the volunteers handling any shelving, I was left with little to do. Of course, there was always reading book reviews to earmark items for acquisition, but my curiosity drove me to undertake a little online sleuthing at the desk computer instead.

I dove back in where I'd left off the other evening, searching for articles or any other information on Nate Broyhill and Meredith's ill-fated dance company, Habitus. The results, while plentiful, were long on puff pieces about the two dancers but short on details about the collapse of the company. The only item of interest was an article from around four years ago that mentioned the art thefts at the Lance family's horse farm and included a quote from Meredith.

So the theft happened while they were still married, I realized, tapping the eraser end of a pencil against my chin. *That's an interesting coincidence.*

I stepped back and considered the possibility that Meredith had somehow been involved in stealing from her husband's family. Not that I suspected her of physically taking art from the Lance family home, but what if she'd arranged the theft, or at the least provided the thieves with easy access? The company her husband had founded to showcase her had been floundering, and a cut of the profits from an illegal sale could've seemed alluring.

And maybe her soon-to-be ex had only recently discovered her involvement and decided to confront her about it. *Now you're really reaching,* I warned myself, aware that my desire to remove Conner Vogler as the prime suspect was coloring my thoughts.

"Hello, Amy," said a deep male voice.

I looked up from the computer and into the piercing blue eyes of Kurt Kendrick. At seventy-four, the art dealer, with his craggy face and mane of white hair, looked every bit as fit as men half his age. In his youth, Kurt had been called "The Viking," and I thought it was still a fitting nickname for the tall, broad-shouldered man who'd made a fortune by mysterious and dubious means. Having shed a darker past, he now owned a few prestigious art galleries along with a townhouse in Georgetown and a gorgeous historic estate located just outside of Taylorsford.

Kurt was related, in a way, to my husband's family, having been the foster son of Richard's great-uncle Paul Dassin. He was also connected to my aunt Lydia through his close friendship with her late husband, Andrew Talbot. These intertwining threads had woven him into the lives of both our families. Absent for decades, over the past few years he'd grown closer to us. He'd often used his wealth and his ties to various shady enterprises and unscrupulous people, as well as to law enforcement, to help and protect me and my extended family.

Which didn't mean I entirely trusted him. "Hi, what brings you into the library today?" I brushed back a straggling lock of hair and straightened to my full height, which still left me standing a foot shorter than Kurt.

"I was in town and thought I'd stop by and say hello since I haven't seen you in some time. My fault, of course. Too much traveling this spring," Kurt said.

"You're here for the weekend?" I asked. Kurt often spent weekends at his estate, Highview, while living in Georgetown during the week. Of course, as he'd mentioned, he also spent a great deal of time traveling the world for business.

"Actually, I'll be in Taylorsford for a week or so. I need a little downtime after all my recent art acquisition jaunts." Kurt smiled, displaying his large, white teeth. "Good for business but a little hard on the bones of an old man."

I made a dismissive noise. "As if you are incapacitated in any way."

"Oh, don't be fooled—time takes a toll on us all, my dear. Anyway, I also wanted to see how you were doing after that unfortunate incident at the theater." Kurt's intense gaze swept over me.

"The murder, you mean," I said.

"Exactly." Kurt's eyes narrowed. "I've seen Meredith Fox dance many times. It's a shame to lose such a talent. Not to mention the havoc it has undoubtedly unleashed on Richard's upcoming production."

"It has, but they've been allowed to return to the theater, so rehearsals are finally back on track." I frowned. "Now the main issue is that all of Meredith's parts have to be danced by others. Not to mention, one of the primary suspects is a young man who was also dancing at least one primary role."

"Ah yes, Conner Vogler. Pity about that as well. I saw him perform in a summer institute last year and thought he was a promising talent." Kurt brushed back the thick fall of hair draping his broad brow. "What makes me think that you aren't convinced of his guilt despite discovering him standing over the body?"

I shrugged. "Maybe it's just wishful thinking. Richard was hoping to mentor Conner, you see. He even thought he might recruit the boy into his university studio. And, I don't know— he struck me as such a quiet, gentle young man. I guess I just can't see him as a killer."

Kurt raised his bushy white eyebrows. "You should know better than anyone that it isn't always easy to tell a murderer from an ordinary person."

"True. Hold on—I need to take care of this patron," I said as one of our regulars, Mrs. Dinterman, bustled toward the desk.

Kurt stepped aside and offered a cheerful greeting to the elderly woman, who simply glared up at him, suspicion glinting in her dark eyes.

"You're that fellow who throws all those elaborate parties with artsy sorts, aren't you?" she said as I finished checking out her stack of books.

"Guilty as charged." Kurt's eyes twinkled as he offered Mrs. Dinterman one of his charming smiles. "I'd be happy to invite you next time, if you'd like."

When Mrs. Dinterman tossed her head, her dyed-black helmet of hair never moved. "As if I'd fit in with your froufrou crowd. No thanks—I prefer my church socials."

"The offer still stands if you ever change your mind. Always delighted to entertain the ladies." Kurt sketched a slight bow.

Mrs. Dinterman sniffed before collecting her books. She wished me a good day and muttered something less enthusiastic to Kurt as she swept past him.

"A real charmer," Kurt said as she exited through the main doors.

"She's probably heard all the salacious stories about you. You know how rumors spread in a small town like Taylorsford," I replied.

"Indeed. Which is actually how I heard about you discovering Meredith Fox's body." Kurt stepped closer, resting his palms on the top of the circulation desk. "Since you didn't bother to inform me directly."

"Was I supposed to? I wasn't aware that I had to report my activities to you."

Kurt's smile tightened. "Only the dangerous ones, which includes finding murder victims."

"I'll try to remember that next time," I said, meeting his fierce gaze with a lift of my chin. "Although, to be honest, I'm not sure what help you could've offered in this instance."

Kurt shrugged. "I could've shared a few facts that might interest you as well as the authorities. Concerning Meredith Fox and her ex-husband, I mean."

"I know she was married to Nathaniel Broyhill. Richard told me that," I said. "Which is a weird coincidence since I saw Nate in the parking lot of the theater around the time Meredith was killed."

"I've heard something about that." Kurt's expression told me this was the real reason he'd stopped by to check on me.

"From your little birds?" I wrinkled my nose. Kurt ran a network of informal spies who provided information on anything and everything affecting his businesses or his friends. "You must know Nate Broyhill, even if only casually, since you follow the arts and contribute money to help support several dance companies."

"Very casually, but yes, I've met him at a few galas." Kurt met my inquisitive gaze with a smile. "I'm actually better acquainted with his mother and half brother."

"You know Glenda and Oliver Lance?" I asked before the realization hit me. "Oh right, they collect art, or have in the past."

"I've brokered some deals for them, as well as sold them a few select pieces."

"Which means you must be aware of the theft that occurred at their horse farm a few years back." I drummed my fingers against the desk. "Could it have been an inside job?"

Kurt looked me up and down. "You're thinking Meredith Fox had something to do with the robbery, and Broyhill or his family decided to off her because of said involvement."

This was so close to my earlier musings that heat prickled the back of my neck. "It's one possible theory."

"Hmm, I don't know. I can't quite see Meredith Fox getting involved in such a scheme. She was a haughty little minx, but hardly the type to dirty her hands with a robbery."

I clasped my hands together on the desktop. "Not even to raise money for her husband's failing dance company, the one that was supposed to make her an international star?"

"You mean Habitus? Sorry, still can't picture it. I can imagine Meredith schmoozing some rich old codger"—Kurt flashed a toothy grin—"because she tried it with me, to no avail. I knew better than to invest in that lost cause. But I don't believe she'd orchestrate the theft of artworks from her husband's family."

Something in his tone made me realize what I'd been missing. "Wait—you're sure she didn't, right? Because you know who did."

Kurt spread wide his hands. "I can neither confirm nor deny that. I simply have rather strong suspicions."

"You should share those with Hugh Chen, then. He'd love a new lead in that case. Fred Nash too."

Kurt crossed his arms over his broad chest. "Should I? Even if it wouldn't be in my best interest?"

"Don't tell me you had something to do with that theft," I said, tightening my hands.

"Of course not. I don't steal art. Never have, despite all my other indiscretions. However, some of my business connections may be a little less honorable."

"I'm sure." I looked up into his weathered but still attractive face. "Just like I'm certain there are some people you wouldn't want to betray, for fear of retaliation if nothing else."

"And not simply to protect myself." Kurt dropped his arms to his sides. "I have others I must look out for now, you know."

"If you mean me or my family, or Richard's family, I think all of us"—I paused, thinking of Richard's parents—"well, most of us anyway, would prefer that you share what you know with the proper authorities."

"Perhaps I will, one day." Kurt studied me for a moment. "I've heard a rumor that you are helping the Sheriff's Department with this murder. Is that true?"

"Just a little research." I looked down at my hands, avoiding his stare. "And maybe talking informally with a few people involved in the case."

"Would that include Glenda Lance or her sons? Because I might be able to help with that."

I immediately looked up at him. "Maybe Nate, since I saw him outside the theater. He's still the ex, and they can always have a motive. As for his family—from what you've said, it doesn't sound like Meredith was involved in the art theft, so there's no reason for Nate's mom or half brother to have wished her harm."

"But are you sure *they* know she wasn't involved?" Kurt tapped his temple with one finger. "I know the truth, but that doesn't mean that either Glenda or Oliver—or Nate, for that matter—do. They may still harbor those suspicions, and if they realized she was in Smithsburg and decided to confront her . . ."

"Bringing a knife along for good measure? Granted, it looked like it could fold up, but it had a wicked blade, so it wasn't simply a little pocketknife just anyone would carry around." I frowned, realizing I hadn't properly thought through this aspect of the case. "That's something I haven't considered, to be honest. If the killer brought a knife along, even one that could be carried in a pocket, it looks like premeditated murder, not an argument that got out of hand."

Kurt nodded. "True, which makes me wonder how the authorities plan to account for that in charging young Mr. Vogler. Why would the boy have brought a knife to the theater? It doesn't make a lot of sense to me."

I snapped my fingers. "Exactly! Especially if they're going with the idea that Conner flew off the handle after Meredith berated him in front of Richard and Karla and the other dancers. Surely they can see how incongruous that is. If he planned to kill her all along and brought a knife for that purpose, why would he have decided to blithely participate in a rehearsal beforehand?"

"It isn't logical." Kurt tipped his head and examined my face for a moment. "Now you have me intrigued. What would you say to accompanying me on a little visit to the Lance farm? I can call Oliver about some artwork that I'd like to show him, and if he plans to be home, we could drive out to the farm tomorrow. I'm not certain that Glenda will be there, but talking to Oliver might still give insight into their involvement, or lack thereof, in Meredith's death."

"That would be great," I said. "Even if it has to be another day, I'd still be interested, although tomorrow would be great, as I'm off work."

"And I imagine Richard will be in rehearsals all day?" Kurt smiled. "I thought you'd rather he not know about this little expedition."

"That's not true. I'll tell him," I said defensively. "We don't have secrets."

"My dear, don't fool yourself—everyone has secrets," Kurt said.

Chapter Eleven

Kurt texted me later that evening. He'd been able to arrange a meeting with Oliver Lance the next day, along with Glenda, who was staying at the farm for the weekend. As soon as Richard got home, I shared these plans with him. He wasn't thrilled with the idea of me continuing to question people who had a connection to Meredith or her possible killer, but agreed that there was little danger as long as Kurt was acting as my escort.

"I know he won't allow you to come to any harm," Richard told me as we'd snuggled together on the sofa, a cat in each of our laps. "If only because he wouldn't want to face the combined ire of Lydia, Sunny, and me if you were to be placed in danger."

"That definitely would provide motivation to be careful," I agreed with a grin.

So late Saturday morning, after Richard had left for rehearsals, I found myself in Kurt's luxurious Jaguar sedan, speeding toward Smithsburg.

"Can you give me any pointers on interacting with Glenda Lance or her son?" I asked as he turned off onto a side road outside of the town. "Are they prickly or friendly or what?"

Kurt grinned. "It depends on which one. Glenda is usually very gracious, although I've heard she can be ruthless if crossed. I'd call her a hothouse orchid, while Oliver fits better into the cactus family."

"Oh dear, I guess I have to watch my words around him then. Let's see, I'm assuming Glenda is about Aunt Lydia's age but that Oliver is somewhat younger than Nate."

"Early thirties, I believe." Kurt swept his right arm in front of me, pointing toward my passenger side window. "This is where their estate starts. As you can tell, it's quite a spread."

I stared out at an expanse of rolling green meadows enclosed by white board fences. The fields stretched from the road to a row of tall oaks, maples, and pines. "I suppose the house and barn are behind the trees?"

"Yes, and it's *barns*—plural. This is big operation. They board animals and provide riding lessons along with training their own jumpers and dressage horses," Kurt said. "A very expensive enterprise, as you can imagine."

"Oliver is an equestrian, right?"

"A very good one. He's been an alternate for the US Olympic team in the past. He's also in charge of managing the farm, the breeding program, the training, and the riding school."

"He sounds a bit formidable," I said, biting my lower lip.

"Don't worry. Unlike some of his beasts, he doesn't bite." Kurt cast me an amused sidelong glance. "As a matter of fact, he might try to flirt with you. He likes his ladies short and curvy, from what I've seen."

"Now you tell me," I said, looking down at my pink cotton blouse and denim shorts. "I would've dressed up a little if I'd known I could use my feminine wiles to extract more information out of him."

Kurt laughed. "Do you really think you have any of those, my dear? Don't you know your charm lies in the fact that you're so direct and lacking in what some would call feminine guile?"

I made a face at him before switching my gaze back to the manicured emerald fields and gleaming white fences that seemed to stretch for miles. In one field, a cluster of tall, leggy horses stood, nose to tail, under a canopy of trees. "Why are their heads covered with those hoods?"

"It's to keep the flies out of their eyes, I believe. Honestly, I'm no expert on horses. I don't even bet on them." Kurt flashed me a grin. "But then, I've never been much of a gambler."

"Too controlling for that," I murmured.

"What?" Kurt shot me a questioning look, but I just shook my head.

"Wow, this is quite an entrance," I said as Kurt turned onto a paved road lined with a colonnade of trees. On either side of a metal gate decorated with cutouts of prancing horses, curved stacked stone walls displayed hand-painted wooden signs identifying the estate as "Blue Haven Farm." I snorted. "A little disingenuous to call this a farm. It's about as close to farms like Sunny's grandparents' place as I am to a swimsuit model."

"It's one of those things wealthy people do—play down the grandeur of things by calling them by unobtrusive names." Kurt leaned out of his window to press a button on the gate intercom. After the system crackled to life and he gave his name, the metal gate swung open, allowing us to drive through.

I peeked over my shoulder, where two rectangular crates lay on a blanket spread across the back seat. "I see you brought alibis for this visit. Paintings?"

"For your information, I'm not being entirely duplicitous by carting those along. I wouldn't mind making a sale."

"Two horses with one lasso?" I asked, with a smile.

"Something like that. I've sold the family a few pieces in the past, so I know their tastes." Kurt used one hand to brush his thick white hair back from his temple. "One word of caution," he added as we passed the screen of trees, and several white-painted barns and dirt paddocks came into view. "You might not want to mention Habitus around Glenda or Oliver. It's my understanding that Glenda, following Oliver's advice, refused to help Nate bankroll that project, which caused some bad blood between the siblings."

"I bet," I said, whistling as I caught sight of what had to be the main house. "It's even bigger than your place."

The house, or mansion as I felt it should properly be called, was built of stone, although this was more modern-looking stacked stone rather than the fieldstone used to build Highview. Like Kurt's home, there was a taller, three-story central section, with a multitude of tall windows framed by shutters, and two shorter wings. But in contrast to Highview's air of well-worn elegance, this house had a sharp-edged, perfectly maintained quality that exuded wealth more than comfort.

"It's not nearly as old as mine, though," Kurt said. "A modern reproduction. The original house burned to the ground back in the sixties. It was big news at the time, and one of the reasons Kyle Lance was able to snatch up this property for much less than it was worth." Kurt pulled the Jag into a paved parking lot next to a large barn with a wide, open corridor separating rows of horse stalls. "I'm going to park here and walk to the house." He motioned toward the barn. "I just noticed Oliver leading his horse toward the barn. Maybe we can split up and question them separately."

"And you think I'll have more luck with Oliver while you use your charm on Glenda," I said, unbuckling my seat belt.

"That's the plan." Kurt cast me a smile. "Might as well take advantage of our individual assets."

"Very clever," I said dryly.

Kurt got out of the car and grabbed the two wooden crates from the back seat. "I'll bring Glenda back here if I can, just so you can meet her," he said before loping toward the house.

As I climbed out of the Jag, the sweet scent of hay, mingled with the acrid odor of manure, assaulted my nostrils. Inside the barn, hooves stamped against straw bedding, and a few nickers and snorts filled the air.

I strolled into the expansive center aisle. The jangle of halters was followed by two or three horses poking their heads over the iron metalwork decorating the top of the heavy wooden stall doors. "Looking for a treat, are you?" I said, staying far away from any equine noses, or teeth. "Sorry, I didn't bring anything."

The horses swiveled their heads toward the far end of the open barn aisle, and nickered. Their attention, like mine, was focused on the man leading in a handsome dappled gray.

The man and his mount created an elegant tableau. He wore tan jodhpurs tucked into gleaming mahogany leather boots and a black jacket over a crisp white shirt. His short hair, mostly covered by his hardhat, appeared to be a caramel brown, and his eyes were almost as dark as his mount's, who was a tall, lanky creature with powerful hindquarters.

A jumper, I bet, I thought as the pair halted a few feet in front of me.

"Well, hello. Are you here for a lesson? I didn't think there was anything on the books for today." The man, who I assumed was Oliver Lance, looked me up and down with an expression of mingled surprise and interest.

"No, I just accompanied Mr. Kendrick today and . . ." My thoughts whirled as I tried to come up with a reason why I hadn't followed him to the house. "Well, I just wanted to see the horses," I said, hoping my words didn't sound as lame to Oliver as they did to me.

"Good, because you certainly aren't dressed properly for riding," he said, smiling. "Although you look quite lovely, all the same."

Remembering Kurt's words about Oliver's preferences, I thrust out my hand. "I'm Amy Muir, by the way. Kurt is a friend. Well, almost family, since he was the foster son of my husband's great-uncle."

"Good lord, Kendrick has family? I thought he must've sprung, fully formed like the Spartoi, from the earth." Oliver's smile broadened. "I'm Oliver Lance, but you probably guessed that. Sorry if I don't shake your hand, but I need to tie off this fellow first."

"No problem," I said, dropping my hand and taking a step back as the gray stomped a hoof against the floor. Oliver chided him gently before grabbing a lead attached to a ring on a wooden pillar. As he clipped the lead to the leather bridle, I noticed an old black landline telephone mounted on the side of the pillar. *For calling the house or the vet, I guess,* I thought, as I admired the rather intimidating horse. "What's his name?"

"Bucephalus, although we call him Ceph most of the time." As the horse bumped Oliver's shoulder with his nose, Oliver pushed his head away. Turning to me, and undoubtedly catching my amused expression, he added, "I obviously had a classical education."

"Obviously." As Oliver gave me a closer examination, I had to admit that the admiration in his eyes was an ego boost. *But you can't allow that to cloud your judgment.*

Oliver pulled off his hat and set it on a wooden shelf that held various brushes and other implements I assumed were needed for tending to horses. "Amy Muir? That name sounds familiar, but I can't place it."

"Well, I'm the library director in Taylorsford, but I wouldn't expect you to know that. I bet you've probably heard of my husband, Richard, though," I replied. "He's a rather well-known contemporary dancer and choreographer, and there've been several articles about him in the local papers, as well as TV interviews and that sort of thing."

"Oh, right. He would be one of Nate's colleagues. I guess I've heard his name mentioned, or even seen him dance at some point or the other." Oliver's smile had faded slightly, and I couldn't help but wonder if it was due to the fact that my marital status had finally sunk in. "Sorry, I should clarify things. I'm

Nathaniel Broyhill's younger brother. Well, half brother," he added, turning back to the shelf. "But we never quibble about that."

"Oh wow, Kurt said something about Nate Broyhill, but I didn't really get the connection until now," I said, playing dumb so Oliver wouldn't realize how much research I'd already done on his family. "I've heard of your brother, although I haven't actually met him. But of course, since he was such a famous dancer, my husband knows him."

"Wait, Richard Muir?" Oliver paused his rhythmic brushing, earning a nicker from Bucephalus. "Wasn't Meredith engaged to him before she married Nate?"

"That's right," I said. "Don't worry—it doesn't bother me. I knew all about it from the beginning. You see, when Richard and I met, he'd just moved to Taylorsford to take over his late great-uncle's house and make a new start of things. I happened to live next door with my aunt, Lydia Talbot—"

"You're related to Lydia Talbot?" Oliver cast me another questioning glance. "Wasn't she the wife of that painter, Andrew Talbot? I believe Kendrick sold us one of his landscapes a while back."

"She was. Of course, Andrew passed away years ago. Before I was even born, actually." I decided this was as good of a segue as any other. "I hope my uncle's painting wasn't one of those you lost in the robbery," I said.

Oliver's brown eyes narrowed. "You've heard about that?"

"I read about it in the paper," I said, not bothering to clarify that I'd pulled the article off our digital newspaper archives, not actually followed the story when it occurred.

"Fortunately, your uncle's painting was not one of the pieces taken," Oliver said.

"Did you ever get any of the artwork back?" From my research, I knew the answer to this question, but thought it might offer a way to discover whether Oliver actually suspected Meredith of having any involvement in the theft.

Oliver slid his hand down the silken, arched neck of his horse. "Not a single piece. And no one was ever arrested either. To be honest, I think the local authorities bungled the investigation." He placed the brush back on the shelf and picked up a large-toothed metal comb. "It was a total disaster, from our point of view. The authorities decided early on that it was a professional job, done by outsiders, and didn't want to consider any alternative theories."

"Such as?" I asked.

Oliver's shoulders visibly tensed. "Oh, I just thought that perhaps the thieves had a connection to someone on our staff, or even . . . Well, just someone on the inside, you know?" He pulled the comb through Bucephalus's mane. "But the good thing is, no one was hurt. That was one benefit of having a robbery committed by professional thieves, I suppose."

I examined his profile, looking for any signs of anxiety, but found none. "True, things can be replaced, but not people. Meredith's unfortunate death is certainly proof of that. Murder is a much worse fate than being robbed."

Oliver tugged a knot out of Bucephalus's silver mane, causing the horse to sidestep. Deftly avoiding getting a hoof planted on his boot, Oliver moved back, keeping his attention focused on his horse. "Yes, such a shame. It's common knowledge that neither my mom nor I were fond of the woman, but I wouldn't wish that end on anyone."

"She and your brother weren't married long," I said, keeping my tone casual despite my interest in his response.

"Could've predicted that." Oliver returned the comb to the shelf and turned to face me. "Honestly, Meredith was difficult, and my brother isn't much better, so the two of them together . . ." He shrugged. "According to Nate, Meredith could be rude to the point of ugliness to other dancers, so I'm not surprised she came to a violent end at the hands of one of them."

"She did humiliate the young man who was found standing over the body," I said, "but my husband and I aren't convinced he's actually the murderer."

Oliver narrowed his eyes. "Why not?"

"He just doesn't seem like the type of person to stab someone to death."

"Is there a type?" Oliver plucked a strand of silver horse hair off his jacket.

"I suppose there really isn't," I said, meeting his gaze with a lift of my chin. "But I can't help but wonder how someone so young was able to act so calmly beforehand. He participated in a rehearsal prior to the murder and showed no signs that he was conspiring to kill someone later, yet he had to have planned the murder since he used a knife." I lifted my hands. "Not that many actual knives lying about theater dressing rooms. Props, yes. Real weapons, not so much."

"I heard it was a pocketknife, and a lot of people do carry those," Oliver said.

"Yes, but this wasn't your typical little pocketknife. It had a pretty serious blade. I doubt most people would carry something like that around on a daily basis."

"You never know. It's an old building, right? And recently renovated." Oliver crossed his arms over his chest. "A workman could've left a knife lying around."

"I suppose," I said. "Anyway, it's a tragedy, however you look at it. Even if Meredith wasn't always the nicest person—and trust me, I've experienced her disdain—she didn't deserve to die. I mean, she wasn't even thirty-five."

"Yes, it is quite sad," said a clear female voice behind me.

I turned to face Kurt, clutching one of his painting crates, and an older woman with a silver bob grazing her sharp jawline. Tall and lean, like Oliver, she was wearing tailored black slacks and a short-sleeved ivory cotton sweater.

"Mom, this is Amy Muir. Library director in Taylorsford and wife of the dancer Richard Muir, whom you've undoubtedly heard mentioned once or twice by Nate," Oliver said. "Amy, this is my mother, Glenda Lance."

"Hello." Glenda extended her hand. "Kurt mentioned that he'd brought you along. I hope Oliver has shown you the horses, since that's why you wanted to visit the stables."

As I clasped her hand, I felt calluses under my fingers. Glenda Lance might be rich, but it seemed she did some physical labor, perhaps with the horses or maybe in the extensive gardens I'd spied near the main house. "Hi, nice to meet you," I replied. "And Oliver has been very gracious, especially since I just appeared out of nowhere, unannounced."

Glenda looked me over, arching her thin eyebrows. Like her son, she had deep brown eyes and a face composed of sharp angles, with hollows beneath her high cheekbones. "That's good. Of course, Kurt should have mentioned that he was bringing a guest, but you know how it is when you get older and forgetful . . ."

I couldn't halt my burst of laughter, earning me a sardonic smile from Kurt.

"It was a last-minute thing," he said, no rancor tainting his tone. "I thought Amy would enjoy seeing your place, and she was rather at loose ends, with Richard tied up in rehearsals all day." Kurt shifted the enclosed painting from one arm to the other. "We're actually family, you see. Richard's great-uncle Paul Dassin was my foster father."

"What a small world," Glenda murmured, flashing a bright smile. "At any rate, it is nice to meet you, Amy. You'll have to come back and have dinner with us sometime. With your husband, of course," she added with a glance at Oliver.

She suspects him of checking me out, I thought, biting my lower lip to hide a smile. *I guess, like Kurt, she knows his preferences.* "That would be great, but of course it will have to wait until after Richard's latest production closes. The one Meredith was working on," I added, interested to see Glenda's reaction.

"Of course. That's why she was back in the area." Glenda's smile faded. "It was generous of your husband to give her a job after she basically ran out on their engagement."

"Oh, that was several years ago. It doesn't bother him anymore."

"Besides, he married Amy instead," Kurt said. "Which was a much better choice, in my opinion."

"Definitely an upgrade." Oliver looked away when his mother shot him a sharp look.

I hoped my cheeks weren't as red as I feared. "It worked out for the best. Anyway, we certainly didn't hold a grudge against Meredith."

"Wish I could say the same, but the way she treated Nate . . ." Glenda's lips thinned. "That's all in the past, but I'm not surprised that someone wanted her dead. She was quite oblivious to the feelings of others, I'm afraid. And she had a rather fast and loose relationship with honesty."

I gazed from Glenda to Oliver. Both of their faces had gone still as stone. *Not surprising if they suspected Meredith of engineering that art theft,* I thought. I laid a hand on Kurt's arm. "Are you ready to leave? I should get back. I promised Aunt Lydia I'd help her test out a new pie recipe this afternoon."

Kurt looked down at me, his blue eyes sparkling with repressed amusement. "Of course, dear. My business here is done. Thank you again," he added, focusing on Glenda.

"I should be the one thanking you," Glenda said, her expression lightening. "I've always wanted to own a Hockney."

"Too bad the de Chirico didn't suit, but of course you must love something to display it in your home," Kurt said, his fingers tightening on the edge of the wooden crate he held against his chest.

Glenda swept one hand through the air. "I'm no expert—that was Kyle's department. But I know what I like."

"Ah yes, always good to know that." Kurt's tone was pleasant, but I spied the sardonic gleam in his eyes. "All right, Amy, let's head out."

"Nice to meet you both," I told Glenda and Oliver as I turned to head for the car.

I waited until we'd pulled away from barn and were traveling toward the end of the long driveway before I posed my question. "So what did you find out?"

"Not much, I'm afraid," Kurt said, keeping his eyes on the road. "The only thing of importance was confirmation that Glenda did suspect Meredith of somehow being involved in the art theft. She suggested that perhaps it was to raise funds for Nate's failing dance company, which neither she nor Oliver were willing to bail out again."

"Again? Had they done so before?"

"Apparently. I guess they decided not to throw more money into that sinking ship, so—according to Glenda—perhaps Meredith was looking for another way to raise funds."

I leaned back against the buttery leather passenger seat. "Oliver didn't say anything that blatant, but I got the impression he felt the same."

"So, there's a motive or two." Kurt cast me a sidelong glance. "If one or the other of them decided to confront her, perhaps things simply got out of hand."

"Or maybe Nate did it for them, having come to the same conclusion about Meredith's involvement in the theft. He was the one at the theater, supposedly planning to meet Meredith to reclaim a piece of family jewelry, so he's the more likely suspect.

Although"—I tapped the door handle as another thought occurred to me—"there was someone in a metallic-blue car that Nate spoke to in the parking lot. It was an older model sedan, but one that's pretty common on the road today, so not really easy to trace. Nate said the driver was just a stranger, asking for directions. The authorities seem to believe him, but I'm not so sure. Which means I still think Nate tops the suspect list."

"Perhaps. But if that was the case, the question would still be, did Glenda and Oliver know what he was up to?"

"And would they flip on him to save their own skins?" I stared out the window, watching the last of Blue Haven Farm's fields disappear from view. "It's a solid line of questioning for Brad and his team, at the very least."

"Indeed," Kurt said, flashing a smile. "A good day's work, then. One sale and two more names for your list."

"It's not *my* list. I'm not in charge of the investigation."

"Could've fooled me," Kurt said.

Chapter Twelve

On a whim, I decided to accompany Aunt Lydia on a trip to the garden center on Sunday afternoon.

"This could be disastrous," Richard said when I told him my plans over breakfast.

Clutching a bottle of maple syrup, I paused by his chair. "What do you mean? I'm unlikely to run into any of our possible suspects at the nursery."

"Maybe not, but I just know what happens when you're let loose among plants or books, especially if I'm not around to monitor your spending." Richard grinned as he held out his hand. "Syrup?"

"I should pour it over your head," I said, plopping the bottle down beside his plate.

Richard looked up at me from under the fringe of his dark lashes. "I'll just take it on the pancakes, thanks."

"Monitor my spending, my foot," I muttered, as I sat down across the table from him. "How about I monitor you in a record store, huh? All those CDs you have to collect, even though you could get the same stuff through streaming."

"It's for work." Richard gave me a wink before popping a forkful of pancake into his mouth.

"Sure, sure." I focused on cutting up my own pancakes before adding, "I just thought it would be nice to spend some quality time with Aunt Lydia. We don't see as much of each other these days, even though we are next-door neighbors."

"All joking aside, that is a good idea. Especially since you know where I'll be." Richard rolled his eyes.

"Rehearsing, rehearsing, and more rehearsing," I said, punctuating this by stabbing another section of cut-up pancakes with my fork.

"As always. At least we'll finish at eight tonight, so I can actually spend a little time with you this evening." After wiping his mouth with a napkin, Richard added, "I mean, if we're speaking about living side by side and still not seeing each other much, I'm the guilty party right now." He stretched his arm across the table to reach for my free hand. "Thanks for putting up with everything associated with this production, sweetheart."

"It's fine," I said, clasping his fingers. "I know how much it means to you. And how much it's going to help Karla's studio as well the local school dance programs." I squeezed his fingers before releasing my grip. "All good causes."

Richard sat back, looking me over with a smile. "And a great foundation for some of the work Karla and I want to do in the future. If we can build up the dance programs in local schools and studios, as well as at Clarion, maybe we can actually establish our own summer dance festival. Something that gives young dancers—"

"A leg up?" I interjected, earning another grin from my husband. "Yeah, I know that's the dream. Maybe even your own company?"

"Hmm, are you reading my mind now?" Richard scooted back his chair and rose to his feet. "I'll clean up. You made breakfast, after all."

"Thanks." I stood up as well, carefully avoiding Fosse, who'd parked himself in a sunny spot behind my chair. "And it doesn't take a psychic to figure out that you and Karla would love to start a dance company, especially if it included a training program for young dancers."

"That's the dream," Richard said, moving close enough to encircle my waist with his arms. "I'd say it was just a fantasy, but I've learned that some dreams do come true."

"Such as?" I titled my chin to look up at him.

"Such as finding lasting love," he said before kissing me.

* * *

As I drove to the garden center, which was located just outside of town, Aunt Lydia chatted about Hugh's latest discovery of a fake Manet in a Washington, DC, art gallery, before asking about Kurt.

"I saw him recently," I said, looking over at her. "Why do you ask?"

"Because Zelda saw you speeding out of town with him in his car yesterday. She was curious about where you two were headed." Aunt Lydia pulled into the nursery's gravel lot, careful to avoid parking too close to the numerous oversized trucks.

"Can't see a thing when I back out if I'm caught between two of those monolithic things."

I unbuckled my seat belt. "Zelda's curious about everything. And all I was doing was accompanying Kurt on a visit to a couple of his clients. He was hoping to sell a few pieces, and I was hoping . . ." I looked away as my aunt fixed me with one of her trademark piercing looks. "We visited Blue Haven Farm, if you must know. I thought talking to Glenda and Oliver Lance might offer some insights into the Meredith Fox murder."

"So Kurt is aiding and abetting your snooping again?" Aunt Lydia sighed as she joined me outside of the vehicle. "It seems you two really are becoming partners in crime."

"It's not like that," I said as I followed Aunt Lydia into the garden center. "He's truly curious about the case and wants to help. Besides, while *he* may still commit a few crimes, *I* only want to solve them."

"But sometimes you cross the line, Amy. In terms of putting yourself at risk, I mean." My aunt paused beside a display of annuals. The slatted wood table was filled with black plastic plant trays overflowing with vibrant flowers. She picked up a cascading violet-and-white petunia. "I've always wanted to do flower boxes, like Zelda's, but I'm afraid there's not enough sun on my porch."

It was obvious that Aunt Lydia had decided to change the subject, which suited me. "You do have that big maple in the front yard," I said. "Maybe some shade-loving flowers would work, like certain types of impatiens or coleus. Or begonias."

"It's just more to water, though." Aunt Lydia set the petunia back into its tray. "I have enough trouble keeping up with the ferns and the backyard garden."

"I should help more," I said, more to myself than my aunt, who shook her head.

"You have enough to do with your own flower and vegetable beds, not to mention working full-time, plus helping Richard with his various projects. Don't worry, I'm not upset about you not having as much time these days. Besides, you and Richard both assist me with the more strenuous chores, and Hugh is always happy to take care of a few things around the house." Aunt Lydia's lips twitched. "He's just not one for working in the yard or garden. A city boy at heart, I'm afraid."

"Which is fine, considering all his other good qualities," I said.

"Which is fine," my aunt reiterated. She motioned toward another section of the nursery. "Look, it's Emily Moore. Let's say hello."

Following the direction of her gaze, I caught sight of an older woman, whose square-jawed face was framed by a sleek brown bob streaked with a few silver threads, and whose brown eyes were encircled by large frames that gave her face an owlish expression. As she waved at us from behind a collection of potted ferns, I was once again struck by the incongruity of Emily Moore's appearance, given her decidedly bohemian background. Dressed simply in worn jeans and a plain white blouse, she blended in with other shoppers. No one would have pegged her as a former member of Andy Warhol's Factory or imagined that her first fame had come from a collection of psychedelic-inspired poetry.

"What a lovely coincidence," Emily said as we approached. "I haven't seen either of you in ages."

I clasped her outstretched hand for a moment. "No worries. I know how busy you've been, since Richard told me you were overseeing a summer writing camp at Clarion. I'm sure that's quite a challenge."

"Too true. It's difficult for a woman over seventy to keep up with high school students." Emily batted away an inquisitive, iridescent dragonfly. "But I have great instructors leading the classes, and of course I love seeing young people so enthused about writing."

"I'm sure," Aunt Lydia said. "It's nice that the university offers programs like that."

"It's actually the first year for any sort of writing camp. I've been lobbying the English department to do something for a while, so it's great to see my badgering produce some results." Emily strolled over to an adjacent table, which held a collection of begonias in shades ranging from salmon to purest white. "Maybe next year we can involve the Taylorsford Library as a partner in the program."

"Sounds interesting." I picked up a blush-pink begonia. "This might work for your porch, Aunt Lydia, if you ever decided to put up flower boxes."

"Possibly." My aunt turned to Emily. "I'm sorry I haven't seen you at recent garden club events. I've missed quite a few, I'm afraid, and can't offer up a good reason. I don't even have Amy's excuse of working full-time."

I knew the reason—Aunt Lydia had spent several weekends out of town, visiting Hugh at his DC condo. But that wasn't my information to share. "Then there's Richard's new choreographic production, which basically takes up all his time—and some of mine as well. But you probably know all about that."

"I should hope so." Emily's thin lips curved into a smile. "Since I'm one of the production's major backers."

I slapped my forehead. "Oh shoot, of course you are. Please forgive me—my brain's a sieve these days. I know how grateful Richard and Karla are for the support of donors like you."

"Think nothing of it." Emily swept her hand through the air, stirring the tendrils of ivy spilling over the edge of the flower pots hanging overhead. "Most of our lives are so busy these days, it's hard to keep track of everything."

"Especially for Amy." Aunt Lydia lightly rested her fine-boned hand on my shoulder. "Along with her library job, she's been assisting Richard and Karla with research for the *Folklore Suite*."

"I'm sure she's been a big help," Emily's smile faded. "I'm so sorry that Meredith Fox's death has cast such a shadow over the entire production."

"It's definitely unfortunate," Aunt Lydia said, her fingers tightening on my shoulder blade. "Amy discovered the body, you know."

As Emily's intelligent gaze raked over me, her expression expressed doubt that I'd been overly traumatized by the murder scene. She knew as well as anyone that I'd encountered similar situations before. "Particularly distressing when one knows the victim."

"I didn't actually know her that well. We were simply acquainted through her work with Richard." I drew a circle in the packed dirt with the rubber-tipped toe of my sneaker. "I'm sorry, I guess I should've asked if you knew Meredith from her short teaching stint at Clarion."

"We met a few times at faculty parties and a few dance recitals. But we didn't really socialize. Honestly, most of what I knew about her came through my friendship with Riley Irwin, and that didn't inspire me to seek a closer bond with the woman." Emily pushed her glasses up her nose with one finger. "But to be fair, I expect a lot of Riley's information was biased, and not in Meredith's favor."

I stepped forward, breaking free of Aunt Lydia's grip. "Meredith Fox was connected to Riley? In what way?"

Emily's eyebrows rose above the top rims of her tortoiseshell frames. "You didn't know? I thought Richard would've heard the rumors. Then again, he isn't one to pay much attention to gossip, so perhaps not." She tossed her head, swinging her smooth cap of hair. "Riley and Meredith were in a relationship for a while. A very short while, but it was definitely a significant experience, at least on his side."

"Really?" I took a breath before modulating the incredulity in my tone. "I wouldn't have thought . . ."

"That Meredith Fox would date someone like Riley?" Emily shrugged. "Neither did he, to tell you the truth."

Aunt Lydia adjusted the collar of her turquoise linen blouse. "Why was that so strange? I've gotten the impression from Richard that Meredith flitted in and out of relationships with great regularity. Unless Mr. Irwin is married?"

"No, no, nothing like that." Emily looked around, as if making sure no one was in earshot. "The truth is, Lydia, that Riley isn't terribly rich or handsome or famous in any way."

"Not Meredith's type, in other words," I added with a sideways glance at my aunt.

"I see." Aunt Lydia's thoughtful expression told me that she understood all too well. That didn't surprise me. I knew she'd had to endure resistance to her marriage to Uncle Andrew from the grandmother who'd raised her and my mother after their parents died. While photos of Andrew showed him to have been good-looking, and he was undoubtedly talented, he certainly wasn't wealthy or, at the time, famous in any way. *Not Great-Grandmother Rose's type at all.*

"Riley and I became friends through a project involving my poetry students. He provided musical accompaniment for some of the readings." Emily studied my aunt's pensive face for a moment before turning her intelligent gaze on me. "I guess he saw me as someone he could confide in. Anyway, he played for some of Meredith's studio classes and fell hard for her. He was over the moon when she seemed to reciprocate his feelings. But of course, it couldn't last." Emily shook her head. "To be honest, I expect Meredith was using him for some reason. I imagine she encouraged the relationship because she wanted something from him, although I never figured out what that was."

"He didn't have any idea either?" I asked. "I mean, after their romance was over, surely he had some suspicion of what she was after."

Emily frowned. "If he did, he never told me. All I know is that, after the fact, he felt completely used and betrayed."

I shared a look with Aunt Lydia. "He held a grudge?"

Taking a step back, Emily looked us both up and down, lines creasing her brow. "I hope you don't think anything I've said means I'd suspect Riley of harming Meredith, much less killing her. He isn't that sort of person, and besides, he genuinely loved her."

Swallowing a comment along the lines of—*anyone could be that sort of person, given enough provocation*—I lifted my hands, palms out. "Please don't worry. I certainly wouldn't accuse someone of murder simply based on a failed romance. Heaven knows, I had a few of those myself and never felt like resorting to murder as retribution."

"I just wouldn't want to get Riley in trouble." Emily's worry lines deepened.

"If, as you believe, he had nothing to do with Meredith's death, there's no way anything you've told us could implicate him," Aunt Lydia said, her tone calm as a still pond. "In any case, it was good to see you, Emily. I hope to make it to the next garden club meeting. Perhaps we can catch up some more then. Right now, I should go and track down the items on my list." She pulled a scrap of paper out of her pocket and fluttered it. "I desperately need some organic pest spray. The Japanese beetles are chewing my rose leaves to lace."

Emily nodded and wished us a good day before we turned and walked away.

As we entered the enclosed section of the garden center, I cast Aunt Lydia a questioning glance. "I won't mention Emily's name if I don't have to, but I really think I need to share with Brad her information about Meredith and Riley's relationship.

Just so he can pose some follow-up questions. It shouldn't seem that strange, since Riley *was* one of the people near the murder scene around the time that Meredith was killed."

"Just like you," Aunt Lydia said dryly before she turned and headed for the shelves holding various types of pest control.

Chapter Thirteen

Since Sunny was working a full day on Monday, and Samantha was also covering the desk in the afternoon, I decided to take a little time to do some research in the library archives.

Making my way outside, I crossed the gravel parking lot to reach the archives, which were housed in a small stone building behind the library. Once the home of the original library director, it had been converted to hold town papers and memorabilia, and served as a record repository for the town and surrounding area as well as the library.

Before unlocking the door, I studied the bronze plaque that had been installed on the side of the building. The larger inscription read "The Greyson-Frye Archives." It was followed by a smaller script that declared "Honoring Town Residents Ada Frye and Violet Greyson, Who Tragically Lost Their Lives in 1879." That plaque always made me recall the events that had led to the archives, and the library, receiving a substantial donation from one of our older community residents, Delbert Frye.

Entering the single-room building, I immediately flicked on the overhead fixture. There was no natural light, as shelving stuffed with archival-grade bankers boxes lined the walls of the interior, covering the windows. Although some of the information on Taylorsford's history had been digitized, much of the material was still only available in paper formats.

My search today was focused on discovering more about the art theft at Blue Haven Farm, which my internet research had already told me occurred around four years ago. Even though it was a long shot, I wanted to see if any print clippings existed. The incident had apparently happened around the time I had first taken the job of library director in Taylorsford, when some of our volunteers were still clipping items from the local and regional newspapers instead of scanning them. It was possible that such print articles could fill in the information I hadn't been able to find online.

Since I'd told Sunny to call or text if I was needed in the library, for reference assistance or anything else, I pulled my cell phone out of my pocket and checked for any messages. Seeing none, I laid the phone down on the large wooden table the dominated the center of the room and strolled over to the shelves. I pulled down a gray banker's box labeled with the appropriate time period and set it on the table as well. Slipping on a pair of white cotton gloves, I flipped through the acid-free folders, hoping to find any articles referencing the theft.

At first, all I found were clippings on events like the Harvest Festival and the county fair, as well as puff pieces on local people. I was amused to discover an article profiling me on the occasion of my first day on the job at the Taylorsford Public Library. The piece included coverage of my background, including my years working at Clarion University, as well as my master of library science degree and my original bachelor's degree in art history. Of course, it also mentioned my family heritage. My ancestors on my mother's side, the Bakers, had been some of the wealthiest members of the Taylorsford community. Aunt Lydia still lived in the house my great-grandfather had built around the turn of the century. Unfortunately, once they sold off their lumber holdings and mill, the family's wealth had slowly dwindled away, leaving my aunt nothing more than the family home and a small trust. My mom, who earned money from her own career as a marine biologist and also had my dad's computer programmer salary, had been happy to relinquish all claims to the family inheritance, allowing my aunt to have enough to live on.

But only just, I thought, aware that Mom and Dad had surreptitiously added some funds to the trust over the years. Of course, they'd sworn me to secrecy on that point.

I gazed back at the article, pursing my lips over the picture that accompanied it. I appeared withdrawn and slightly sad, as I had in most photos from that time. *You just didn't know what good things the future had in store,* I told my former self before refiling the article.

Continuing my search finally turned up something useful. The article was brief, but it confirmed the fact that Nate and Meredith were visiting the family farm when the art theft occurred.

However, they had gone out for a late dinner with Glenda and Oliver Lance, only returning to the farm when Oliver received a phone call about the break-in from the Smith County Sheriff's Department. Apparently, the alarm system at the main house had been disabled. At the time the article was written, it hadn't been determined whether this was done accidently by one of the family members or staff, or intentionally by the thieves.

There wasn't much more to the article, just some speculation that it had been a professional job, undertaken by a criminal gang from DC or Baltimore. One of the neighbors was quoted as saying, "It was a slick operation. No one saw or heard anything. Of course the Lance place is secluded, but it still seems like it had to have been done by professionals."

That may have been so, but I bet they also didn't want to believe that sort of people lived around here, I thought, shaking my head as I slipped the clipping back into its acid-free plastic sleeve. I knew better. Crime could happen anywhere, and did.

Flipping through additional folders in the box, I finally unearthed one more article about the Lance family, only this time it concerned their horse operation, not the art theft. "Deadly Illness Strikes Local Horse Farm," the title read.

I laid the clipping down just as my cell phone buzzed, its vibration sending it skittering across the hard surface of the wooden desk. Peering at the screen, I noticed a recent text notification and swiped to access it.

Kurt's here, the text said. *Do you want to come inside to talk to him, or should I send him to the archives? —S*

Curious as to why he felt the need to speak with me directly, I texted back that she should tell him to meet me in the archives building. Kurt appeared a minute or two later, his large frame filling the doorway.

"Hello, again," I said. "What brings you here today?"

Kurt strolled inside, ducking to avoid hitting his head on the dangling lightbulb overhead. "Nothing much. I was headed back to Georgetown and just decided to stop by and see if you needed me to do anything else to aid your little investigation."

I gazed up into his craggy face, noting the sparkle in his blue eyes. "If you can use your network of spies to find out more about that art theft at Blue Haven Farm . . ."

Kurt grinned. "Spies? I wouldn't call them that."

"What would you call them, then?" I sat back in my hard wooden chair.

"Colleagues. Associates. Frenemies, perhaps?" Kurt stared down at the article lying on the table. "I see you're looking into the Lance family's background."

"Yes, but there's not much here. This article"—I held up the clipping—"isn't even about the art theft. It's just a brief mention of the loss of a couple of horses."

"I don't remember hearing anything about that, but of course I may not have officially moved into Highview at that time. When was this?"

"About four years ago." I skimmed through the short article. "There aren't many details, just a mention of Blue Haven Farm losing some horses to an infectious disease. I guess it was written as a warning to other local equestrians, as much as anything else." I squinted as I read the last few lines of the article. "Some vet named Winston Duran is quoted as saying that everything was under control, and there shouldn't be any concerns for other farms or stables, but that Blue Haven would be quarantined for a few weeks due to an abundance of caution."

"Who was that vet again?"

I looked up and met Kurt's intent gaze. "Winston Duran. Why? Do you know him?"

Kurt shook his head. "The name seems familiar, but I can't place it. Perhaps I sold him artwork sometime in the past. Those names always stick in my mind, even if I don't remember the details without consulting my records."

"Well, I scarcely think it's connected to the art theft, or Meredith's murder, in any way, but maybe you could check? Just to see how you know him, I mean."

"Because if his name rings a bell with me, he might be a criminal?" Kurt's bushy eyebrows disappeared under the white hair falling over his forehead.

I couldn't avoid a smile. "That thought may have crossed my mind."

"I'm hurt, truly," Kurt said with a toothy grin that belied his words. "Anyway, I'll see what I can find out about the art theft as well Dr. Duran. As I mentioned before, I have some inkling of who may have been involved in organizing the robbery at the Lance farm, although I've never uncovered solid proof. Or at any rate, not yet. As for the good doctor—he's probably just a former client, although there's something else tickling my brain." Kurt tapped his forehead with one finger. "I'll just have to check my records and see what I can find. Most of my recent ledgers are at the Georgetown gallery, so I'll take a look at those today. But if it was an older sale, it may take longer. I sent my back files to a secure storage facility last year."

"You don't keep your business records in a database?" I asked as I refiled the newspaper article into the box.

"Heavens no. That just makes them too easy to access."

There was definitely a devilish gleam in Kurt's eyes. "You mean, for law enforcement or tax authorities."

"Perhaps," he replied with a shrug of his broad shoulders. "I also broker deals with certain individuals who are, shall we say, not the most reputable people in the world. They prefer that their purchases and sales are not traceable. They'd be displeased if my records were easily hackable."

Thoughts of tax evasion schemes and hot merchandise flooded my mind. "I thought you told me you'd never been an art thief."

"That's absolutely true." Kurt dramatically sketched a cross in the air. "I will swear on your aunt's most charming but disapproving glare that I've personally never stolen a piece of art. Have I dealt in questionable merchandise without checking too closely into its provenance?" He gave me a wink. "Well, what do you think?"

"I think you've danced on the edge of legality plenty of times," I replied, pushing back my chair and rising to my feet. "Now, if you'll excuse me, I should reshelve this material and head back into the library. I've spent too much time out here as it is."

"Very well, I'll leave you to it." Kurt turned and crossed the room, but paused with his hand on the doorknob. "You know," he said, glancing back at me over his shoulder, "sometimes you play a little fast and loose with legalities too, my dear. Especially when it comes to your amateur investigations. Chasing down suspects and questioning them without any legal authority present, for example."

"I'm just talking to people as an interested private citizen," I said, not bothering to temper the sharpness of my tone.

Kurt didn't respond to this comment. He cast me a sardonic smile instead. "Goodbye, Amy. I'll let you know when and if I find anything interesting," he said.

I huffed, unable to think of an appropriate response. Of course, I came up with the perfect comeback as I fastened the lid on the banker's box and carried it to the shelf, but by then, Kurt was long gone.

Chapter Fourteen

I was alone at the library on Tuesday, having given both Samantha and Sunny the day off. Bill Clayton, one of our library volunteers, was scheduled to come in around noon to cover the desk so I could grab lunch, but in the morning, it was just me.

I didn't mind managing the library solo. It allowed me to indulge in one of my favorite fantasies—that the collection of books and other materials, as well as the comfortable, well-worn space, were all mine. My own private sanctuary, filled with light and enough reading material to keep me entertained and informed for years and years.

Of course, this dream was shattered by the arrival of a cluster of patrons, including Mrs. Dinterman and a chattering group of parents herding their toddlers into the Children's Room. *So much for pretending to be the owner of some grand private library,* I told myself. *This isn't yours and never will be. It belongs to the people of the town and surrounding county. As it should.*

"So you ran up on another murder, I hear," said one of our regular patrons, the eccentric older woman we called "The

Nightingale." She'd been given this nickname because of her habit of "helping" the library staff by reshelving books. Unfortunately, she usually stuffed them in the wrong locations, which just made our lives more difficult.

I looked up from the stack of books I'd pulled from the outside book drop. The Nightingale was tall and gaunt, with thin gray hair she typically wore pulled away from her sharp-featured face. Today she'd slicked it back into a tight bun, like an aging ballerina.

Aware that The Nightingale had a tendency to gossip, I chose my words carefully. "I did stumble on the scene, but I really don't know much more than what's on the news." I offered her a tight smile, hoping she'd simply accept my white lie and move on.

The Nightingale audibly sniffed. "I heard tell that it was some young man that did the deed. I swear, I don't know what this world is coming to when you've got kids running around with knives and guns, stabbing and shooting and such."

"I did walk in on a young man standing over the body, gripping a knife," I replied, straightening to my full, sadly not that impressive, height. "But that doesn't mean he was the murderer. He told me he was just trying to help the victim."

"Help her into the next world, it seems like." The Nightingale clasped her knobby-knuckled hands together and pressed them against the desktop. "But what can you expect from young folks these days, what with the violence on TV and those video games they play day and night."

I swallowed a sharp retort before answering. "I don't think we can draw any conclusions yet. The authorities are still investigating the crime." *As am I, but I'm certainly not going to tell you anything about that,* I thought as the muscles around my mouth twitched.

The Nightingale leaned over the desk, her watery eyes gleaming. "Heard another little juicy bit of news. Seems the victim was once engaged to your husband. That kind of puts him in a bad spot, I bet."

I took two steps back. "That was several years ago, and if you must know, *she* broke off their engagement to marry another man." Realizing that this could add fuel to the fire of The Nightingale's speculations, I hastily added, "Not that it matters anymore. Richard was over her even before he met me, and now we're happily married. Not to mention, he and his dance partner were leading a rehearsal on the stage, far from the murder scene. They and the dancers they were training are totally in the clear."

"What about you?" The Nightingale pressed the tip of one knobby finger to her chin. "You must've been in the area where the poor woman was killed, since you discovered the body and all. I hope the detectives aren't hounding you too much."

"No, they aren't." I pulled one of the books off my stack and ran it over the sensitizer to reactivate the hidden tag. "I guess I have an honest face."

The Nightingale looked me up and down. "Or maybe they figured you've helped with enough of their investigations to know better than to stab someone in a public space."

"Could be," I said, grabbing another book from the pile. "Is there anything you needed?"

"Naw, I'm just gonna go look for a book or two. I'll let you know if I hear anything else interesting," she called over her shoulder as she stalked off toward the stacks.

"Gee, thanks," I muttered, making a mental note to check the shelves later, to ensure she hadn't reshelved cookbooks in the fiction section again.

The rest of the morning was relatively peaceful. I kept busy with checkouts of picture and chapter books and one reference question concerning the tax implications of setting up a trust. Although, not actually being a lawyer, I couldn't give legal advice, I could point patrons in the direction of the best information, as well as provide lists of local attorneys.

After lunch, I relieved Bill from his stint at the circulation desk and asked him to reshelve the books I'd carried in from the book return earlier. "And double-check to make sure there aren't any books stuffed into the wrong call number sections," I told him as he rolled the cart away from the desk.

He lifted his salt-and-pepper eyebrows. "Ah, The Nightingale has been in today?"

"You guessed it," I said with a smile.

After Bill disappeared into the stacks, a handsome, well-built young man approached the desk. "Hi, Amy," he said.

"Hello, Ethan, how are you?" I replied, looking him over, A firefighter and EMT, Ethan Payne had once rescued me from a dangerous situation. He'd subsequently become a casual acquaintance, and then a little more than that when he'd started dating my younger brother, Scott.

"Good. Keeping busy."

I often thought that Ethan's rugged good looks were the perfect foil for Scott's leaner, professorial style, although both men were equally physically strong. *And brave,* I thought, flashing Ethan a bright smile. "Seen my brother lately? 'Cause I sure haven't."

"Not for a couple of months." Ethan shook his head. "He's been on assignment. Somewhere. Doing something." He shrugged. "You know how it is."

"I do." Scott worked for one of the US intelligence agencies. Although my parents and I had always thought he had a desk job, we'd recently learned he conducted plenty of fieldwork too. "I hope he stays in touch with you from time to time."

"He occasionally contacts me via text." Ethan flashed a grin. "We have a code. Not very high tech, but it works."

"That's more than I get. Although I do think he lets the parents know that he's still alive, at least."

Ethan took a deep breath before speaking again. "Talking of life and death, I hear you were the one to find the body of that poor dancer."

"Unfortunately. I was at the theater when she was killed and just happened to stumble over the murder scene. It was during rehearsals for the dance production Richard and others are putting on over at the new theater in Smithsburg. Richard had hired Meredith as one of the principal dancers."

"Right. Meredith Fox." Ethan's hazel eyes narrowed. "She was once married to Nate Broyhill."

"How did you know that? Do you follow dance?" I asked, fighting to keep the surprise out of my tone. Although I'd spent a little time around Ethan, I had to admit I didn't actually know that much about him in terms of his hobbies or interests. I was aware he was an avid outdoorsman, but it was possible he was also a dance aficionado.

"Not really. I mean, I admire what people like your husband can do. They are true athletes, no question." Ethan shifted his weight from foot to foot. "But I'd actually heard about Meredith Fox before, from my younger sister. She used to work for them."

"For Nate Broyhill and Meredith?" I asked, widening my eyes.

"No, no. For the Lance family. Out at their spread—Blue something Farm."

"Blue Haven Farm." I tipped my head and studied Ethan's face for a moment. "What did your sister do for them?"

"She worked with the horses. She's a teacher and trainer. A good one." Pride gleamed in Ethan's eyes. "She was younger back then, of course. Just out of college and looking to start her career. Oliver Lance gave her a job as a riding instructor, with some promise of eventually making her a trainer." Ethan shook his head. "But that never happened. Monica left after only nine months."

Resting my arms on the desktop, I leaned forward. "What happened?"

"I'm not really sure. Monica doesn't like to talk about it." Ethan frowned. "She was honestly kind of messed up when she left the Lance place. Emotionally, I mean. I tried to talk to her, but she refused to discuss it."

"She worked at Blue Haven when Nate and Meredith were still married?"

"Yeah. She used to talk about them, along with some of the other people who lived or visited there. That's why Meredith's name clicked with me when I saw her death mentioned on the news."

"Interesting." I looked up into Ethan's face, noticing the question in his eyes. "The truth is, I'm helping our local Sheriff's Office with the investigation. Well, mainly the chief deputy, Brad Tucker. I'm conducting a little research and talking to a few people. Nothing dangerous," I added, just in case Ethan talked to my brother in the near future.

"You think Nate Broyhill or his family had something to do with the murder?"

"Maybe. Or maybe not. It's hard to say. It's just that I saw Nate at the theater the day Meredith was killed. Outside the theater, anyway. He claims to have a good reason for being there . . ."

Ethan's lips quirked. "But you aren't so sure?"

"I'd just like to know more about his relationship with Meredith. Whether he was ever violent or anything like that. It might give the authorities an additional reason to question him." I tapped the top of the desk with my short fingernails. "I'm not convinced the young man they have in custody is guilty, you see."

"Well, I wouldn't really know anything useful. Monica mentioned Meredith and Nate a few times, but she never went into detail. I don't know if she ever saw them fight or anything like that."

"Monica would know a lot more," I said, more to myself than Ethan. Looking back up at him, I said, "Do you think she would speak with me? On the phone would be fine if she no longer lives in the area."

"She's still here. She manages the stables at Brentwood Farms, just outside of Taylorsford," Ethan said. "But I don't know if she'll want to talk to you about the Lance family. I think that whole experience left a bad taste in her mouth."

I almost batted my eyes, but remembering Kurt's words about my lack of feminine guile, adopted a thoughtful expression instead. "Would you mind asking her, all the same? I'd be very grateful if she'd be willing to meet with me. And let her know she might be able to help a young man with a bright future avoid being wrongly convicted."

Amusement lit up Ethan's face. "You really are a determined amateur detective, aren't you? I guess I shouldn't be surprised. Scott's told me how dogged you can be, especially when you're trying to make sure justice is served."

"Scott talks entirely too much," I said darkly, earning another grin from Ethan.

"That's not really true, now, is it? I'm the chatterbox in our relationship." His expression sobered. "But sure—I'll talk to Monica and see what she says. Can't promise she'll agree to speak with you, but I'll do my best."

"That's all anyone can ask." I frowned as I noticed Mrs. Dinterman making a beeline for the desk. "Uh-oh, you'd better make tracks. Or you're going to be grilled by someone who is even more dogged than I am."

Ethan glanced over his shoulder before looking back at me in mock terror. "Not her. She's always going on about her great-niece and how we'd make the perfect couple. No matter what I say about being in a relationship with Scott, she chooses to mis-understand me and insist that it's fine to have my guy friends, but I need a good woman to make my life complete." Ethan rolled his eyes.

I choked back a giggle. "Make a run for it then. I'll cover for you." I hurried out from behind the desk to intercept Mrs. Dinterman before she could waylay Ethan.

"How can I help you?" I asked her as Ethan turned on his heel and strode toward the exit.

Mrs. Dinterman tried to slide around me, but I sidestepped and kept her in place until Ethan left the library.

"Darn it," she said, her dark eyes snapping. "I wanted to speak to Mr. Payne. I'm having a little party for my great-niece's birthday and wanted to invite him." Focusing on me, her angry expression morphed into a simper. "A nice fireman like that deserves to have someone special in his life, don't you think?"

Recalling my brother's intelligent face and gentle smile, I nodded. "I couldn't agree more."

Chapter Fifteen

B ill helped me check over the library to make sure all of our patrons were gone before he left at around 4:50.

"Happy to hang around until five," he said, loitering near the entrance to the workroom.

"Don't worry—I've closed the place down plenty of times before. Besides, we've cleared the building and locked everything except the front doors. There's no need for both of us to wait around just to count down the minutes," I replied, keeping a lookout from the desk as he headed for the workroom and the staff exit.

I waited for the loud click of the lock to engage on the staff door before leaving the desk and crossing to the doors leading into the narrow lobby. The keys on my heavy work key ring jangled as I gazed at my wristwatch. With no one in the building, I could've locked up early, but I always made it a point to keep the library open until the actual closing time. *A matter of principle,* I reminded myself.

One I instantly regretted as the outside doors swung open and a man stormed into the lobby. I stepped back, wishing the interior doors locked or that I had gone ahead and secured the outer doors.

Or anything that would've kept an obviously incensed Nate Broyhill out of the building.

"We're closing," I said as he pushed his way past the lobby doors and stopped short in front of me.

Nate flipped his silky blond hair away from his forehead with one hand. "Go ahead and lock up. I'm not here to use the library anyway. I just want to talk to you."

"You could've done that during the day, when we're open. Or on the phone," I said, crossing my arms over my chest.

"Didn't want to share my business with the whole world." Nate's eyes were an unusual color—they appeared to shift between blue and green as he turned his head.

He is a handsome devil, I thought as I considered my options. I knew the sensible thing to do was to dash into the workroom, where my cell phone was stashed in my purse. *And where I can make a run for the side exit.*

But I still needed to lock the main doors, which had to be done from inside the lobby. I couldn't leave the building unsecured.

And, admit it—you want to hear what he has to say.

"Wait here," I told him before stepping into the lobby and locking the doors.

When I walked back into the main part of the library I noticed that Nate had wandered over to a seating area near a bank of computer workstations. Set up as a place for parents to wait and keep an eye on their children while the kids used the public computers, it consisted of a couple of small round tables and a few rolling task chairs.

Nate was already slumped down in one of the chairs, his long legs stretched out across the dark gray carpet covering the area. He lifted his head as I approached and fixed me with an intense stare that did little to relieve my anxiety.

Idiot, you really should've grabbed your phone, I chided myself as I sat down in the chair across the table from Nate. But gazing into his fine-boned face, with his slightly hooked nose offset by high cheekbones and a surprisingly full-lipped mouth, I decided that he seemed far too intelligent to attempt any sort of violence in full view of any passersby. Granted, the doors were locked, but the library's windows and doors were not covered by any blinds or shades, allowing anyone on the street to see inside. Given the long June days, and how warm and sunny it was outside, numerous locals and tourists were still strolling the streets of my historic town.

"Nice evening for a walk," I said, pointing toward the main doors. "I imagine you saw plenty of people outside."

Nate's lips rolled back, displaying his perfect, obviously capped, teeth. "If you're concerned about me hitting you over the head with some hard object, you can rest easy. I'm not here to attack you. Violence is not really my thing."

"Good to know," I said, eyeing him with distrust.

"You look dubious. Trust me—if I wanted to harm you, I wouldn't have made such a grand entrance. I'm sure several of the joggers and others outside noticed me barging into the lobby. They could easily identify me if anything happened to you." Nate ran his fingers through his golden hair. "Not to brag, but I'm told I'm rather hard to miss."

"No doubt," I said dryly. Adjusting the set of keys so that one poked through two of my fingers, I slid back in my chair.

"So what is it that brings you here today, Mr. Broyhill? I doubt you require reference assistance that badly."

Nate lips twitched. "I see the reports of your sassy attitude are on point, Mrs. Muir."

"Amy," I said automatically. Despite being happily married, I found being addressed as "Mrs.," as if that was my only attribute, unappealing. *Especially from someone I suspect of being a male chauvinist.*

"Then you must call me Nate. After all, we've been thrust into a rather distasteful situation together, haven't we? The unfortunate murder of my ex, which you sadly stumbled over."

"I didn't see the actual murder," I said. "Only the aftermath."

"But you saw the killer, right?"

"If you mean did I see a young man standing over Meredith's body? Yes, I did. But I don't believe that automatically makes him her murderer." I shifted in the chair as I tightened my grip on the keys. "There were other people in the area."

"That you saw?" Nate's tone was light as a meringue.

"I didn't necessarily see any others, although I know an accompanist and two dancers were in the basement not long before Meredith died." Examining Nate's face for any reaction, I noted the flicker of interest in his eyes. "And of course, there was the maroon SUV I noticed in the parking lot around that time. Along with a metallic-blue sedan." I tossed off these last statements with an accompanying flick of my free hand.

"The SUV was mine, but of course you already know that." Nate's gaze swiveled to focus on the READ posters hung on the wall behind the circulation desk. "The blue car . . . Well, as

I told the authorities, that was simply a stranger asking directions. Not that I could help much, since I barely know the area."

I studied his aristocratic profile but couldn't read his expression. "Your mother owns an estate right outside of Smithsburg. You must've toured the town once or twice."

"I typically drive directly to the farm when I visit, which isn't often." Nate turned his head to face me again. "You told the detectives about seeing me in the lot behind the theater, I assume?"

"Yes. But I didn't know how long you remained parked there, which I also told them." I met his intent gaze with a lift of my chin. "I heard you told the authorities that you were there to meet Meredith, that she was supposed to return a piece of family jewelry to you."

"It's true. I chose an unfortunate day to do that, as it turns out, but that was the only reason I was at the theater."

"Did you actually meet?"

"Not that it's any of your business, but no—I never saw her. She was supposed to connect with me outside, in the parking lot. I waited for some time and she never came out." Nate narrowed his eyes. "I was pretty angry about that until a couple of sheriff's deputies tracked me down and I learned what had happened." He shrugged. "I suppose it is difficult to keep an appointment when you've been stabbed."

Taken aback by his flippant comment concerning his ex-wife's death, I remained silent.

"And now you think I'm a real jerk." Nate templed his fingers and rested his chin on his hands. "Did you know Meredith?"

"Not well," I said. "Only through her work with my husband."

"Oh, right, her ex-fiancé," Nate said. "I don't suppose you'd ever suspect him of being the killer? Heaven knows he had reason to hate her."

"Of course not. For one thing, he doesn't—didn't—hate her. He actually gave her this job to help her out, since she was having difficulties . . ."

"Getting hired elsewhere?" Nate's sardonic smile raised the hair on my arms. "Not surprising. Despite her talent, she wasn't easy to work with. I should know."

"Anyway, Richard wasn't anywhere near the murder scene. He and his partner, Karla Tansen, were working with a group of dancers on the stage, so they both have airtight alibis." I shifted my keys to my other hand.

"So you went downstairs alone? That means you could also be considered a suspect," Nate said, narrowing his eyes. "I imagine Meredith didn't treat you too well whenever you were required to socialize with her."

"She was a bit disdainful, but that's scarcely a motive for murder."

"No?" Nate arched his pale eyebrows. "Didn't she ever attempt to regain your husband's affections? I know for a fact that she eventually regretted dumping him for me."

This was news to me, but I wasn't about to let Nate know that. "If she tried such a thing, it wouldn't have gone anywhere. Richard would've made sure of that. He was totally over her, even before we met."

"Right. Richard Muir, the perfect gentleman." Nate looked me over, his lips curling into a sneer. "He wasted a lot of opportunities when he was single, you know. Or so I'm told. Not one to take advantage of all the women throwing themselves at him. Meredith said she had to seduce him rather than the other way around. Strange, don't you think?"

"No, and trust me, he pursued me quite vigorously," I said, unsure of what point Nate was trying to make. Perhaps he, like Richard's dad, had suspected that Richard was not really interested in women just because he wasn't one to fool around with every available female. "Anyway, I don't think that has anything to do with the point of our discussion. Which is what, exactly? We seem to be veering off into random topics. Honestly, I'm not really sure why you were so eager to talk to me."

Nate dropped his arms and straightened in his chair. "I just wanted to inform you about a few facts that might change your perception of Meredith's case, that's all. Since you've been so determined to inform the investigators about my presence near the murder scene, perhaps you'd like to know who *I* saw in the same area."

"Two men and a woman?' I asked, leaning forward. "That would've been Riley Irwin, the accompanist, and two dancers, Tamara Hardy and Davonte Julian. I know they left the theater at some point for their dinner break, so if you were still in the parking lot at that time, you probably saw them."

"Yes, and I told the authorities as much. I also let them know that after I finally left the parking lot, I spied Tamara Hardy several blocks away and stopped to talk to her. I worked with her in the past, you see, and wanted to say hello." Nate threw out this bit of information so casually that it immediately attracted my attention.

"You saw her farther up the street?"

"Which is how I knew she couldn't have been involved in Meredith's death. Tamara even got into my car. We sat there on the street and chatted for quite a while. Then we heard sirens and a couple of sheriff's deputies actually tracked us down to tell us what happened and ask us a few questions." Nate's blue-green eyes glinted with suppressed emotion as he met my surprised gaze. "So, you see, both Tamara and I are in the clear."

But she never mentioned anything about this to me, I thought, with a frown. "You said you saw some other people near the theater before you drove off. I assume one was Conner Vogler?"

"The blond boy who's been arrested for the murder?" Nate crossed his arms over his chest. "Yes, I did. Although, as I told the authorities, I drove off before I saw anyone actually enter the theater, I did see Vogler, as well the accompanist and other dancer you mentioned earlier. And actually, one more person."

"Someone else was there?" I asked, my curiosity piqued. Although I didn't entirely trust Nate's account, I still wanted to hear what he had to say.

"Yes, a dark-haired woman who actually left her car on the adjacent street and crossed the parking lot to reach the theater."

A dark-haired woman . . . Recalling what I'd heard about her movements from Shay Green, I immediately thought of Janelle DeFranzo. "Was the woman rather slight? Maybe a bit drawn-looking, but not that old?"

"Exactly. I had no idea who she was, of course, but I did give the detectives a good description. If you think you know who she is, perhaps you could pass that information along."

"I think they may already have an idea," I said, making a mental note to share this confirmation of Janelle's return to the theater with Brad. That was it, then—the best information I'd probably get out of Nate. *Time to put a halt to this little convo.*

As I rose to my feet, my chair rolled back and banged into the adjacent table. "Is this what you came here for? To let me know that plenty of other people were in the area, and I shouldn't encourage the authorities to focus on you?"

"That was part of it." Nate stood, looming over me. I felt another frisson of fear. He was slender, but it was clear he was all lean muscle. And much taller than me. "I also wanted to let you know that, along with me, Tamara Hardy shouldn't be the focus of your amateur investigating. As I've said, I know she never returned to the theater before Meredith was killed."

"If that's the case, you've achieved your purpose." As I squeezed the key ring, the notched edges of the keys bit into my palms. "Now I'm asking you to leave. My workday is over, and I'd like to head home, sooner rather than later."

"No problem at all. If you'll just let me out the front doors . . ."

I complied with this request with alacrity. After I'd ushered him outside and relocked the doors, I took a moment to breathe deeply before heading for the workroom. Grabbing my purse, I left through the staff door, which locked behind me.

I paused behind the large forsythia bush that shielded the side door from the street and turned on my cell phone.

Clicking on a message from Ethan, I was pleased to see that he'd arranged for me to meet with his sister at his house on Wednesday afternoon.

I looked up at the sound of an engine revving. Screened by the shrub, I stared directly at Nate's maroon SUV, which he'd parked on the street.

Someone was sitting in the passenger seat. As Nate bent over to adjust something on his dashboard, I was able to see past him to the other occupant of the vehicle.

Tamara Hardy, I realized, almost dropping my phone. Nate had admitted that they knew each other, of course, but it looked like they weren't simply past acquaintances. Judging by the kiss Nate planted on her cheek before they sped off, it seemed they might be more than friends.

Which meant they could also be accomplices.

Chapter Sixteen

I shared this latest information with Brad as soon as I got home. Even over the phone I could sense his frustration with the way Meredith's case was being handled.

"I was never told about Tamara Hardy and Nate Broyhill being found together in his SUV when the deputies located them after the murder," he said. "Now I need to go back to those deputies and find out if those two were actually parked on the side of the street or were stopped as they were leaving the area."

"Because if they were driving away and pulled over, it might show that they were trying to flee the scene?" I asked, absently stroking Loie, who'd jumped into my lap as soon as I sat on the sofa.

"Right. And so we know how credible Nate Broyhill's statement is." Brad's sigh reverberated through my phone. "Obviously, Ms. Hardy lied to us. Well, I suppose it wasn't an outright lie, but she certainly withheld information."

"She never mentioned seeing, much less talking with, Nate Broyhill?"

"Not in any statement I've seen," Brad said. "Thanks for gathering this information, Amy. It can't be part of the official investigation, of course, but it does provide me with some good leads. I'm definitely going to push for another round of questioning for Broyhill and Hardy, as well as the DeFranzo woman."

Fosse, leaping up on the sofa, swatted Loie with one paw. "What about Riley Irwin and Davonte Julian? Their stories don't match up either," I said as I attempted to separate the two cats before they launched into a wrestling match on my lap.

"I've already convinced the Smithsburg department to follow up with those two. Should happen in the next couple of days," Brad cleared his throat. "You know, it concerns me a little, these folks being questioned again after you've talked to them. I worry that if any of them are the killer, they might put two and two together and come after you."

"I doubt that," I said, grunting as Fosse's back paws slammed into my stomach before he bounded off the sofa. "Sorry—trying to wrangle cats."

"I thought that was a losing proposition from the start." Amusement lightened Brad's voice. "Anyway, I just want you to keep an eye out for anything that feels off, like weird text messages or calls, or the sense that someone is following you. Let me know immediately if that sort of thing happens, okay?"

"Don't worry—you'll be the first to know," I said, leaping to my feet at the sound of a crash. "Sorry, got to go. I think the cats are running amok in the kitchen. Talk to you again soon," I added, then hung up and ran down the hall.

Loie and Fosse looked up at me from the base of one of the cabinets, their faces and paws dusted with white powder. I soon discovered the cause of this indoor snowfall—the metal flour canister lay on the floor, its contents covering the wood-toned tiles as well as the cats.

"Gee thanks, you guys," I said, trying to decide what to do first, clean the cats or the floor.

That decision was made for me when Loie dashed out through the cat door onto the screened back porch. Fosse quickly followed her, leaving the mess they'd made behind.

I sighed and grabbed a hand broom and dustpan from the small closet beside the back door. As I knelt down to sweep up the drifts of flour, a wave of dizziness swamped me, forcing me to drop back into a sitting position.

"Well, this is just great," I said, setting the dustpan and broom on the floor until my head cleared. "Can't even bend down without wimping out. Must have so much swirling around in my mind, it's making me tipsy," I added as Fosse pushed his head through the cat door and stared at me. "What do you think?"

Fosse didn't reply; just pulled his head back and left me to clean up the mess.

Unfortunately, I was already asleep when Richard got home that night, so I didn't get a chance to talk to him until the next morning. After breakfast, when I finally shared the news of Nate's visit to the library, Richard was ready to track down the former dancer and, as he quite forcefully put it, "give him a piece of my mind."

"I'd rather you didn't. You need all your faculties right now, with everything you have going on." I wrapped my arms around him, feeling the tension vibrating through his body.

"Very funny," Richard said without pulling away. "But seriously, sweetheart, you need to be more careful. What if Nate is a killer? Wouldn't put it past him," he added darkly.

"I didn't think he'd murder me in broad daylight, with people on the street able to watch everything that went on in the library. Besides," I said, "I gathered some more useful information for Brad, which I call a win."

"Hmm, not so sure anyone is winning in this situation." Richard pulled me in for a kiss before speaking again. "Promise me you'll be more cautious from here on out."

I laid my head against his shoulder. "I will. I mean, later today I'll be talking to someone but it's just Ethan's sister at his house, so hardly anything dangerous."

Richard's sigh lifted my head. "You're impossible, you know that."

"I know," I said, rising up on tiptoe to kiss his mouth. "And you're impossibly patient. And talented. And smart. And sexy. And . . ."

But I didn't get to finish my sentence before he kissed me again—this time silencing me for quite some time.

* * *

With Sunny working until eight, and Zelda and another volunteer available to cover the desk so she could have a dinner break, I left the library at three on Wednesday.

"All for a good cause," Sunny said as I apologized for taking more time off to follow my amateur investigation. "Besides, you covered for me often enough when I was called away on mayoral business."

I climbed into the car I shared with Aunt Lydia, which I'd taken today so I could head to Ethan's directly from work, and drove outside of town. After a few turns, I ended up on Logging Road, one of the many gravel-covered roads that led up into the mountains. Having traveled this route a few times before, I was prepared for its bumps and ruts, but still swore a few times when my small car's tires bounced into particularly deep holes.

The farther I drove up into the mountains, the thicker the frieze of pines lining the road became. Like silent sentinels, their dark branches created a wall that blocked all sunlight except the beams falling directly over the road.

Slowing down when I reached the mailbox marked with Ethan's house number, I turned onto his dirt lane. As I rounded the corner in the drive, his house, screened from the road by the pines, came into view. It wasn't a log cabin, but rather a simple brick ranch with a wooden deck that ran from the front door around the side of the house.

I parked in the spacious lot, noticing the compact car sitting next to Ethan's truck. Bright copper, shiny as a new penny, it appeared to be a hybrid. *Must be Monica's vehicle,* I thought. I glanced up at the deck.

Ethan was waiting, holding the front door open with one foot as he pushed a large collie behind him with his hands. I hurried up the steps to meet him.

"Hey there," I said as I slipped through the door.

"Unfortunately, Cassie remembers you and won't settle down until you pet her," Ethan said, releasing his hold on the dog's collar.

"No problem." I allowed the collie to sniff my fingers before I stroked her head.

I gazed around the long, narrow living room. There was no one sitting in the worn leather recliner by the brick fireplace, the adjacent wooden rocker, or on the sofa. "Is your sister here? I thought I saw her car outside. Anyway, I assumed it was hers."

"You mean the little hybrid? Yeah, that's hers. I wouldn't be caught dead in that thing," Ethan said.

"Right, 'cause you're more likely to turn up dead in that monster truck of yours," said the woman who appeared in the archway that led into the kitchen. "It's more of a rollover risk, you have to admit."

I turned to face the speaker, who was almost as tall as her brother and had the same strong, attractive facial features. A pair of aviator sunglasses were perched on top of her golden-brown hair, which was pulled back into a loose, low ponytail. Dressed in jeans so worn that the knees were white, a plain aqua T-shirt, and battered sneakers, she exuded an air of coiled energy, as if she was prepared to take off at a sprint at any moment.

"Hello," I said. "You must be Monica. I'm Amy. Thanks so much for agreeing to speak with me."

"I can tell you're Scott's older sister." Monica's smoky voice reminded me of a singer's in a jazz lounge. "There's not only a physical resemblance, but you both also get right to the point."

Ethan gestured toward the rocking chair and recliner. "Why don't you have a seat? I'll grab some water or wine or whatever else you want."

"Come on, bro, you know I want a beer," Monica said, rolling her amber-flecked hazel eyes. She sauntered over to the rocking chair with a swinging gait.

Hours in the saddle, I thought, remembering that she was an equestrian.

"Beer it is," Ethan said equably. "How 'bout you, Amy?"

"Just water, thanks. I do need to drive home, and the roads up here aren't really that forgiving."

"Tell me about it," Monica said as she settled into the rocker.

Ethan flashed a grin before disappearing into the kitchen, Cassie at his heels.

I sank down into the recliner. The slightly stiff leather crackled as I adjusted my position. "You're probably wondering why I wanted to talk with you," I told Monica, who was examining me with interest.

"Not really. Figured it had something to do with the murder of Meredith Fox, since Ethan's filled me in on how you've helped the Sheriff's Office with some research and stuff in the past." Monica pushed off the floor with her foot to set her chair rocking. "He's talked about you a lot, actually. How he had to rescue you that one time and how well you run the library, and all that." A slow smile crossed Monica's square-jawed face. "I think part of it is just an excuse to bring Scott into the conversation. Like Ethan going on and on about your wedding, as if he cared about such things."

"He cares about Scott," I said, offering her a smile.

"Bingo. And strangely enough, when Ethan speaks about you, the conversation always comes back to your brother."

Monica gave me a wink. "I guess it's time we met, since we might end up as relatives someday, don't you think?"

"Maybe." As I sat back in the recliner, my feet lifted off the floor. I hadn't thought about a possible family connection to Monica when I'd asked Ethan to set up this meeting. My realization of the truth of her words made me resolve to be a little more careful in my questioning. I didn't want to sour any future relationship with her by coming across as some sort of Grand Inquisitor.

Ethan returned with a glass of water in a plastic tumbler and two frosty cans of beer. After handing us our drinks, he paused in the center of the colorful braided rug that covered the pine plank floor, clutching the second beer to his chest. "I can disappear if you'd rather talk privately," he said as Cassie padded over to her dog bed by the hearth and flopped down with a grunt.

"Nah, it's okay with me if you stay." Monica shot me a swift look. "If it's all right with Amy, of course."

"No worries," I said, waving my hand through the air. "Have a seat, Ethan."

He popped the top of his can as he plopped down on the sueded sofa. "Just let me know if you ever do want me to vamoose. I won't be offended."

"Good to know. I'd hate to offend you." Monica took a swig of her beer.

"Liar," Ethan said in a tone that told me how much he loved his sister. "You usually revel in my embarrassment."

Monica made a face at him before turning her focus on me. "Sorry, Amy. But you have a brother, so you know how it is."

"Indeed I do," I said. "However, I don't want to take up too much of your time, so let me get right to the reason I asked to speak with you. It involves Nate Broyhill and Meredith and the Lance family."

Monica's expression darkened. "Should've figured that, I guess. What do you want to know?"

"Your impressions of them, mostly. Whether you thought they were on the up-and-up in terms of their business dealings and that sort of thing."

"You mean whether I suspect Meredith and Nate of engineering that art theft?" Monica asked before taking another sip of beer.

I closed my open mouth and swallowed before replying. "Exactly that."

"Not surprised at the question." As Monica waved her beer can through the air, Cassie opened her eyes and let out a low growl when a few droplets splashed on her head. "It was something several of the detectives were looking into at the time, believe you me."

"You never told me that," Ethan said.

"You know I don't like to talk about that time too much." Monica stared down into her beer can. "The thing is, teaching riding and training horses for Blue Haven was kind of a dream job. I learned so much, especially from . . ." She cleared her throat and took another swig of beer.

"Oliver Lance?" I asked, keeping my tone light. "I know he's a pretty big star in the equestrian world."

"Yeah, him. Oliver freakin' Lance," Monica said, drawing out his name like a curse.

I pressed my fingertips into the leather arms of my chair. "You didn't like him?"

"Oh, I liked him all right." When Monica met my inquisitive gaze, her morose expression told me everything.

"A little too much, maybe?" I asked, offering her a sympathetic smile. "It's okay. We've all been there."

"Oh boy, have we ever," Ethan said, earning a sharp glance from his sister. "I just mean, no judgment, sis."

"Well, I was young and stupid and thought, you know, if I liked someone enough, surely they had to like me back." Monica's sharp bark of laughter brought Cassie to her feet and sent the dog trotting over to sit on the floor near Ethan.

"It doesn't really work that way, does it?" I said, recalling some of my own unrequited loves.

"Nope. I wasn't his type at all." Monica's laser-like gaze focused on me. "You're more the kind of girl he goes for, Amy. Not a tall, rangy gal like me."

I shifted on the recliner cushions. "So I've been told. But all that aside, did you ever hear Oliver, or his mom, say anything about suspecting Meredith and Nate of being involved in the art theft? Or even Meredith alone?"

"As a matter of fact, I did hear them whispering together in corners and shooting daggers at both Nate and Meredith. Picked up a few words, here and there. Enough to say they did have their suspicions. Especially Oliver. He seemed determined to throw shade their way."

"But nothing was ever proven," Ethan said, laying his hand on Cassie's head.

"It wasn't." Monica shrugged. "Nate and Meredith stopped visiting the farm, though. I thought that was a little suspicious."

"Playing devil's advocate, maybe they just didn't feel welcome anymore," I said. "And I guess they didn't stay married long after that either."

"Nope. Which didn't surprise me." Monica tipped up her beer, obviously finishing it off. "They fought all the time. Not physically, but man, did they have some vicious verbal arguments. Glenda and Oliver jumped into a few of those, especially when they were talking about that dance company that Nate was trying to get going. It was a real four-way free-for-all whenever that topic came up."

"What about other financial stuff—did the family ever argue over things like jewelry or land or other property?" I asked, hoping to glean some information linked to Nate's mention of family jewelry.

"Not really." Monica tossed her head, swinging her long ponytail over her shoulder. "Oliver was very meticulous about financial stuff, along with all the records connected to the horses and the farm. He actually kept print ledgers documenting everything. Didn't trust computers, he said."

"So he was in charge of the finances?" I asked.

"For the farm, yeah. He once showed me a whole set of ledgers in the main house's private library. He said they held all the information about the horses—when they were purchased or sold and for how much, when they were bred, their foals, and all that sort of thing. He was planning to train me in how to keep the records, but"—Monica squeezed her beer can so hard it crumpled—"then we lost two of our best mounts, and I got fired."

I scooted to the edge of the recliner seat. "Lost? How?"

"Some sort of sickness, right, Monica?" Ethan cast me a warning look. "Something no one could really control."

Monica hunched her shoulders. This was obviously a touchy subject. "Equine Influenza. Everything actually happened when I was on vacation, so I wasn't around when our horses became infected and two of them died. But Oliver blamed me anyway."

"Why was that?" I asked, deciding not to let on that I'd read about the deaths of the horses in that article from the archives. I thought it best to allow Monica to tell her side of the story without me interjecting anything extraneous into it.

"Because I'd okayed the transfer of two new horses into our herd before I left for vacation." Monica set the dented beer can on the raised bricks of the hearth. "They were new boarders. Oliver had asked me to take over that aspect of the business— boarding horses for other people in the area. These particular horses seemed fine and had been checked over by our vet recently. They were even vaccinated against influenza as well as other equine diseases, or so their records said. I didn't expect any problems."

"And maybe there wasn't one." Ethan turned to face me. "Oliver claimed that the two boarders brought in the influenza, but who knows? Monica wasn't around to see what actually transpired. All she knew was that somehow, despite also being vaccinated, two of the Blue Haven Farm horses got sick and died."

"It happens," Monica said with a shrug. No vaccine is one hundred percent effective. Although it was odd that the new boarders recovered while our horses did not. Still, I had to accept what had happened and move on. At least Oliver gave me a decent reference for my next job." Monica looked up from her tightly gripped hands. "Sorry, I guess we've veered way off subject. You wanted to know about Meredith and her relationship with the Lance family, not my unhappy past."

"I think you've covered that," I said. "It seems Glenda and Oliver could easily have held a grudge against her, and even suspected her of robbing them. Or arranging a robbery at the very least. Maybe with Nate's help, maybe not."

"It wouldn't surprise me if they felt that way. But I really don't think either one of them would kill her over such a thing." Monica's gaze was fixed on her hands. "I mean, I wouldn't want to be the reason they got in trouble. I just have my impressions, you know. No hard facts."

Something in Monica's troubled expression alerted me to her real concern. *She doesn't want to throw Oliver under the bus,* I realized, *even if he did fire her. I think she's still carrying a torch for him.*

"Well, I've taken up enough of your time." I set my water glass on a side table and stood up. "I should be going. Thanks for your insights, Monica. It does seem to solidify the possibility that Meredith was involved in that art theft in some way. And maybe, if Nate was also part of the scheme, she'd finally threatened to expose him or was blackmailing him or something."

"That could be it," Monica said, her eyes brightening. "It might have nothing to do with Glenda or Oliver."

Since I could tell that this was her preferred scenario, I simply nodded and wished both Ethan and Monica a good day, gave Cassie another pat, and left.

But when I called Brad after driving home, I presented the information without speculating on anyone's innocence. As far as I was concerned, every member of the extended Lance family was equally suspect.

Chapter Seventeen

O n Friday evening, with Richard once again tied up in rehearsals, I had dinner at Aunt Lydia's house.

"Here we are again, just the two of us," I said when my aunt informed me that Hugh was off on another work assignment, this time in South America. "What I don't understand is why you don't travel with Hugh more. It seems to me it'd be fun to visit all those places."

"I don't want to interfere with his work." Aunt Lydia set a casserole dish on the kitchen table. "This is a cold rice pilaf thing, by the way. I didn't think we'd want anything hot, as warm as it's been outside."

"Looks delicious, as usual," I said, examining the dish, which featured rice studded with veggies, dried fruit, and almonds. "And you're exactly right about the heat. I've actually felt a little nauseous just smelling some cooked food lately. Especially anything greasy. Not that I need that anyway," I added, patting my stomach.

"It isn't anything I want in the summer," Aunt Lydia said, ignoring my jibe at my weight struggles as she sat down across the table from me. "Grilled meats are okay, but I'm not interested in anything fried when the weather turns hot."

When I plopped a spoonful of the rice mixture on my plate, my stomach rolled. *No, this is ridiculous,* I told myself. *There's nothing in this dish that should upset your digestion or give you acid reflux or anything else. You've just worked yourself into a nervous frenzy over this latest murder. Time to take a deep breath and calm down.* I took a bite of the pilaf, reassured when my stomach didn't protest.

"So tell me more about this conversation you had with Ethan's sister," Aunt Lydia said. "Did it give you any useful information to share with Brad and his team?"

My mouth full, I simply nodded. "It certainly keeps Nate Broyhill and the rest of his family on the list of suspects," I said after swallowing.

"Speaking of which"—Aunt Lydia tapped her fork against the edge of her plate—"in a strange coincidence, I'll be visiting Blue Haven Farm tomorrow. Glenda Lance has invited the garden club to a party. I didn't mention it before now because . . ."

"You didn't want me to beg to tag along?" I asked, pointing my fork at her.

"That may have had something to do with it." Aunt Lydia's lips twitched. "Mainly due to the fact that I thought it was going to be a more intimate affair, and you'd stand out like a sore thumb. But Zelda's informed me that it's actually a fundraiser for the regional society, so several different garden clubs are invited."

"Which means I could blend in more easily." I grinned. "So can I come? I know I'm not a member of any club, but since it's a larger group, I could probably mingle without much notice."

Aunt Lydia scooped up a forkful of rice. "You can accompany Zelda and me, I suppose. We can introduce you as a future garden club prospect, if anyone asks."

"That would be fantastic. I know Richard will be busy with the production, since they're starting tech week, so it's not like I have anything else planned."

"Not that I want to encourage you to pester the Lances, but this might be the safest way for you to observe them again, on their own turf. So to speak," my aunt said with a smile.

"I see what you did there," I said. "Horses and turf. Very *punny*."

"I have my moments," Aunt Lydia said before taking another bite of her meal.

After we finished our dinner and cleaned up the dishes, we carried our glasses of iced tea out to the sunroom. Aunt Lydia sat in her favorite wooden rocker while I chose the fan-backed wicker chair.

"I have to agree with Richard about this view," I said as I settled into the chintz cushions. "It makes me want to enclose our back porch so that it can be used year-round."

"Wasn't the plan to make that space your dining room?"

"Since Richard took over the original dining space for his studio, we kind of need to do that, sooner or later." I sipped on my tea as I contemplated the birds converging on one of Aunt Lydia's feeders. "But with just the two of us, we don't need a dining room all the time. I think what I'd really like is something that could be used as a sitting area most of the time but could also be converted into a dining room when we have guests."

"You could buy a table with several leaves, like the one I have," Aunt Lydia said. "That way, the table could remain fairly compact unless you needed to expand it."

"Good idea." I swirled the ice cubes in my glass. "We've actually been saving some money for renovating the porch. Almost have enough unless something comes up." I reached over and rapped my knuckles against the surface of the small wooden table next to my chair. "I probably shouldn't say anything like that aloud. The house and cars are probably listening."

Aunt Lydia cast me an amused glance. "You think they schedule their need for repairs based around your desire to save money for something else?"

"Don't you?" I asked with a lift of my eyebrows.

"It does seem that way sometimes," Aunt Lydia said, her expression growing thoughtful. "I'm afraid I'm going to need a new furnace before this winter, and can't help but shudder at the likely cost."

"We can help, if you need it," I said, pushing the thought of our porch renovation out of my mind. My aunt had done so much for me—allowing me to live with her for several years when I'd first moved to Taylorsford was the least of it—that I felt I should consider her needs before my wants.

"That won't be necessary. Like you, I've been saving a bit for just this sort of thing. And Hugh will probably insist on contributing something as well." Aunt Lydia smoothed a strand of her silver hair behind her ear. "I'd say no to that if he didn't live here sometimes. But since I do feed him when he's here . . ."

"And quite well too," I said.

Aunt Lydia smiled. "He doesn't complain, that's for sure. So, given that, I don't mind him helping out with some of the house expenses." She took a sip of tea before adding, "I may be proud, but I'm not foolish."

"Just let us know if you ever need additional funds," I said, setting my empty glass on the side table. "It's our family home, after all. I mean, your family's and mine."

"Which Richard is a part of now," my aunt said firmly.

I studied her profile for a moment, happy to hear her confirm this. "True. He always says he feels closer to you and Mom and Dad than his own parents."

"Having met Fiona and Jim Muir, that doesn't surprise me," Aunt Lydia said with a roll of her eyes.

"That's for sure. Although Fiona has mellowed a teensy bit."

A loud crack followed by a rush of wings as the birds fled the feeder made me leap to my feet. "What the heck was that?"

"I'm not sure. It certainly disturbed the birds," Aunt Lydia said, standing and following me to the porch door. "Perhaps a large dog leaping through the garden?"

"Or a deer, although they don't tend to wander out of the woods until later in the evening." I peered through the glass of the door into the garden, but it was too lush for me to see anything except the first few rows of beds. "Tell you what—let me go out and take a look. I think whatever it was, it was closer to the woods, 'cause I can't see anything from here."

"All right, but take the spray bottle," Aunt Lydia said. "It's still in the garden bin."

I nodded and headed outside. At the foot of the concrete steps leading down from the porch stoop, I paused to open the bin where my aunt kept some of her gardening supplies, and grabbed a plastic spray bottle she kept filled with a mixture of water and hot pepper sauce.

Since our gardens were bordered by a ribbon of woods that connected to fields rolling up into the forested foothills, it wasn't uncommon to encounter wildlife that had wandered down from the mountains. Although I knew that most of the creatures were more afraid of me than I should be of them, and that they were unlikely to attack without provocation, there was always the chance that a racoon or fox could be rabid. In that case, all bets were off, which was why Aunt Lydia kept the spray bottle handy. It could scare off a creature or, at a minimum, force it to keep its distance without actually harming it. When we heard or saw any indication that a larger animal might be wandering out of the woods, we carried the bottle as a precaution.

I crossed the small patch of grass and entered the garden. Walking slowly down the white pea-gravel-covered paths, I swept my gaze over the beds of flowers, herbs, and vegetables, looking for any sign of what had caused the earlier commotion. There was nothing amiss with the front beds, but as I strolled past the decorative bird bath and fountain in the center of the garden, I noticed broken flower stalks and pieces of limbs from flowering shrubs littering the path in front of me.

A few more steps and a scene of devastation came into view. The flowers in the back, which were screened by tall lilacs, weigelia, and mock orange shrubs planted in the beds in front of them, had been sliced off at the base of each plant. The spear-like leaves of irises and fountains of daylily foliage lay in heaps on the ground, and two of Aunt Lydia's prized shrub roses were chopped to pieces. Gazing up, I noticed indentations in the dirt, and a broken tree limb lying across the path that led into the woods.

It looks like someone fell, grabbing a low-hanging branch as they went down, I thought, assuming that had caused the noise we'd heard from the porch. Standing with my balled fists on my hips, the spray bottle dangling from my hooked thumb, I stared around in disbelief. Not only because of the vandalism but also because someone had been bold enough to wreak havoc on my aunt's garden before the sun went down.

I stared into the woods but knew it was useless to try to track down the perpetrator. I was sure they'd already fled the area, slipping through the woods to reach one of our neighbors' backyards and then make their getaway. They'd probably parked a vehicle up the road so they could drive off before we even realized what had happened.

Footsteps crunched the pea gravel. I turned to face Aunt Lydia.

She stopped short in front of me, her gaze taking in the destroyed garden beds. But instead of expressing anger or grief, she held up her cell phone, screen facing out.

"I received a message," she said in a hollow tone. "You should read it."

I took the phone from her hand, noticing the slight tremble in her fingers. That was enough to warn me that the message was nothing good.

Tell your niece to stop helping with the investigation, or your plants won't be the only thing you lose, it said.

I sucked in a sharp breath. "You just got this?"

"A minute ago." Aunt Lydia's blue eyes were clouded with anxiety. "I don't like this, Amy. They know you're helping the detectives working on this case and that you're my niece."

"And where you live, which means they probably know I live next door," I said grimly.

"What do you want to do?" my aunt asked, exhaling a breath as she surveyed the damage to her garden.

She's just realized the extent of it, I thought. *She was consumed with concerns about me and didn't really take it in before this.* "I think we have to take your phone and let Brad and his team check it out. Sorry."

"It's okay. I can call Hugh on my landline and let him know what's going on. I don't use my cell for much else," Aunt Lydia said. "And you don't have to worry—I know you have to work, covering the Saturday shift at the library, so I'll take the phone down to the Sheriff's Office tomorrow and make a report about the damage to the garden."

As I stared at the mangled flowers and shrubs, a cold chill ran down my back. "This is someone who has a temper. Even if they hired someone else to do the actual deed, they wanted us to know that they are willing to tear things apart to make their point."

"Which concerns me more than anything," Aunt Lydia said. "You're going to tell Richard about this, I hope?"

"Of course," I said. "But please don't worry—I've already spoken to all of the people that were on the extended suspect list. So I can comply with our vandal's request."

My aunt frowned. "Not if you accompany me to that garden party."

"Oh that." I swept my hand through the air. "Who's going to question me attending a party with you and Zelda? Especially if we say I want to join the garden club someday. Besides, I probably won't even ask any questions. I'll just observe Glenda for any signs of nerves or guilt or whatever."

"I doubt you'd see any, even if she did whack Meredith," Aunt Lydia said dryly. "She's been a wealthy society matron for a long time. No doubt she's learned to cover her emotions well."

"Whack?" I asked, with a grin. "Why, Aunt Lydia, if I didn't know better, I'd suspect you of watching some of those mob-inspired TV shows."

"I may have seen one or two," she replied airily, "but also plenty of noir films from the forties. There's sadly no time-frame limitation on crime and violence, you know."

"I guess not." As I took a deep breath, the scent of crushed vegetation filled my nostrils. "I should gather up this debris and toss it on the compost heap. Fortunately, even though the vandal made hash of your plants and shrubs, they didn't pull things up by the roots. So it should all come back."

"Stronger than ever." Aunt Lydia laid a gentle hand on my shoulder. "Just like us."

Chapter Eighteen

"I agree that the young man doesn't seem like the most likely suspect. If you ask me, the Smithsburg Sheriff's Department could be doing a better job. Too much jumping to conclusions too fast," Zelda said as she helped me collect books from our outdoor book drop.

Zelda was working the Saturday morning volunteer shift at the library, with Dawn Larson, another one of our volunteers, covering the afternoon hours. I'd given both Samantha and Sunny the day off, since they'd been working some extra Saturdays for me recently.

"Brad is doing what he can, but he's not in charge," I said. "I'm relieved that Conner is out on bail now and safely in the custody of his parents." I unlocked the staff door and used my foot to hold it open until Zelda could grab the upper edge with her free hand.

"Too bad. Brad's a lot more thorough than some," Zelda said. "Really pursues the facts."

I shot her a sidelong glance as I set my stack of books on the workroom table. Zelda had experienced her own run-in with the law less than a year ago. While everything had turned out well, I knew she undoubtedly sympathized with Conner's situation. "Let me grab a cart. Then we can work on processing these at the desk."

Zelda placed her stack of materials on the table. "I can do that, if you need to take care of other stuff before we open up."

"Thanks. I do want to give all the areas a once-over before I unlock the front doors."

After I'd walked through the building, making sure all the lights were on, the tables were clear, the chairs were in their proper positions, and no books had been left lying about from the day before, I turned on our bank of public computers. Peering at my watch, I hurried over to the lobby to open the building precisely at ten. While no one was waiting outside, I expected some of our regular patrons to show up soon.

By the time I returned to the desk, Zelda had placed all the returned books on the cart in call-number order. "Should I check these in, or do you need me to do some shelf reading?"

"I think the shelf reading can wait. Just wand those in with the portable barcode reader and reactivate the security strips. I'm going to check the circ system for any overdue notices or other messages."

Zelda's blonde curls bounced as she nodded her head. "By the way, Lydia told me what happened to her garden. I sure hope someone can catch that hooligan, sooner rather than later."

I bit my lip to stop myself from saying anything about the cell phone message my aunt had received. She'd apparently not shared that tidbit with Zelda, allowing her friend to assume the garden destruction had been an act of random vandalism.

"Aunt Lydia was going to stop by the Sheriff's Office today to make a complaint, so we'll see. It'll probably be next to impossible to track down the culprit, though."

"I can't understand why anyone would do that to Lydia," Zelda said, looking up from the book cart to fix me with a sharp stare. "She doesn't have any enemies, or at least none that I know of."

Noticing a young woman entering the library with two toddlers in tow, I pressed a finger to my lips. "Let's discuss this later. I don't want the news about the garden to spread too freely. In case that might muddy the investigation," I added when Zelda widened her eyes.

"Okay, boss," she said under her breath before turning back to the books on the cart.

I spent the rest of the morning alternating between helping patrons find books and other materials, and covering the circulation desk while Zelda reshelved the books we'd brought in at the start of the day. By one, my stomach was audibly growling, which made Zelda suggest I take a lunch break.

"To tell you the truth, you look a little peaked," she said, examining me with a critical eye. "Maybe pop outside for some fresh air and take your full hour too. I can cover the desk and keep an eye on everything, especially since Dawn should be here within a half hour or so."

I didn't argue. Eating outside sounded much more pleasant than sitting in our small, windowless staff breakroom.

Grabbing my reusable lunch bag and a bottle of water from the refrigerator in the breakroom, I slipped out the back door of the library. We'd recently installed a picnic table under one of the large maples that bordered our gravel parking lot, next to the stone archives building.

The weather was sunny and hot, with banks of clouds piling up like snowdrifts in the pale blue sky. It looked like the prediction for thunderstorms later in the day was on point. I spread a napkin across the wooden surface of the table and laid out my raw veggies along with some slices of cheese, whole-wheat crackers, and a ripe pear. Having put on a few extra pounds lately, I was trying to eat lighter. *And healthier,* I reminded myself as I nibbled on a carrot stick. Not that I'd actually been overindulging recently, which was a little frustrating. *Probably not enough exercise,* I thought, vowing to skip an hour of reading or watching TV to take an extra walk in the evenings.

A breeze rustled the leaves overhead. I gazed up into the tree canopy, noticing how the wind blew back some of the foliage, exposing a silvery underside. *Like minnows darting and shimmering through a forest of seaweed,* I thought. Allowing this fancy to lull me into a daydream, I closed my eyes for a moment, enjoying the warm breeze.

Words broke through my reverie. "Ms. Muir," said a male voice. "Sorry, I didn't mean to disturb you."

I opened my eyes and looked up into the face of Conner Vogler.

"Oh, hello," I said, offering him a bright smile. "Don't worry—you aren't bothering me. I was just resting my eyes for a second."

"You're eating your lunch." The color was high in Conner's smooth-skinned face.

"I have plenty of time for that. Please, have a seat." I motioned toward the bench on the other side of the table. "I'm very happy to see you out and about."

"It's sure better than where I was for a while," Conner said as he sat down.

"I bet." I examined him, noticing the dark circles under his eyes. "How are you holding up? I'm really sorry you've had to endure so much trauma recently. I kind of wish I hadn't walked in on you that day."

Conner shrugged. "If it hadn't been you, it would've been someone else. At least you didn't jump to the wrong conclusion."

"If you mean I didn't immediately assume you killed Meredith Fox, that's absolutely true," I said.

"Well, that makes six people who think I'm innocent." Conner rested his tightly clasped hands on the tabletop. "You, Mr. Muir, my parents, and my two sisters. Everyone else is sure I did it."

"I don't think that's actually true." I stretched out my hand to bump his clenched fists. "I've talked to several people who are questioning your guilt. And there are other suspects, you know."

"But they weren't found standing over a dead body with a knife in their hand," Conner said morosely.

"What happened exactly? I know you had to have discovered Meredith's body in that dressing room, but what occurred before that?"

Conner lowered his head. "That's the problem—I don't remember things very clearly. Once I saw Ms. Fox lying there on the floor, I was so in shock, everything became a blank."

"Well, why don't we walk through it? I mean, from the time you came back to the theater after your break until you ended up in that dressing room." I held up my hands. "I know, I know—you've already told the authorities all of this. But let's face it, they can be intimidating. It's hard to think clearly when a bunch of deputies and detectives are staring you down."

"You've got that right," Conner said, meeting my gaze with a wary smile. "Okay—you know about the encounter I had with Ms. Fox on the stage."

"Right. She was incredibly rude to you."

"Didn't surprise me, really. I mean, it did make me mad, but I didn't expect anything better from her. For some reason, she took a dislike to me during that one competition. Anyway, I wasn't happy, but like I told the investigators, I sure wasn't mad enough to kill someone." Conner loosened his clenched hands and shook out his fingers. "I just took Mr. Muir's advice to go get something to eat before the evening rehearsal. Which really helped. It felt good to walk it all off, you know?"

"I imagine it did. So you grabbed something to eat, and then what?" I tempered my tone when Conner winced. I didn't want to come across as an official interrogator. "You walked back to the theater, I guess?"

"Yeah. I still had plenty of time before the rehearsal was supposed to start, so I thought I should probably stretch and warm up. Which is why I ended up downstairs. I was planning to use one of the rehearsal rooms."

"But before that," I said, thinking of the stories I'd heard from others, "you tried to enter the building through the back door."

Conner shot me a sharp look. "How do you know that?"

"I've heard a few people mention seeing you near the building," I said lightly.

"I did try to get in through the loading dock door, but it was locked, so I went around to the front of the building and entered through the lobby. No one was around right then, or at least I didn't see anyone at first." Conner frowned. "Like I told the detectives, I never saw many other people, although I noticed one lady out in front of the theater. She was walking away and turned the corner of the block before I could get a good look at her, but she kind of reminded me of Mrs. DeFranzo." Conner rubbed his forehead with the back of his hand. "Only, I don't see how it could've been her, since I saw her leave with her daughter earlier, before I even headed out for my supper break."

I opened my mouth but snapped it shut again before saying anything about Janelle returning to the theater. If Conner hadn't been told about that, I didn't feel it was my place to add another confusing element to his story. "You went inside, through the lobby, at that point?"

"Yeah. Like I said, at first I didn't see anyone else, although I could hear some noise coming from the auditorium. I guess that was the rehearsal Mr. Muir and Ms. Tansen were leading with the university dance group."

"Yes, it would've been," I said with an encouraging smile. "Then you must've headed downstairs."

Conner shook his head. "Not immediately. I had to go to the restroom. Too much iced tea," he said with a shy smile. "Anyway, after I entered the building, I did notice someone across the lobby. Well, I really just caught a glimpse of their back. They were wearing dark clothes and a cap. I thought they were probably a dancer, in sweats over their dance clothes, or something. They slipped through the lobby doors and into the hall that runs alongside the auditorium, the one that leads to that exit alcove near the stage."

"And the stairs that lead to the basement," I said thoughtfully.

"But I didn't follow them because why would I? I didn't think anything was wrong at that point, and I really believed they were just another dancer. Anyway, after I used the restroom, I took that same hallway to reach the basement stairs." Conner's pale lashes lowered, veiling his eyes. "This is where it gets hazy. I remember going downstairs, but after that, it's all a blur."

"You didn't see anyone at this point?"

"Not that I remember. I mean, I didn't check every space, and you know there are emergency exits down there. Stairs that lead up and out in case of fire or whatever."

"Right, there'd have to be more than one set of exit stairs, by code," I said, talking to myself as much as Conner.

"Yeah. Ms. Tansen gave a safety talk to all of us when we first started working in the theater. Showed everyone all the exits." Conner rolled his shoulders, as if relieving tension.

"After you got downstairs, what drew you to that dressing room?" I asked.

"Some sort of noise. I guess it might've been Ms. Fox, groaning or something. I dunno." When Conner looked up, his expression conveyed the horror of his next words. "I don't remember it well. I just found myself in that dressing room, seeing all the blood, and the knife in her chest . . ."

"And you tried to help her."

"I think so. I mean, I'm sure I wanted to. I remember kneeling down and trying to stop the bleeding, but it just wouldn't." Conner dropped his head into his hands. "And then I must've pulled out the knife, which I now know I shouldn't have done, but right then I guess I wasn't thinking clearly—or at all. I pulled out the knife and tried to stop the blood, but it kept bubbling up, until it didn't, and I felt for her pulse, and there wasn't any."

"You didn't yell out for anyone? Yell *help*, I mean?" I asked, keeping my voice as gentle as possible.

Conner looked up at me, tears beading his lashes. "I thought I did, but I don't know. Maybe it was like in a nightmare—you try to scream, but nothing comes out. Then, next thing I knew I was on my feet, and you burst into the room, and then the deputies were there, and . . . that's it. That's all I know."

"And of course your fingerprints were on the weapon," I said. "Have you heard whether there were any other fingerprints found?"

"There weren't." Conner expelled a breath. "Seems like whoever actually stabbed Ms. Fox wiped the handle or was wearing gloves, or something."

"That's unfortunate." I inched forward on my bench. "I assume you told the investigators about the person you saw outside as well as the one in the lobby?"

"I did. It didn't seem to make much of an impression, though." Conner rubbed at his eyes. "Didn't mean to get all weepy again. It's just hard to talk about."

"I can imagine," I said, pressing my fingers over the hand he'd rested on the tabletop. "I hate to make you relive it. But in case you didn't know, I've been helping one of the deputies from the Taylorsford area. We're trying to make sure every angle is investigated. We don't want there to be any rush to judgment about you."

Conner offered a wan smile. "I know. Mr. Muir called me when I made bail. He told me you were doing that. Thanks."

"He believes in you too." I patted Conner's hand.

"That means a lot. I really admire him. He's a great dancer and choreographer."

"I think so," I said, lifting my hand and sitting back.

"Everybody does. Well, everyone who knows anything about dance. He's a demanding teacher, but fair, and he never yells at us or belittles anyone." Conner flipped the hair out of his eyes with a toss of his head. "Can't say that about all the dance instructors I've worked with."

"I know he sees great promise in you. So hang in there. Once this mess is all cleared up, you can get back to your life, including your dancing."

"I'm still practicing," Conner said. "Ms. Tansen said I could use her studio when she wasn't teaching classes. She's pretty cool too."

"Yes, she is." I looked Conner up and down as he slid out from behind the table and stood up. "Stay strong. We're going to get to the truth, one way or the other."

A blush tinted Conner's cheeks. "Thanks again. I'll let you get back to your lunch now." He turned to go but paused to face me again and add, "Oh, one more thing I told the detectives: I think some of them thought I was lying, but I swear I wasn't. I saw that knife, the one that killed Ms. Fox, earlier in the day. I noticed it because it was open, even though it was a folding knife, and the overhead light was glinting off the blade. It was in the exit alcove, near the stairs to the basement, stuck behind a fire extinguisher in a niche. I figured some workman had dropped it there or something, so I left it alone." He frowned. "Of course the deputies think I grabbed that knife before I headed downstairs, but I didn't. Someone else might've done that, though. Seen the knife and taken advantage of the opportunity, I mean."

"Or they stashed it there to use later," I said, giving him a thumbs-up gesture. "Another clue I'll share, in case my deputy friend hasn't heard about that yet."

"Okay. Not sure how it will help, but that's what happened. See ya." Conner gave me a wave and headed off toward the side road that led to a walking path behind the library.

I called Brad again before finishing my lunch. As I'd expected, he hadn't been informed about Conner seeing the knife earlier in the day, before the murder.

"You're right—it could've been stashed there ahead of time," he said. "Although a workman accidentally leaving it behind is also a possibility. It's the sort of thing a construction worker, or even someone building theater sets, might use for various purposes."

"Worth checking out, though, either way, don't you think?"

"Absolutely. I'll see what any of my colleagues may have done, in terms of that lead. If anything," he added with a sigh. "But regardless, I'll look into it, as well as follow up on the individuals Vogler says he saw both outside and inside the theater around the time of the murder."

"Thanks. That will be a big help." I took a swig from my water bottle before adding, "You're a stand-up guy, Brad Tucker."

"I do my best," Brad replied, a touch of embarrassment coloring his tone.

"If only everyone did," I said, then wished him a good day.

Chapter Nineteen

I decided that I was going to stay up Saturday evening until Richard got home, so I could share my conversation with Conner.

Which is how he found me asleep on the sofa with one cat tucked behind the crook of my bent knees and the other plastered up against my back.

"Should've taken a picture," he said as I struggled to sit up. "You three were just too cute, snuggled up like that."

I swished some saliva around inside my mouth, realizing that I hadn't brushed my teeth after my dinner. I could still taste the two slices of leftover margherita pizza. "Oof," I said, running my fingers through my tousled hair. "I'm sure I look a lot more rumpled than the cats. They stay nice and sleek despite rolling around on the sofa, while I go all frumpy and frowzy."

Richard grinned and bent down to kiss me on the forehead. Before he could go in for a kiss on the mouth, I pressed my hand over my lips. "You don't want to do that. I have garbage breath right now. Let me go brush my teeth and throw on my pajamas while you put your dance bag and other stuff away."

Richard stepped back as I stood up. "I'm sure it's not that bad," he said while Loie and Fosse, who'd leapt off the sofa the minute I'd moved, weaved around his ankles, meowing pitifully. "What's this? Didn't your mother feed you?"

"Of course I did. But now that you've come home, they expect a treat." I grabbed the shoes I'd kicked off before I'd fallen asleep on the sofa, balancing them on the book I'd left on the coffee table. "See you in a minute."

I hurried upstairs, setting the book on my bedroom nightstand and tossing the shoes into our walk-in closet. Changing into my shorts and a cami, I ran into the bathroom and brushed and flossed before heading back downstairs.

"Better now?" Richard asked, meeting me at the foot of the steps. Before I could answer, he pulled me in for a kiss. "Yes, that's quite nice," he said when he released me.

I wrinkled my nose at him. "Meanwhile, I can tell you've been drinking coffee."

Richard shrugged. "Late night, semi-long drive. I didn't want to fall asleep at the wheel."

"Good thinking," I said, slipping my arm around his waist as we strolled toward the living room area. "Did you give the beasts their treats?"

"Do you see them pestering us?" Richard led me back to the sofa. "You didn't need to stay up and wait for me. I know you were working at the library all day."

"But something else happened. While I was eating lunch outside, behind the library, Conner Vogler showed up, and we had an interesting chat. I wanted to tell you about it." I rubbed my bare arms. "But first, I need some sort of wrap. Maybe it's from just waking up, but I feel kind of chilled."

"Sure thing," Richard said as he took a seat on the sofa. "I believe your cotton sweater's still hanging on the coat tree, if that will work."

"Good idea." I trotted over to front door, where a tall wooden rack held a variety of light jackets, hoodies, and other outerwear. Grabbing the cotton sweater I'd carried into the theater the day Meredith was killed, I strolled back to the sofa. "Fortunately, it isn't stained with any blood splatter. I guess I should've checked that sooner, but I honestly forgot all about it after we got home that day."

"Not surprising," Richard said as I slipped on the sweater and plopped down next to him. "So, what did Conner tell you? Anything that you think might help his case?"

"Maybe. I already shared some of the info with Brad, and he's going to look into it." Snuggling up against Richard, I laid my head against his chest before detailing the story Conner had told me.

"So there were other people in the area," Richard said thoughtfully. "That means Conner could've actually seen the killer."

"But not clearly, unfortunately. He said it was someone in dark clothes, but since a lot of dancers wear black rehearsal togs, that doesn't narrow things down too much."

"What about Nate Broyhill? What was he wearing when you saw him outside?"

"A charcoal-gray shirt and black pants," I said, sitting up. "If he'd simply thrown on a black sweatshirt and cap, he could've been the person Conner spied leaving the lobby."

"But would he have known about the emergency exits?" Richard leaned back into the sofa cushions, staring up at the beadboard ceiling. "Conner and all the other dancers and their parents were given a safety tour and talk by Karla, but Nate wouldn't have been privy to that information."

"Unless he studied the floorplans ahead of time," I said. "They were available on the theater website as part of the fundraising campaign for the renovation."

"True." Richard stretched out his legs, pushing back the coffee table. "Sorry, cramping tendons."

"You need to take a long hot shower or an Epsom salt bath," I said, patting his muscular thigh. "All that standing around on hard wooden floors, as well as the dancing, is bound to take a toll."

"On an old man, you mean?" Richard met my raised eyebrow look with a grin. "It's all right, sweetheart. I know I'm not getting any younger, and I'm afraid a dancer's life doesn't get easier as you age."

"I think you've still got a few good years left," I said mildly as Loie sauntered in from the hall. "Had your snack, did you? Where's your brother?"

As if in response to my question, Fosse barreled down the hallway, leaping over Loie, who hissed her disapproval. The orange tabby paid no attention to this, instead jumping up onto the coffee table to survey Richard and me with his wide golden eyes.

"Watch out, he's going to make the leap sooner or later," Richard said.

"But Loie's going to beat him to the punch." I motioned toward the tortoiseshell, who'd slinked under the coffee table and now sat on her haunches at the edge of the sofa. She sprang up in a graceful arc, landing on the cushion on the other side of Richard.

"A sneak attack," Richard said, petting her head. "Very clever, girl. I guess age and guile sometimes wins out over youth and impetuousness."

I giggled as Fosse, looking hurt, turned his back on us. "And now we'll be spurned, having made fun of his highness," I said, absently thrusting my hand into one of the sweater pockets.

My fingers encountered a hard lump of paper. Sliding it out, I realized it was the crumpled notecard I'd stuffed into the sweater pocket on the day Meredith died.

"For goodness sake, I'd forgotten all about this," I told Richard as I smoothed the card flat. "It was tossed in the corner of one of the rehearsal studios at the theater. I found it when I was checking the rooms downstairs, right before I discovered Meredith's body. I grabbed it, thinking I would reunite it with its recipient. But then it completely slipped my mind."

"Not surprising, considering what came next." Richard leaned in closer. "What is it?"

"Some sort of note. Looks like it was deliberately crumpled." Having flattened the notecard back to something close to its original square shape, I opened it up. "Let's see what it says."

With Richard's head close to mine, we read the short note together.

M.—You've manipulated and used me for the last time. Back off or prepare to pay the price.

The note was printed in block letters that looked like someone had tried to disguise their handwriting. There was no signature.

"Wow," I said. Richard let slip a swear word that made Loie lift her head and stare balefully at us. "*M* has to mean Meredith, right?"

"It could be." Richard spoke slowly, as if he was still processing the implications of the note. "Although that's not something we can be absolutely sure about."

"But I found the note tossed in the corner of a rehearsal studio that Meredith had used, giving a warning to someone with an *M* initial." I picked up the note, holding it by one corner. "There's probably no DNA left on it, is there?"

"You mean other than yours? Who knows? I suggest bagging it and handing it over to Brad. See what he can make of it." Richard jumped up, striding toward the hall. "I'll grab a plastic bag from the kitchen."

I stared at the note. The way it was worded made me reconsider Riley Irwin as a more viable suspect. He had been dressed in black on the day of the murder, and a spurned lover could easily have written that text. *Or an ex-husband,* I thought, considering Nate Broyhill's dark clothing along with Conner's description of the individual he'd seen in the lobby. He thought the person could've been a dancer, and Nate would definitely move in that manner.

Nate was outside, with his vehicle, earlier. But after you went inside, you watched the rehearsal from backstage for a while. Probably long enough for him to head into the theater, kill Meredith, and flee in his SUV. He could've known where the emergency exits were if he'd studied the floorplans ahead of time. Now, whether he somehow got into the theater earlier to stash that knife or simply found it, who knows?

Richard returned with the plastic bag, holding it open while I dropped the note inside. He sealed the bag and carried it over to an end table with a drawer. "I'm putting this in here until you can take it to Brad, or have him pick it up," he said. "One of the few places the cats can't get to."

I nodded, before expounding on my Nate theory while Richard sat down beside me. "He told the authorities that he stopped up the street, a few blocks away, to talk to Tamara. But what if he actually fled in the SUV and then met Tamara along the way and stopped so she could give him an alibi?"

"Because you think they're having a romantic relationship?" Doubt clouded Richard's gray eyes. "I don't know. I'd have thought Tamara was too smart to get involved with Broyhill. She has to have heard all the stories. It's not like he has a sterling reputation in dance circles."

"Maybe it isn't a romance," I said, my mind racing with other possibilities. "He did try to create a dance company once before. Perhaps he's thinking of trying again and is recruiting principal dancers ahead of time."

"I suppose it's possible. Let me ask around and see if there's any chatter about that."

I looked up into Richard's handsome face. "Good idea. By the way, I met a voice teacher at Clarion who said you don't listen to gossip much, so you definitely may have missed any rumors about such a thing.

"Oh? Who was that? I didn't realize many people at the university were even aware of my existence."

I pressed my fingers over the hand he laid on his thigh. "A Ms. Holt. And I bet you're talked about throughout all the various departments at Clarion—at least all the artsy ones. An attractive and talented and famous dancer in their midst? Pfft— you're probably a common topic of conversation."

"Not that famous," Richard said, turning his hand so he could clasp my fingers.

I flashed him a smile. "I bet it was even worse when you were single."

"But I wasn't really ever single when I was working at Clarion, now was I?" Richard lifted our clasped hands and kissed my knuckles. "Since I met you when I first moved to Taylorsford, before I even started my teaching job there."

"We weren't married, or even engaged, for a year or so," I said. "You were fair game then."

"Maybe in their minds. Not in mine," Richard said firmly. He released my hand and slipped his arm around my shoulders. "Now, getting back to our discussion about the cryptic note— who could've sent it if it wasn't Nate? Any ideas?"

"Riley Irwin, perhaps?' I snuggled up closer to Richard, blinking to keep my eyes open. I was tired. Exhausted, actually.

Which was silly. I'd worked plenty of Saturdays without becoming so drained. "I told you what Emily Moore said about him having a relationship with Meredith."

"One that didn't end well," Richard said thoughtfully. "I suppose that could fit with the 'manipulated and used' line."

"Exactly. Maybe he didn't actually head to that café when he left Tamara and Davonte in the parking lot. He could've circled around to the front of the theater and reentered through the lobby, or something. He knows the building, so he'd be able to get away and reappear outside later without much trouble."

A piercing meow drew my attention to the foot of stairs, where Loie and Fosse had gathered. "Not so patiently waiting, are you, guys?" Richard gave my shoulder a squeeze before pulling back his arm. "I think they want us to go to bed. Which seems like a great idea. I'm worn out, and you look like you're still half asleep. What do you say we head upstairs and talk about this again after you share the note with Brad?"

"Sounds like a plan," I said, yawning.

Richard helped me to my feet, keeping a hold on my hand as we crossed the room. He also followed behind me as I climbed the stairs, claiming he didn't want me to tumble backward.

"I'm not that out of it," I said, although I was grateful for his concern.

"All the same, I'd rather be safe than sorry," Richard said as we reached the hallway at the top of the steps.

Instead of walking into our bedroom, I stopped and turned around as a new thought hit me. "Come to think of it, that note could've also been written by Davonte or Tamara. We don't know about all of their interactions in the past. Maybe Meredith did manipulate and use them. In terms of career-related stuff, I mean. It wouldn't surprise me."

Richard placed his hands on my shoulders and spun me around before giving me a little push forward. "Bed. Now."

"All right, all right," I mumbled. I crossed the room, shedding the sweater and tossing it over a chair along the way. Fosse and Loie were already waiting, curled up on the coverlet I'd pulled back to the foot of the bed. "But you know I'm going to be puzzling over this half the night."

"Then I'd better find a way to distract you," Richard called out as he headed into the bathroom.

Chapter Twenty

One of the deputies from the Taylorsford Sheriff's Department stopped by to pick up the note just as I was preparing to leave the house on Sunday. After handing it off, I locked the front door and hurried down the steps to join Aunt Lydia and Zelda at the car.

"What was that all about?" Zelda, who was sitting up front, turned her head to look at me in the back seat.

"Just some info for Brad. I'm helping him with research on the Meredith Fox case," I said, widening my eyes as Zelda turned back around and my aunt glanced at me in the rearview mirror. I certainly didn't want to discuss my latest clue with someone who was simply incapable of keeping such news to herself.

"I hope they clear that up soon. I want to see that young man exonerated." Zelda pursed her lips as she checked her makeup in the visor mirror.

"So do I, which is the main reason I'm helping Brad," I said.

Aunt Lydia shot me another quick look via the rearview mirror. "Amy's convinced he's innocent, and I tend to agree with her."

"Well, it wouldn't be the first time an innocent person was arrested." Zelda closed the visor with a loud click.

"You're absolutely right," Aunt Lydia said. "But why don't we change the subject? I'm a little weary of all this talk about murder."

After that, we chatted about gardening—or rather Aunt Lydia and Zelda did. I stared out the side window instead, focusing on calming my rolling stomach. Getting carsick was the last thing I needed. I wanted to keep all my wits about me so I could observe Glenda Lance, and perhaps Oliver, in their natural habitat.

When we reached the entrance to Blue Haven Farm, Zelda oohed and aahed over the beauty of the estate. "Never been here before," she said. "I've met Ms. Lance at several regional garden club events, but this is the first time she's hosted anything at her place."

"It's quite impressive," Aunt Lydia said as she sped the car down the long, paved driveway. "Even bigger than Kurt's place."

"And more ostentatious." I stared out at the trees lining the drive and the expanse of white fence behind them. Clusters of horses dotted the emerald-green fields. "They run a riding school along with training and boarding horses. Glenda's son, Oliver, is in charge of all that."

"He's on the show circuit, isn't he?" Zelda asked. "I've seen articles on his riding success in the paper."

"Yeah, he was even an alternate for one of the Olympic show-jumping teams." I smoothed out the full skirt of my sunflower-patterned dress. "He's a trainer as well as a rider. An all-around equestrian, I guess." Staring out my window again,

I noticed a gravel lane leading to a small parking lot off to one side of the house. It was partially hidden by a garage, which I assumed was where the family parked their vehicles. Behind the garage, all I could see were rows of cars and trucks. "I think we should just park in front of the house, if there's a space. Looks like the guest lot is full."

"Just one left," Aunt Lydia said as she maneuvered the car into a tight open spot in the circular driveway in front of the house.

"Better you than me squeezing into this space," I said, unbuckling my seat belt.

"They sure must be rolling in the dough to be able to maintain this house and run a horse farm," Zelda said as she opened her door. "I've always been told that keeping horses costs a fortune."

"It's like what Dad says about boats—be prepared to throw money into a bottomless pit."

As we both climbed out of the car, my aunt cast me a smile. "Nick only says that because your mom wants a boat so bad."

"I know. And just between you and me"—I met her gaze with an answering smile—"he's going to relent sooner rather than later. He's actually stashed away some of his bonuses so he can buy her a boat as soon as she retires and no longer has access to one through her work."

"Good for Nick." Aunt Lydia tugged down the short sleeves of her pale lilac linen jacket, which she'd paired with a deep purple skirt. With her string of pearls and taupe pumps, she was the perfect image of a garden club lady.

Zelda, on the other hand, had chosen to wear a vivid geometric-print tunic over a pair of crimson palazzo pants. Standing side by side, she and my aunt offered quite a contrast—like scarlet poppies arranged in a vase filled with lilac branches.

"Shall we? From the sound of voices, I assume the event is taking place around back." Aunt Lydia led the way onto a flagstone path that encircled the house.

When we reached the backyard, I paused to survey the landscape. The lawn was a long rectangle of perfectly manicured grass surrounded by flower beds. A white, open-sided party tent had been set up in the center of the lawn. Large, stoneware urns overflowing with fountains of brightly colored flowers had been placed at each tentpole. Most of the guests milled around inside the tent, examining the potted plants and vases of flowers that adorned white linen-draped banquet tables.

Aunt Lydia's low heels clacked against the flagstone patio that stretched out in a wide arc from the back of the house. The roofed section of the patio held an outdoor living area, complete with a kitchen, a large-screen TV hung over a stone fireplace, and numerous sofas and chairs.

"How the other one percent lives," I said under my breath, earning a sharp glance from my aunt.

"If you want to learn anything useful, I'd suggest you keep such thoughts to yourself," she told me.

I wrinkled my nose at her but didn't really take offense. She was right. I needed to be quiet and gracious, listening rather than saying too much. *You're just here to observe,* I reminded myself, as Aunt Lydia, Zelda, and I made our way over to the table holding various drink options.

Pouring myself a glass from a dispenser that held water infused with fresh cucumbers and strawberries, I gazed around the space, looking for Glenda Lance. I finally spotted her standing inside the tent, chatting with a group of men and women dressed in dark suits.

"Those are the judges," Zelda said, nudging me with her elbow. "Apparently, in addition to this being a fundraising party, it's also a competitive event."

"You didn't enter anything?" I asked.

"The judged event was only for Ms. Lance's club." Zelda's eyes sparkled with mischief. "I guess she figured she might as well take care of two hosting responsibilities with one party. From what I hear, she's pretty reluctant to do much entertaining outside of her own social circle, which is based more in the city than out here in the boonies."

"That's right, she doesn't live here full-time," I said, squinting to get a better look at Glenda Lance. Today she was dressed like the quintessential garden club grande dame, in a periwinkle-blue silk sheath dress and a straw hat decorated with creamy silk flowers.

"Just off and on, from what I hear," Zelda said. "Oh, there's a bunch of our club members, Lydia. Should we join them?"

My aunt turned away from the young woman she was speaking with. "All right. Nice to meet you," she told the woman before introducing Zelda and me. "And Amy, this is Gina Smithy. She just mentioned a possible book donation to the Taylorsford Library. I thought you two should talk."

"Sure, that sounds good," I said, studying the young woman, who appeared to be in her late twenties or early thirties. Short and plump, she was casually dressed in a white cotton top and black slacks. "I'll catch up with you two later."

"So you're the library director for Taylorsford?" Gina tipped her head to one side, exposing a florescent green streak in her short, dark hair. "I remember an older gentleman who used to run the place when I was a kid."

"I took over a little more than four years ago," I said, marveling, as always, over how much had changed in my life during that time. "Do you still live in Taylorsford or nearby?"

"No, a couple of counties over. My garden club is in the region, though, which is why I'm here." Gina grinned. "You probably think I don't look like the garden club type."

"Is there one?" I asked with a smile. "I love to garden, and I'm not sure I fit the mold either. Certainly not the stereotype. But then again, I don't fit the librarian stereotype either."

Gina looked me up and down. "No, you don't. Anyway, as I was telling your aunt, I have a collection of vintage gardening books that need a home. I was planning to donate them to my local library, but they really didn't have the room to take anything right now. I don't know your situation, but I thought I'd offer."

"I'd be glad to take a look at them. We don't have much on that topic, and I know several of our patrons would be interested." I brushed back a tendril of hair the warm breeze had blown into my face. "A lot of people are trying to restore older homes right now, and understanding vintage gardens could be quite useful to their landscaping projects."

"Great," Gina said with a broad smile. "I'll bring them by one day soon. Can I just call the library ahead of time?"

"Sure, or call me directly." I fished a business card out of my purse and handed it to Gina. "How did you come by these books anyway? Are you a horticulturist?"

"Heavens no. I'm actually a small animal vet. I work with my dad's practice. Dr. Mitchell Smithy—maybe you've heard of him?"

"No, I'm afraid not. My husband and I have two cats, but we take them to the vet in Taylorsford."

"They're very good." Gina fiddled with the collar of her blouse. "Anyway, the reason I have the books is because someone gave them to my dad. He's an equine specialist, so he works with a lot of the horse farms in the area. One of his clients who recently passed away left him the books because he was gracious about allowing her to ramble on about her roses." Gina grinned. "I think the lady believed that Dad was into gardening, which he most certainly is not."

"Does he take care of the animals here?" I asked. "I mean, the Blue Haven Farm horses?"

Gina's bright expression instantly darkened. "No. Not anymore." She turned away for a moment to grab a glass of white wine from the drinks table. "Which is one reason why I was actually hesitant to come today. I don't much care for the Lance family, to tell you the truth."

"What happened?" I asked, before taking a sip of my water.

Gina faced me again, cradling her wineglass between both hands. "Basically, Oliver Lance fired him."

"Whatever for?"

"Nothing, really. Anyway, nothing my dad understood. He'd been their vet for years, treating all their horses, including the boarders. No complaints in all that time, and he was working with some high-value horseflesh, so a lot was always on the line."

Recalling Monica's story about being fired, I frowned. "Was this about four years ago?"

"It was. My dad had just given some new boarders a clean bill of health, which allowed them to be brought here. Then, before he knew it, he heard that some of the Blue Haven stock had fallen ill. He was pretty frantic over that." Gina squared her shoulders. "Dad loves horses, you see. It isn't just a job to him. He really cares. So when he heard the news, he was ready to jump into his truck and head over here as fast as legally possible. But Oliver Lance told him not to bother."

"Why would he do that?"

Gina shrugged. "Who knows? It didn't make any sense. Dad told me that Oliver had brought in another vet. After that, Oliver said my father's services were no longer needed. Ever." Gina sniffed. "It was ridiculous. Dad knew those horses and had all their medical records. He was the person who should've attended them. Maybe they would've lived if he had."

"Did Oliver Lance give a reason for this change?"

"Not really. Dad figured it had something to do with him okaying those new boarders. He assumed Oliver believed that those horses carried in the influenza. But Dad was certain they were healthy. He also knew for a fact that they were vaccinated, just like the Blue Haven horses." Gina shook her head. "It didn't make any sense. Dad's been kind of haunted by the whole mess ever since."

"Did your dad work with a young woman at the farm named Monica Payne?" I asked, trying to piece these two stories together.

"Yeah, I know Monica. She works at another farm now—Brentwood, I think it is. Anyway, Oliver fired her too, over the same situation. I didn't think that was fair either."

223

"I can see why you aren't particularly fond of the Lance family." I finished off my water and deposited the empty glass on a small table set up to collect used tableware.

"Oh, crap, speak of the devil," Gina said, motioning toward the backyard.

Oliver Lance was strolling across the lawn, heading in our direction.

"Sorry, I really don't want to speak to him. I'll give you a call about the books sometime soon." Gina scurried off, clutching her wineglass to her chest.

When Oliver reached me, Gina had already disappeared into a group of people hovering over the buffet table. "Hello, Amy," he said, his expression offering no clues to his feelings about Gina's rapid departure. "I wasn't expecting to see you here today. For some reason, I don't picture you as the garden club type."

"I'm actually here with my aunt, Lydia Talbot, and our friend, Zelda Adams. They've been trying to recruit me into their club for some time now." I hoped my smile didn't look quite as plastic as it felt. "I must confess—I enjoy gardening, but the club aspect isn't something that I'm particularly interested in."

"Me neither. I'm just supporting Mom today." Oliver's hair gleamed with golden highlights, but his deep brown eyes seemed shadowed. "I tell you what, how about a tour of the house? We do have a rather nice private library."

I studied his handsome face for a moment, puzzling over his intentions. He knew I was married, but I was savvy enough to realize that didn't mean anything to certain people. *And the look he's giving you is a little more than friendly.*

"That sounds interesting," I said, keeping my tone neutral. I didn't want to lead him on, but the opportunity to learn more about his family and their possible connection to Meredith's death overwhelmed my concerns over his flirtatious attitude.

"Great. We can go in through the family room," he said, striding across the patio to a set of glass doors that could be folded back like the accordion pleats of a paper fan. Oliver simply opened one panel, allowing me to walk into the house in front of him.

The "family room" was larger than the entire first floor of my house. Anchored at one end by an enormous stone fireplace and at the other by a kitchen whose expanses of white quartz sparkled under gold-colored light fixtures, it could easily accommodate the entire cast of the *Folklore Suite*.

"Very nice," I said, assuming it was only polite to say something.

Oliver shrugged. "It works well for events, like hosting fundraisers or when I entertain my horse show colleagues. But I actually prefer the library when I'm here alone."

I looked up at him as we crossed the room and entered a wood-paneled hallway. "It's a big house for one person."

"It is." Oliver gazed down at me with a warm smile. "Mom is here part of the time, of course, and I occasionally have houseguests, but I often feel like a pea rattling around in a rather gigantic pod."

Unsure whether this declaration was meant to arouse my sympathies for his single state or simply confirm that he had no live-in girlfriend, I just nodded my head and smiled.

"Here we go—the library," Oliver said, throwing his hand out with a flourish as he opened the door.

"I can see why you love this room," I said as I stepped inside.

With its tall ceilings, white-painted wood paneling and trim, and floor-to-ceiling bookshelves, it was definitely a reader's haven. Not as large as many of the other rooms I'd glimpsed on our short walk through the house, it was warm and cozy, its solid wood and damask-cushioned furniture elegant but worn. A huge desk dominated the center of the room, complemented by a high-backed, rolling wooden chair and a Tiffany desk lamp.

Probably a real one, I thought as I crossed over to the desk.

"We have quite a few first editions of classics," Oliver said, motioning toward the bookshelves. "As well as some wonderful old atlases and bound maps. My father was the collector," he added, pride evident in his voice. "He was a world traveler and adored anything to do with geography or other cultures."

"I'd love to spend some time examining his collection," I said with absolute honesty. The beautifully bound volumes that filled the shelves were calling to me—a siren song I could never resist.

"You're welcome anytime," Oliver said, turning away at the sound of someone calling his name.

"Sorry sir," said a young woman in a plain white blouse and tailored gray slacks.

Staff, I thought as Oliver walked over to the open doorway. "What is it?" he asked, not bothering to temper the irritation in his tone.

"Phone call on the landline," the young woman said. "Something I think you need to take, sir, as it has to do with the sale of the bay gelding."

Oliver made an exasperated noise before agreeing to take the call. "Stay here and look around. I'll be back in a few minutes," he told me as he left the room, closing the door behind him.

Chapter
Twenty-One

I couldn't believe my good luck. Here I was, given free rein in the very library where Monica had told me Oliver Lance kept his records.

Crossing to the bookshelves, I surveyed the rows of books until my gaze finally landed on a set of tall, narrow, gray suede volumes that lacked print on their spines. *The ledgers,* I thought, hurrying over to that section of the shelves.

I pulled down the first volume in the set and opened it. On the title page, handwritten dates informed me that this was far too old to contain the records I wanted. But it also told me that each ledger represented one year of Blue Haven's operations. Replacing that volume, I counted down the row until I found the volume I thought would contain records from four years ago.

Opening the ledger, I sped through its pages, looking for any mention of the influenza outbreak or the death of the horses. I kept an eye on the door to the hall too, not wanting Oliver to return and find me rifling through his records. I was sure that, despite his apparent attraction to me, he'd be angry at such an invasion of privacy.

All for a good cause, I told myself as I flipped through the ledger. Reaching the pages covering the summer of that year, I finally noticed a mention of two new horses being brought in as boarders. In the column dedicated to medical notes was a notation of the horses having a clean bill of health, signed off by Dr. Mitchell Smithy.

But just a page later, two other horses were marked as deceased. The vet confirming their deaths was not, as I already knew, Dr. Smithy, but rather a Dr. Winston Duran.

The guy quoted in the article in the archives, I thought. I skimmed through the rest of the pages in the ledger but never saw Dr. Duran's name again. Another veterinarian was mentioned once or twice—Dr. Kiner, who was someone I'd actually met at one of Kurt's parties. She was a pleasant woman who still practiced in the area and had, as far as I knew, a spotless reputation.

I flipped back to the page that included Dr. Duran's name. Pulling my cell phone from my purse, I took a couple of quick snaps of the relevant entries before closing the ledger.

The library door opened just as I shoved the ledger back in place on the shelf. I turned to face the door, expecting Oliver.

"Sorry, I wanted to take a few photos of the library," I said, waving the phone I hadn't been able to stash in time. "I know I should've asked first . . ."

"What are you doing in here?" asked Glenda Lance.

I swallowed and shoved my phone into my purse. "Your son was showing me the library, but he got an important phone call and told me to wait and . . . well, being a librarian, I got a little carried away looking at all these wonderful books and wanted to get some photos." I realized I was babbling, but hoped my obvious embarrassment would be enough to placate my hostess.

Glenda's eyes narrowed. Tapping the toe of one of her navy pumps against the hardwood floor, she raked her gaze over me. "Oliver left you in here?"

"He was giving me a brief tour of the house, but I was most interested in this room, being a librarian."

"Yes, yes," Glenda said with a dismissive wave of her hand. "You mentioned that before."

The hair on the back of my neck stood at attention as Glenda stepped into the room, closing the door behind her. "I'm very sorry if I wasn't supposed to be in the house. I know the party is actually outside. But since Oliver invited me, I thought it would be okay."

"Oh, that part is fine. It's Oliver's home as much as it is mine, so he can do as he pleases about who comes and goes. It's just that"—Glenda crossed to the desk and picked up a glass mosaic paperweight—"I don't like people taking photos of the interior of my houses, unless I've arranged it beforehand. I hope you can understand."

"Of course," I said, stepping away from the bookshelves. "I'm sure it feels like an invasion of your personal space."

"Exactly." Glenda bounced the paperweight from one palm to the other. "And I don't particularly like snoops either. That was one of the things that always annoyed me about my ex-daughter-in-law, Meredith, rest her soul. She tended to be a little too nosey. Always poking around in other people's business."

I opened my mouth but snapped it shut without saying anything. Glenda Lance was staring at me in a way that made my heart feel like it was bouncing off my ribs. There was a ferocity in her gaze, like a caged wild animal. *She'd spring on me if she could break convention's leash,* I thought, inching sideways in the direction of the exit.

"I truly am sorry," I said. "I should've known better."

"Indeed, you should have." Glenda clunked the paperweight back down on the desk. "I suppose I shouldn't keep expecting young people to have any manners, though. That seems to have gone out with video cassettes."

The door opened again, revealing Oliver, who looked from me to his mother and back again. "Ah, how nice, you two having a little conversation."

I could tell by the set of his shoulders and jaw that he was not actually thrilled by this development, but decided to play along. "Yes, it was great to have a chance to chat again."

Glenda turned her intimidating stare on her son. "You really shouldn't abandon our guests when you've promised them a house tour. I thought I'd taught you better than that, Oliver."

"Forgive me, I was detained longer than I expected," Oliver said, keeping his gaze fixed on me. "I hope you were able to examine some of our more interesting volumes."

"She also appears to have taken some pictures," Glenda said, causing Oliver's focus to immediately snap to her.

"Nothing wrong with that, is there? Amy's the library director in Taylorsford. She has a great interest in books." Oliver kept his tone light, but I could see tension tightening the lines around his mouth.

"No, of course not. It's simply that, as I told her, I prefer no one take photos inside our house. Without our permission, I mean." Glenda strolled over to stand in front of her son. "Unless you gave her permission? In which case I must apologize."

"Not explicitly," Oliver said. "But I also didn't tell her not to."

"Well then, we'll just call it a mistake and let it go, shall we?" Glenda flicked her wrist in the slightest semblance of a wave. "Goodbye, Amy. Oliver can show you out."

She sauntered out of the room, brushing past her son without an apology.

"I am sorry about the pictures," I told Oliver as soon as his mother disappeared. "I wasn't thinking. Your library is just so lovely, and I wanted to be able to show it to a few people who appreciate books like I do." I kept my head down, hoping Oliver would read this as evidence of my embarrassment instead of the duplicity it really was.

"It's not a problem," Oliver said. "You'll just have to send me copies of the photos when you get a chance."

There was something different in his eyes—a calculating gleam that matched his mother's piercing gaze. "Sure, I'll do that," I said, not intending to do any such thing. "But for now I guess I should be getting back to the party. My aunt will be wondering where I am."

"Understood. Well, come along then. A more complete tour of the house will have to wait for a future visit."

I flashed him a bright smile before I followed him into the hall. Of course, I had no intention of visiting Oliver's home again, but there was no point in making such a declaration now. Following him back outside, I thanked him again for showing me the library before I made a beeline for the party tent.

"And where have you been?" Aunt Lydia asked, side-eyeing me.

"Oliver Lance offered to show me the family's private library. You know I can't resist that."

My aunt arched her pale eyebrows. "And did you find anything interesting?"

"As a matter of fact, I did," I said, closing my lips over my next words when Zelda bustled up to join us.

"You'll never believe what I just heard," Zelda said, her expression barely containing her excitement. "Remember that woman who told us she'd won awards at the National Flower Show in the UK?"

Leaving Zelda excitedly explaining to Aunt Lydia that this claim was, as they had expected, a fabrication, I wandered over to one of the display tables to examine some flower arrangements. But although I admired the beauty of the plants, and the skill required to achieve the floral designs, my mind was actually focused on my recent encounter with Glenda Lance.

Does her barely repressed anger, directed at Meredith as well as you, mean she could be the killer? But why? Could it be that Meredith, whom she accused of snooping, discovered some secret Glenda wanted to keep buried?

I paused in front of an artful arrangement of peppermint-striped carnations and rosy pinks in a vintage ceramic milk bottle. As I inhaled the spicy scent of the flowers, I once again considered the possibility that Meredith had been a black-mailer. If she'd uncovered some information her ex-husband—or someone else in the Lance family—desperately didn't want to come to light, had she forced them to pay for her silence?

"That would explain the note I found," I said to myself.

"Excuse me?" someone at my elbow asked.

I shifted my gaze to the speaker—a slender, gray-haired gentleman wearing silver-framed glasses and leaning on a cane. "Sorry, just muttering to myself," I said, mustering up a smile.

"I don't think I've seen you at any of our events before," the man said, his watery pale eyes sweeping over me. "What club are you with, if I may ask?"

"None, actually. I'm a guest of Lydia Talbot, who's part of the Taylorsford area club. I'm her niece," I added, as the man's expression brightened.

"Ah, dear Lydia. I knew she had a niece, but I'd never have picked you out as her relative. You look nothing alike."

"I know. I take after my mother, Lydia's younger sister."

The older man's eyes sparkled behind the lenses of his glasses. "That's right, there was a sister. Deborah, wasn't it?"

"Yes, but she goes by Debbie, and it's Debbie Webber now. I'm Amy Webber. Well, Amy Webber Muir, actually." I extended my hand. "You must've known my family in the past."

"Jerome Kline," the man said, briefly clasping my fingers with his free hand. "I was a fresh-out-of-college teacher at the high school when your aunt and mother were students of mine. English class," he added, with a thin-lipped smile. "I taught your aunt's future husband too. Andrew Talbot." Jerome's expression grew distant. "Unlike Lydia and your mom, he wasn't much for reading, but he certainly was a talented artist. I wish I'd picked up a few of his early paintings back then, when they were affordable. I bought one much later at a considerably higher price."

"Well, even I only have one, and that was a gift from my aunt. I certainly couldn't purchase any on the open market these days. Where did you find yours?" I asked, always on the lookout for dealers in my Uncle Andrew's work. Aunt Lydia still owned a lot of it, but there were other pieces floating around the art world. I knew my aunt liked to keep track of where they were and who owned them.

"At a gallery in Georgetown. A place owned by that Kendrick fellow who has an estate outside of Taylorsford." Jerome's expression turned sly. "At any rate, he calls himself Kurt Kendrick these days, although I remember him by another name."

"Really?" I kept my tone light, hoping it wouldn't betray my interest. "And did you make a good deal?"

"I did. Once I reminded him of our past association, that is." Jerome studied me for a moment. "Taught him too, for a brief time. Karl Kloss he was called back then. Bad apple, I'm afraid. I was surprised to discover he'd become so successful. Figured he'd be in jail by the time he was in his twenties."

Of course, I knew about Kurt's name change as well as his past adventures on the wrong side of the law, but I wasn't about to confess that to Jerome Kline. "He must've turned his life around."

Jerome tapped his cane against the short-cropped grass beneath our feet. "Maybe. I just remember he and Andrew Talbot were thick as thieves, and that always concerned me.

Andrew was a good kid. I didn't want to see him get tangled up in whatever illegal activities that Kloss boy was into."

Knowing the less than reputable activities my late uncle had ended up getting drawn into—none of which was really Kurt's fault—I just murmured something noncommittal before changing the subject to ask Jerome about his involvement in garden clubs.

"I'm part of the Smith County group," he told me. "I moved to a senior living community here a few years back. Luckily, I was able to get a cluster home that does have a small backyard so I could continue to grow things."

"You must know our hostess then," I said.

"Glenda? Only casually. She's not the most chummy sort, and if you ever get on her bad side"—Jerome cast a withering gaze over my head—"she can be ruthless."

I turned to follow his gaze. Glenda, deep in conversation with other guests, fortunately didn't notice us. "I've gotten that impression."

"All I did was to question whether she'd actually grown one of her exhibited flowers from seed. It was one where that's extremely difficult to do, you see," Jerome said, his frown curling into a smile as he looked back at me. "You would've thought I'd insulted her family name, the way she reacted. She's been cold as an icicle to me ever since."

"So, not the forgiving sort?" I asked, mulling over this confirmation of my suspicions. It seemed that if Meredith had done something to anger Glenda Lance, the older woman could've still been furious with her, even years later. Which, to my mind, pushed Glenda up the suspect list.

"Hardly. She's the type to hold a grudge until the end of time. But enough of such unpleasantries," Jerome said, straightening his back. "I'd really rather talk about flowers."

We chatted briefly about his gardening exploits before I excused myself and located Aunt Lydia standing by the buffet table.

"I need to ask Ms. Lance for the recipe for these delicious lemon tarts," she said before dabbing her lips with a napkin.

"You think she'll share?" I asked. "Besides, I'm sure this was catered."

"True." Aunt Lydia stared over my shoulder. "There's Zelda. Why don't we round her up and make a graceful exit? I'm certainly ready to leave. I can only take so much schmoozing. I showed up today, and I've already made my rather meager contribution to the fundraising campaign, so I think I've done enough."

After we collected Zelda, we sought out Glenda Lance to express our thanks for the party. I couldn't help but notice the warm wishes she extended to Aunt Lydia and Zelda were not offered to me. I received a curt *goodbye* without so much as a smile.

"Glenda didn't seem very fond of you, Amy. What did you do to tick her off?" Zelda asked as we reached the circular driveway.

"I was too nosy, I think," I said. *Just like Meredith . . .*

Once we were in the car, heading back to Taylorsford, I slipped my cell phone from my purse and examined the photos I'd snapped of the ledger pages.

It was evidence I needed to share with someone who might know more about a veterinarian named Dr. Winston Duran. I texted Monica Payne, asking her to meet me at the library as soon as possible.

She texted back, offering to stop by the next day, although she wasn't sure of an exact time.

Doesn't matter, I told her. *I'll be there from eight to five. Anytime during those hours is fine by me.*

She sent back a thumbs-up emoji.

I turned off my phone and settled back in my seat, hoping I could at least clear up the confusion around Monica's firing. Even if it didn't have anything to do with the murder case, it would be one positive thing to come out of all my recent research.

And one question I could answer was always better than none.

Chapter
Twenty-Two

M onday was the start of tech week for the *Folklore Suite*, which meant, as I told Sunny, that I probably wouldn't see Richard for more than ten minutes each morning.

Sunny, checking in some books, cast me an amused glance. "He does come home at night, I assume?"

"Well, sure. Although I'm often asleep before he gets back from rehearsals. It doesn't help that he's supervising the lighting as well as directing the show."

"And dancing in it." Sunny flipped her single braid behind her shoulders. "I swear, that man has more energy than I've ever even imagined having."

Having known my vivacious friend for over twenty years, I could've challenged that statement, but I concentrated on checking a few new records in our online catalog instead. "Speaking of being busy—are you sure you don't mind covering Samantha's hours this week? I want to give her a break, since she'll be ferrying Shay to and from a lot of rehearsals, with some running late into the night. But if you have a paper or project due for school . . ."

"It's fine," Sunny said, cutting me off with a wave of her hand. "I can always work on my coursework when it's quiet here. As long as you don't mind me using the circ computer for my online classes, that is."

"No problem with that. I've also doubled up on the volunteers, which should help with any busy periods." I straightened the flyers in a plastic holder on the desk.

"You aren't working backstage after all? I remember you mentioning something about being asked to help out after Karla had to take over Meredith's part in the production."

"No, some of the dance moms volunteered. They're going to take turns working backstage over the run of the production, so they can all see the show from the audience, of course, but said they thought I should have the opportunity to watch from the audience on opening night, which was really nice." I handed Sunny an item from the book drop at the desk. "By the way, I've secured two tickets for you for Saturday night's premiere performance. Will Fred will be in town? I hope so. Aunt Lydia said that Hugh was planning to accompany her."

"Yeah, first real date in a while." Sunny rolled her eyes. "I guess I'll have to get all dolled up to celebrate the occasion."

"I'm sure Fred will appreciate that," I said with a smile.

"Oh, he likes me just as well in sweats." Sunny gathered up her stack of books and turned to the book cart parked behind us. "Just so you know, we're looking at houses together."

I couldn't see her face, which I suspected was her intention. "Really? To buy or to rent?"

"Buy, I think. No use throwing money away on a rental." Sunny began arranging the books on the cart in call-number order. "Doesn't mean we're getting married, if that was your next question."

I lifted my hands. "It wasn't, but now that you've brought it up . . ."

Sunny looked over her shoulder. "Nope, no wedding. And I still don't want to have kids either. If you can spread that news around so people stop asking, I'd definitely appreciate it."

"You know that won't do any good. They're always going to pester you about that sort of thing. But I will mention it to Zelda, which should be enough to relay your message far and wide."

As she turned to face me, Sunny's serious expression morphed into a grin. "Perfect way to make any news go viral," she said. "Now, tell me more about this garden party you crashed yesterday. Was Lydia upset over having to leave early?"

"Speaking of news traveling fast—no, not really. She was actually the one to suggest it. And once I explained why I was snooping in the library, which I'm sure you also heard about, she was okay with that too. Except for worrying about me possibly placing myself in danger, of course."

"That concerns me as well." Sunny narrowed her eyes. "You've shared your suspicions about both Glenda and Oliver Lance, who were at the party. As well as Nate Broyhill, who could certainly have heard about your antics from the others. If any of them actually killed Meredith, you could've just painted a bright red target on your back."

"I don't know—none of them strike me as the impetuous or foolish type. With most of the attention focused on Conner Vogler, whoever murdered Meredith has escaped detection so far. Would they really risk exposing themselves by harming me?" I shrugged. "I know I've been warned off, but the authorities haven't been able to identify that person yet either. The phone message was untraceable. As careful as the culprit's been, I just don't think they'll take impulsive action at this point."

"I hope you're right." Sunny examined me, frown lines bracketing her mouth. "You look really tired. Are you feeling okay?"

"Gee, do I look that bad?" I made a comical face. When Sunny didn't smile in response, I laid a hand on her forearm. "I'm fine. There's just been a lot going on recently, and I've had some trouble turning off my brain at night, so I've been sleeping rather fitfully."

"Okay. I'm just glad you don't have to take on that backstage work this week. At least you can rest after work, even if you aren't sleeping so great."

"And thankfully, the parents of the dancers from Karla's studio have arranged a reception following the Sunday afternoon performance, so I don't have to deal with that either." I rubbed a flyaway strand of my dark hair between my fingers. "Normally we'd have some sort of afterparty Saturday evening, but Richard and Karla thought Sunday afternoon would work better since they have younger performers in the cast."

"I bet Richard will appreciate just being able to go home Saturday night. Karla too."

"Absolutely. I'm sure they'll both be exhausted once the show is over on Saturday." A bang like an elbow hitting glass made me glance over at the lobby doors. "Oh, it's Monica Payne. She promised to stop by today, although she never said when."

"Do you need me to disappear?" Sunny asked as Ethan Payne's sister paused just beyond the doors and allowed her gaze to sweep over the library. Dressed in tan jodhpurs and a navy polo shirt emblazoned with some sort of logo, as well as ankle-high riding boots, Monica looked like she'd just strolled out of the stables.

"Thanks, it might help if I can speak with her alone. But I'd like you to meet her, so stay long enough to be introduced. She might end up being part of my extended family one of these days."

"Ah, Ethan and Scott." Sunny shared a knowing look with me as Monica strode toward the desk. "Gotcha."

"Hello, Monica," I said as the tall young woman reached the desk. "I'm glad you could stop by." I introduced her and Sunny before adding, "I hope I'm not interfering with your work schedule."

Monica tucked the lock of honey-brown hair that had escaped her loose bun behind her ear. "It's fine. One of my riders didn't show up for her lesson, so I thought I'd take the opportunity to talk to you, sooner rather than later."

"It was nice to meet you, Monica, but I need to head out into the stacks to reshelve these books." Sunny rolled the book cart out from behind the desk.

"I've seen her somewhere before," Monica said as she watched Sunny disappear into the stacks. "Something connected with fruit and vegetables, somehow."

"Maybe you've visited Vista View, her grandparents' organic farm, or seen their booth at the farmers' market?"

"That's it," Monica said with a snap of her fingers. "She was manning their booth at the market one Saturday. I remember because she suggested that I try a new variety of apple, and I ended up really liking it." Monica switched her focus back on me. "Anyway, you said you wanted to share some information?"

"And see what you make of it." I leaned over the desk, resting my forearms on the worn surface. "It's related to the time you worked for Oliver Lance. Sorry to bring up a sensitive topic, but you told me that those horses you okayed as boarders were cleared by a vet, right?"

"That's right." Monica looked puzzled. "What does that have to do with anything?"

"Do you remember which vet?"

"Sure, it was Mitchell Smithy. He took care of all of the horses at Blue Haven Farm. At least, he did when I was working there."

"Then why didn't he sign the death certificates for the horses that died from the influenza?" I asked.

Monica took a step back. "What? I assumed he did."

"Nope." I slipped my cell phone out of my pocket and turned it on. "I was at Blue Haven yesterday, in the library . . ." Noticing Monica's confusion, I clarified my actions. "Okay, so I was there with my aunt and her friend for a garden club event. But what I really wanted to do was see if I could gather any more information on the Meredith Fox case. I know that sounds strange . . ." The arch of Monica's eyebrows confirmed this, but I forged ahead. "Oliver was there and we got to talking, and he invited me to check out their family library."

Monica's eyes widened. "Really? Was it sort of a 'let me show you my etchings' type of invitation?"

"No, it wasn't anything like that. At least, not on my part. Anyway, while we were in the library he was called away, and I noticed a couple of those ledgers you'd mentioned. So I . . . opened up one of them that was labeled with dates from about four years ago."

"You found the entries for the horses who died?" Monica, who'd inched her way closer to the desk, leaned forward until we were almost nose to nose.

"I did. There was a column for notes associated with each entry." I swiped to the proper photo.

Monica nodded. "A lot of times that was used for notes from the seller or buyer, or the vet, depending on the situation."

"Well, in this case it was the vet, documenting the cause of death. Only it wasn't Dr. Smithy. See?" I handed her the phone.

Monica peered at the photo, her eyes narrowing. "Winston Duran," she said in a low voice.

"Do you know him?" I asked.

"Never heard of him," she replied, thrusting the phone back at me without meeting my eyes.

That was odd. Monica had composed her expression by the time she finally looked up at me, but I could've sworn I'd seen a flash of anger in her eyes. "Funny thing is, he was quoted in some article I read about the outbreak of equine influenza at Blue Haven Farm. It was in the archives." Noticing Monica's confusion, I added, "We maintain historical papers, town records, old newspaper clippings, and other materials in a building out back."

"I see." Monica took a deep breath before speaking again. "Sorry, that name rings no bells, and I know all of the big animal vets with practices in this area." Straightening, she met my inquisitive stare with a lift of her chin. "But maybe Dr. Smithy wasn't available, and Oliver just called in someone he knew from the show circuit."

I studied her face for a moment, observing the tightness of her square jaw and the slight flutter of her eyelids. *It feels like she's lying, but why?* "The thing is, I actually spoke with Dr. Smithy's daughter yesterday at the garden party. She said that when the horses got sick, her dad was ready to attend to them, but Oliver told him his services weren't needed." I lifted my hands in a questioning gesture. "It just seems odd, and I thought maybe you could explain why Oliver might do something like that."

"I have no idea. Like I said, I wasn't even in town when the horses fell ill. I just assumed that Dr. Smithy had handled the case." Monica bit her lip, as if holding back a curse word or perhaps a sob. "Honestly, I was so devastated by the whole situation I never read that article—or any other reports, for that matter." Monica's lips trembled. "I mean, I came back to work, and two of our best animals were dead, and then Oliver says it's mostly my fault and fires me."

"I know it had to be devastating," I said, reminding myself that Oliver had given Monica a good reference despite firing her. Another peculiar aspect of a situation that frankly didn't make much sense.

"I did land on my feet, though." Monica pressed two fingers over the symbol on her shirt, which I realized was the logo for Brentwood Farms. "I've got an excellent job now. So no hard feelings, I guess."

Pursing my lips, I swallowed back a comment concerning Oliver Lance lying to her about the horses who'd died. Or, at a minimum, not telling her about some new vet he'd brought in to replace the man she'd relied on. "Still, it's a little odd, don't you think? I mean, this Dr. Duran just appearing out of nowhere and then apparently disappearing again."

"Oh, I don't know." There was a forced lightness in Monica's voice that made my shoulders tighten. "Oliver would've known a lot of people from his travels on the show circuit. I'm thinking maybe this new vet was just someone he felt he could call on for a serious emergency."

"As opposed to the vet his family had used for years?" I closed my lips over my next words, realizing there was no point in badgering Monica any further. "Anyway, I wanted you to know what I'd found out, but as you've said, you really don't know anything more about the situation. So we can let that go."

"I think that's best," Monica said, the tension draining from her face. "I'm glad you shared that photo with me, though. If nothing else, it makes me feel better about working with Dr. Smithy in the future. I've been hesitant to recommend him to my current employers, but I'm not too fond of the practice we're using now, so maybe we should give him a chance."

"Happy I could help," I said, even though I wasn't entirely sure that I was pleased with Monica's reaction to my information. She'd put on a good show of not being upset by the reveal of the mysterious vet and Oliver's obvious obfuscation of the truth surrounding the deaths of the horses, but I sensed something off about her response.

Like she's pretending everything is fine, when she's actually angry enough to spit tacks, I thought as Sunny reappeared, pushing the cart back toward the desk.

"Did you get everything sorted?" Sunny asked brightly.

"I think so." I studied Monica's calm face. "We just shared information and clarified a few facts."

"Yes, it was quite illuminating." Monica flashed a broad smile. "But I'd better go. I don't want to be late for my next lesson. Hope to see you both around," she added, as she left the desk.

Watching her leave, worry lines crinkled Sunny's forehead. "What in the world did you tell her? She was practically vibrating with energy, like she might explode at any second."

"I'm not really sure. But whatever it was, it was too much, I'm afraid," I said.

Chapter
Twenty-Three

I'd just gotten home and given the cats their treats on Tuesday evening when I got a text from Kurt, asking if he could stop by to talk to me in person. He'd apparently uncovered some information concerning the art theft. *And one other thing,* he'd added at the end of the text, making me even more interested in hearing what he had to say.

An hour later, I welcomed him into the house, suggesting that we sit on the screened back porch. "It's not so hot out this evening," I said as I led the way through the kitchen. "And I like to enjoy our view of the woods and mountains whenever I can."

"I can understand why," Kurt said, surveying the view of our backyard through the screened-in windows, while Loie and Fosse, who were cuddled up together on a wicker settee, eyed him with suspicion. "And honestly, I'd rather sit out here. I always think fresh air is preferable to air conditioning."

"Can I get you something to drink?" I asked, hoping he wouldn't ask for wine. I knew his cellar was filled with high-end vintages, while all we had to offer were supermarket specials.

"Just some water will be fine," Kurt said. "I've decided to limit my alcohol consumption to the weekends, and not too much even then. Trying to keep the old brain sharp," he added, tapping his temple with one finger.

Relieved, I smiled. "Sounds like a good plan. I've cut back too. It's a lot of empty calories. I think I'd rather eat more and drink less."

"You're not on a diet, I hope," Kurt said, looking me over as he took a seat in one of the wicker armchairs facing the settee.

"Not really. Just cutting back a bit on things like alcohol and sweets," I replied.

"Glad to hear it. You don't need to starve yourself to look good, you know."

"Trust me, I'm not doing that," I told him as I headed back into the kitchen.

When I returned with two tumblers filled with ice water, I was amused to see that Fosse had abandoned his sister to jump up into Kurt's lap. "That's a real compliment," I said as I handed Kurt a glass. "He doesn't usually take to strangers like that."

"He recognized me as a cat lover." Kurt scratched behind Fosse's ears.

I studied Kurt with a bemused expression before sitting down in the chair next to him. "I'm always learning something new about you, it seems. I had no idea you liked cats, or any animals, really. You don't have any pets at Highview."

"Because I'm not living there all the time." Kurt stretched out his long legs, allowing Fosse to curl up on his thighs. "I don't actually live anywhere consistently enough, to be honest. I'm in Georgetown sometimes and at Highview sometimes, and then traveling the rest of the time. It isn't the best life for a cat or dog. They crave routine."

"Well, color me surprised. I just thought you didn't care for animals," I said, taking a sip of my water. "But it sounds like you care a little too much."

"Always my flaw," Kurt said with a grin. But as he set his tumbler on the side table between our chairs, his expression sobered. "I should get to the reason I'm here. I don't want to outstay my welcome. I'm sure you'd like a little peace and quiet after working at the library all day."

"It's okay. I actually enjoy the company. Richard won't be home until late, and while the cats are always happy to sit with me, they aren't much for conversation."

"All the same, let me get to the point." Fosse meowed as Kurt adjusted his position, causing Loie to jump off the settee and pad over to investigate. "It's okay," Kurt told Loie as she stared up at him, her emerald eyes narrowed into slits. "I'm not harming your brother. He's just a little heavy on the leg muscles."

"He is that," I said, patting my own leg to draw Loie to my chair. After shooting Kurt a disdainful stare, she finally acquiesced and leapt up into my lap. "So you found out something about that art theft at Blue Haven Farm?"

Kurt leaned back in his chair. "Let's just say I confirmed a suspicion I had concerning the person behind it."

"Information that you plan to share with Hugh and Fred or others investigating that cold case?"

"Yes, although I don't know what good it will do. The artworks are long gone, I'm afraid. Sold on the black market as soon as they were acquired."

"Stolen, not acquired," I said absently as I stroked Loie's sleek fur.

"Well, semantics aside, they probably can't be recovered. They've undoubtedly passed through several hands on their journey to wherever they are now."

I studied Kurt's stoic face for a moment. "It was some sort of professional heist, then?"

"Absolutely. Well orchestrated and undertaken with great care. Of course, someone at the farm was probably involved in disabling the security system, but I doubt the authorities can figure out who at this late date."

I scooted forward in my chair, disturbing Loie, who glared up at me as I used one hand to keep her balanced on my lap. "A member of the family?"

"Doubtful." Kurt met my inquiring gaze with a shake of his shaggy head. "I didn't come across any chatter that linked Glenda or Oliver Lance, or Nate and Meredith, to the art theft. No, it was probably someone who worked for them at the time. I doubt whoever it is remained in their job very long after the robbery. Not if they were smart, that is."

I thought of Monica but immediately dismissed the idea. "The authorities could investigate that angle."

"They could, but again—even if someone confessed, I doubt the person who disabled the system actually knew who'd hired them to do so. There would've been a middleman, likely using an assumed identity."

"You know this type of operation," I said, staring at his rugged profile.

"All too well, I'm afraid." Kurt looked over at me, the brightness in his blue eyes dimmed. "I also know some of the players. I don't engage with them if I can help it, but I'm aware of their methods. And how dangerous interfering in their business can be."

"So it doesn't seem like Meredith's death was connected to the art theft after all," I said, talking to myself as much as Kurt.

"Not sure that's true." Kurt laid one of his large hands across Fosse's back. "As I've said before—we may be convinced that neither Meredith nor Nate had anything to do with the robbery. But does Glenda Lance realize that?"

"Or Oliver," I said, my attention distracted by a flock of crows descending on my garden.

Loie saw them too. Her ears swiveled forward as their caws filled the air. She bounded off my lap and flew over to the screened portion of the porch. Fosse immediately followed suit, leaping off Kurt's legs and skittering across the concrete floor.

"Sorry, birds over bros," I told Kurt, with a smile. "Anyway, getting back to our theorizing—what if Meredith was blackmailing Nate for some reason? Despite what you think, he could've been the one to disable that alarm system, and maybe she knew it."

"Or perhaps he'd engaged in some other sort of illegal activity that she knew about." Kurt grabbed his tumbler to take a long swallow of water. "He was struggling to keep his dance company afloat. Who knows what financial shenanigans he dabbled in during that time?"

"I hadn't thought of that, but it's certainly possible," I said. "From what I've heard, Nate Broyhill isn't the most honest individual on the planet."

"Hardly." Kurt cast me a sardonic smile. "I could tell you stories, things I've heard from Adele Tourneau and others . . . But I'm not sure that's relevant at this point, when we don't have any real evidence linking Broyhill to his ex-wife's murder."

"Not yet, anyway." I stood up and walked over to where both Fosse and Loie were perched on the ledge formed by the solid wall under the screens. "A murder of crows," I said, more to myself than Kurt. Remembering my hostess duties, I looked back at him. "Can I get you more water, or anything?"

"I'm fine." Kurt rose to his feet, his gaze seemingly focused on the azure mountains rising above the trees. "There was one other thing I wanted to share with you. I don't think it has anything to do with the murder of Meredith Fox, but I did find it interesting, to put it mildly."

"Oh? What was that?"

Kurt crossed the porch to join me at the window wall. "It actually involves that veterinarian you saw mentioned in the article about Blue Haven Farm—the one who was quoted about the equine influenza outbreak four years ago."

"Winston Duran?" I laid my hand on Loie's haunches, which were vibrating with her desire to spring forward and attack the crows. Fortunately, the sturdy screens were in the way.

"Right. The good Dr. Duran. Who is, apparently, slipperier than an eel in seaweed." Kurt shot me a tight smile. "Not a sterling individual, according to my sources."

"What's he done to earn that reputation?"

"What hasn't he done?" Kurt lifted his hands. "It's all whispers and innuendo, but my informants who are familiar with the horsey set tell me he's known to have falsified a medical report or two. Or three or four. Apparently he was the guy to call on if you wanted to cover up an equine health problem, or even a mysterious death."

Monica's reaction to Duran's name flashed through my mind. *She knew about him. What he was, what he did,* I thought, my heart lurching. *She pretended ignorance, but she knew.* "People in the horse world would've heard of him? I mean, anyone who deals with horses on the show circuit?"

"I would be surprised if they hadn't," Kurt said.

I swore, earning an amused smile from my guest. "Sorry. It's just that I may have done something really stupid. I was only trying to help, but . . ."

Kurt cast me a raised eyebrow glance. "You're afraid your good intentions have paved a path to Hades?"

"Yes," I said morosely. "I'm afraid of exactly that."

* * *

After Kurt left, I grabbed my cell phone and tried calling Monica, only to reach her voicemail. I left a message asking her to call me, hoping I could speak with her before she did anything to act on the knowledge I'd accidentally given her.

I ate a simple dinner consisting of a tuna salad sandwich and fruit. The tuna had the cats circling the kitchen table like sharks, but I refused their attempts to con me into giving them a taste, telling them they had plenty of cat food in their feeder and would get treats later.

When I finished eating, I wandered into the living room to read for a while. The cats followed me, leaping up to bookend me on the sofa.

But after I'd finished a couple of chapters in my book, I set it down on the coffee table next to my cell phone and sat back with my eyes closed. I was so tired that the words had seemed to flutter like butterflies on the page.

Why so exhausted? I asked myself, pressing a hand to my forehead. *You're not hot, so no fever or anything, and you really haven't been doing that much. Just your typical routine. You haven't even spent much time gardening or cleaning the house. I mean, it's been weeks since you vacuumed . . .*

An entire month. I sat bolt upright, earning a glare from Loie and wide-eyed surprise from Fosse. Grabbing my phone, I checked the calendar app.

"Really?" I said aloud. Loie slapped me with one paw, but I ignored her, too focused on counting back. "Okay, this is something I need to check out, guys. This could change things."

As I stared blankly at the screen, my phone chimed with the musical snippet of folk music I'd assigned to Brad Tucker's calls. When I answered, Brad apologized for bothering me in the evening.

"I just wanted to let you know that you can probably remove Janelle DeFranzo from the suspect list," he said. "She stopped by the department today to speak with me. Apparently, her daughter urged her to come forward and clarify her story."

"She told you that she'd driven back to the theater, didn't she?"

"Yes, how did you know that?" Brad's sigh filled my ear. "Never mind, I'm sure you talked to her and got it out of her at some point. We really should put you on the payroll."

My lips twitched. "Actually, I didn't hear it directly from her, and I didn't get any details, so I'm still very interested in what she told you."

"She said she dropped off her daughter and drove back to the theater, planning to confront Meredith Fox again. She parked on a side street behind the theater parking lot so she wouldn't be noticed."

"That gives credence to Nate Broyhill's account, I guess. He told me he saw her crossing the parking lot and then walking toward the front of the building."

"Yes, that part of his story does seem to check out," Brad said. "Anyway, Ms. DeFranzo claims that once she reached the main doors of the theater, she had a change of heart and walked away."

"Which explains why Conner Vogler thought he saw her leaving."

"Right. She was undoubtedly the person he said he observed disappearing around the next block. Ms. DeFranzo says she didn't notice him, though. She was too focused on getting back to her car and leaving the area as soon as possible."

"So you're convinced she didn't go inside the theater at all when she returned?" I asked, scratching behind Fosse's ear.

"I'm inclined to believe her story at this point. Especially since she shared another tidbit of information that might help the case."

Fosse's purr rumbled against my fingers. "Oh, what was that?"

"She said as she was driving away, she noticed someone running—from what looked to her like the direction of the theater."

I switched the phone to my other hand so I could pet Loie, who bumped my thigh with her head to let me know that I shouldn't ignore her. "Let me guess—this individual was dressed in dark clothes and was wearing a cap, like the person Conner says he glimpsed in the lobby?"

"Exactly. Which is a new lead I hope will force Smith County to dig a little deeper into other suspects rather than simply focusing on Vogler."

"That would be great." I leaned back against the sofa cushions. "Did Janelle DeFranzo say why she hadn't shared this info before now?"

"She was afraid to mention coming back to the theater because she thought it would make her appear a more likely suspect. Which it does, of course. But I'm pretty confident that she'll be quickly cleared of any suspicion. We'll still need to do some follow-up, of course, but she appeared quite remorseful and honest, at least to me." Brad cleared his throat. "Of course I did read her the riot act for withholding information earlier."

"Of course you did. As you should." Tapping my phone against my opposite palm for a second, I carefully considered my next words. "By the way, I have some information that probably has nothing to do with the murder but might be something you should know." I told him what Kurt had shared with me about the art theft, then added, "And I may have done something foolish, alerting Monica Payne, Ethan Payne's sister, about some possibly nefarious goings-on at Blue Haven Farm around the same time. Not connected to the robbery, though. This involves a couple of the farm's horses dying under somewhat questionable circumstances."

"Why are you concerned about that?" Brad asked, his tone taking on an edge.

"It's just the thought that Monica might confront someone, like that mysterious veterinarian, Dr. Duran, looking for answers. I'm not sure I like that idea."

"It doesn't sound like the best scenario, but I wouldn't worry too much. I doubt Duran is that easy to find."

"I suppose not." I hesitated, wondering if I should mention Oliver Lance's possible involvement with Duran. But, surely, Brad and his team were already looking into Oliver's past, since he was on their suspect list, if only tangentially. "Anyway, thanks for the update. I'm glad that Janelle is no longer high on the list. I didn't really want her to be seen as a top suspect any more than I've wanted Conner Vogler placed in that category."

"Unfortunately, Smith County is still focused on Vogler," Brad said. "Motive, means, and opportunity, you know. But this new info from Ms. DeFranzo might shake things up."

"I hope so," I told him before asking him to give my best wishes to Alison.

"Thanks," he replied. "Baby shower's being planned, so expect an invite soon."

"Sounds like fun," I said, managing to wish him a good evening despite my thoughts being distracted by the mention of babies.

I wasn't sure I was ready to embark on that adventure, but after my recent calendar calculations, I had a suspicion I'd better start considering the implications of it all the same.

Chapter
Twenty-Four

T he following day I took an extended lunch hour to drive to a drug store close to Clarion University. Not that I suspected that anyone noticing me buying pregnancy tests in Taylorsford would be inclined to spread that news . . . Well, actually, that *was* my concern. I wanted to make sure I knew for certain before sharing the news with Richard, much less the entire town.

But as luck would have it, as I left the check-out counter, I noticed someone I recognized. Fortunately, I was able to shove the plastic bag with my purchases into the large purse I'd carried for just that purpose.

"Hello, Riley," I said, approaching him in the hair products aisle.

"Well, if it isn't our local version of Nancy Drew," Riley said, sarcasm dripping from his words. "Are you tracking me down to ask more questions just so you can set your deputy friend on me again?"

"That was never my intention," I said, taking a step back.

"It's what's happened, intention or not." Riley's grip on a bottle of conditioner visibly tightened. "I keep being called into the Smith County Sheriff's Department to answer more questions, even after I've assured them over and over that I've shared all I know."

"Perhaps this isn't the best place to have this conversation," I said, looking around. The other customers appeared far too interested for me to feel comfortable saying anything more.

"Let's meet in the parking lot out back, then. I just need to pay for this, and then I can catch up with you," Riley said. The glare off his glasses hid his expression, but I could tell by the set of his jaw that he was still seething.

"Out front," I said. "There's a bench in front of that ice cream parlor across the street."

"What's the matter? Are you afraid I'm dangerous?" Riley's bark of laughter turned a few more heads in our direction. "All right—if you insist, the bench it is."

After I left the store and made my way across the street, I pulled my cell phone out of my purse and made sure it was turned on. Sitting down on the bench, I placed the phone in my lap, hidden under the folds of my mango sherbet–colored sundress's full skirt.

Riley joined me a few minutes later. "Let's escort the elephant out of the room right from the start," he said, keeping his gaze focused on the street. "That note you found in the rehearsal room—I wrote that."

Having set my purse on the bench beside me, I fiddled with a leather tassel dangling from one of the zippers. "To Meredith?"

"Of course." Riley said, shooting me a sideways glance. "Who else?"

I shrugged. "I suppose something addressed to *M* could've been meant for any number of people."

"But you know it wasn't. Because, from all your sleuthing and snooping, you seem to have discovered my brief romantic relationship with Meredith."

"I did hear something about that," I said, keeping my head down. I was praying that Riley wouldn't ask where I'd gotten this information. I really didn't want to risk implicating Emily Moore. "I mean, you dated while you were both working at Clarion, and you know how gossip flourishes in an academic atmosphere."

"Like bacteria in a petri dish," Riley said morosely. He leaned forward, gripping his knees with both hands. "I gave Meredith that note because I was sick and tired of her attitude and her hurtful games. But, as I told the investigators, I certainly didn't kill her. I was angry with her and deeply hurt by her behavior, but I would never have harmed her."

I studied his profile, noting the quiver in his lips and the gleam of moisture fogging his glasses. "You still loved her."

Riley straightened and cast me a piercing stare. "Yes."

"Despite her using and manipulating you?"

"Love doesn't always make sense." Riley ran a hand through his thinning hair. "I knew that Meredith only dated me because she needed a rebound relationship after her marriage crashed and burned. She wanted a nice guy, one who would treat her with kindness. Unlike that worthless husband of hers," Riley added, bitterness sharpening his tone. "I was available, and I guess I fit the bill. Until I didn't."

"I get the part about her using you, but you mentioned manipulation too. What was that about?" I asked. "I mean, I know Meredith tended to view things from the perspective of what would help Meredith best . . ."

"She made sure Nate knew about us, although she didn't want anyone else to know." Riley tightened his thin lips and stared into space for a moment. "She said we should keep things under wraps because we worked together. That it might look strange if people at the university knew we were dating, since I essentially worked for her when I was playing piano for her dance studios. So we never attended events at Clarion together or went out to eat anywhere near the university or appeared as a couple at any of our colleagues' parties."

You confided in Emily Moore, I thought, but I decided to stay silent on that point. "But she told Nate Broyhill?"

"Of course she did. She wanted him to know that she was in a relationship just months after they split." Riley's mouth twisted as though he was in pain. "I didn't know that at first. There she was, forcing me to stay silent about our relationship around my family, friends, and colleagues, while she apparently kept Broyhill informed about everything."

"Hence the sense of manipulation," I said, more to myself than Riley.

But he obviously heard me and nodded in agreement. "When I gave her that note, during one of the early rehearsals for the *Folklore Suite,* I was just warning her that I wasn't going to stay silent if she didn't stop treating me with such high-handed disdain. I wasn't threatening her." He gave me a sharp look. "Even though that's what the detectives seem to think."

"I'm sorry for shining a spotlight on you, but I honestly didn't know where that note had come from." I pressed my hand over the cell phone hidden in the folds of my dress. "Besides, it sounded pretty ominous. I thought the authorities had better look into it in case it had been a threat from Meredith's killer."

"And now you know it wasn't," Riley said, shifting on the bench to face me. "Anyway, as I've told the investigative team, I know who murdered Meredith."

As I met his stare, I instinctively shrank back. Hectic circles reddened his cheeks, and his eyes, even behind the lenses of his glasses, shone with frightening fervor. "And who might that be?"

"Nathaniel Broyhill, of course. He was always abusive toward her, verbally anyway. Despite his statements to the authorities, I think he actually entered the theater to confront her, and things escalated and he snapped."

If that was the case, Nate could've seen that knife and grabbed it on his way downstairs. I forced myself to offer Riley a gentle smile. "I know it seems like the answer to you, but there are some facts that might not line up . . ."

"Like how he got out of the basement and back to his vehicle before Conner Vogler found Meredith?" Riley leapt to his feet. "That's simple. There are two emergency exits downstairs. They can't be used to enter the building from the outside, but anyone inside can access them to exit in case of fire or anything like that."

As Riley paced the sidewalk in front of me, my thoughts honed in on some holes in his theory. *But Riley, you knew about those exits as well. In fact, while possible, it's much less likely that*

Nate was aware of them. And you were the one working in the theater day after day. The likelihood that you could've spied that mislaid knife is much higher than it would be for Nate to just happen upon it.

The fact was, Riley Irwin was working so diligently to convince me that Nate was the murderer that his efforts had the opposite effect. His overly passionate expression of this theory didn't convince me. Instead, it made me question his own guilt.

But I couldn't allow him to know that. "I suppose you've expressed all this to the Sheriff's Department?"

Riley flung up his hands. "Yes, but they don't seem to be pursuing my leads. They're so focused on that poor boy . . ." Stopping dead in his tracks, Riley turned on me. "I hate that Conner got pulled into this. You have to know that."

I looked up into his flushed face, wondering if this was another slip. If Riley had killed Meredith, it was clear he'd have no compunction about Nate taking the rap. But Conner was obviously another matter. I felt certain Riley would never have wanted Conner to be the one charged with Meredith's murder, and assumed that Conner finding Meredith's body was not part of anyone's plan.

I slipped my phone into my purse and rose to my feet. "Well, I need to be moving along. I took a little extra time for lunch, but I'm still going to be late getting back to work if I don't leave right now."

Riley stepped in front of me, blocking my progress down the sidewalk. "You believe me, right? I'm no killer—you can tell that just by looking at me."

But that's the problem—you can't, I thought as I offered him a forced smile. "I leave those sorts of determinations up to the authorities. But I'm not discounting your theory—about Nate Broyhill being the killer, I mean. I've considered that possibility myself," I added as I backed away and told him goodbye before hurriedly crossing the street.

As well as the possibility that it's you, I thought, my mouth set in a grim line as I climbed into my car and locked the doors.

* * *

When I got home from work later that day, I spent a good deal of time procrastinating—feeding the cats and playing with them, as well as eating a light dinner—before I even looked at the test kits. After reading the instructions several times, I finally set them aside. *Until later,* I told myself, deciding to call Brad and inform him about my encounter with Riley Irwin first.

I only reached his voicemail, which made sense. It was Friday night, after all. If they weren't working a late shift, most people were probably enjoying a date or family time.

Unless they have dress rehearsal, I thought with a wry smile. As I slumped down on the sofa, I sent up a little prayer that all was going well with the *Folklore Suite.* I knew Richard was nervous about this final rehearsal—not because he doubted himself or his dancers, but due to the multitude of moving parts involved with the production.

Picking up my cell phone, I called Brad's number again and left a message asking him to call the next day. No use worrying him with my thoughts about Riley before morning, especially since I suspected he'd probably already developed the same suspicions. If Riley had been as fervent in his accusations against Nate with the authorities, it would only be natural for them—or for a thoughtful officer like Brad, anyway—to question Riley's own involvement in the crime.

Propping my feet on the coffee table, I ignored the sphinx-like stare Loie had fixed on me. "Yes, yes, I'll get to it," I told her as I examined the messages on my phone.

I paused in my scrolling when I noticed that Ethan had texted a few hours earlier, asking me to call him back.

"Hey there," I said when Ethan answered my call. "What's up? Nothing wrong with Scott, I hope."

"No, no, he's fine, as far as I know." Ethan's breathing sounded labored, as if he'd just come in from a run. "Hold on—let me catch my breath. I was out tossing the frisbee with Cassie, and she took off like a rocket after a squirrel."

"Uh-oh. I hope you got her back okay." I grunted as Fosse leapt from the top of the sofa onto my lap and then back off again, landing on the cushions beside me. "Sorry—cat's using me for a springboard."

"Pets," Ethan said in an indulgent tone. "And yes, I was able to corral the dog, eventually. Anyway, the reason I called is to find out if you've heard from Monica lately. A call or text or anything at all. I know she stopped by the library to talk to you the other day because she told me she planned to do that. But since then I've heard nothing. I don't know if she even followed through on that plan."

"She did, but I haven't spoken with her since then." I once again mentally kicked myself for inadvertently cluing Monica in on the unscrupulous Dr. Duran's connection to Blue Haven Farm. "Does she usually ignore your calls or texts for days at a time?"

"No, which is why I'm a little worried," Ethan said.

"Let's not panic. Maybe something happened to her phone. I know I've had that problem from time to time. Why don't you swing by her place and see if she's there?"

"I was holding off on that because she lives in an apartment above the carriage house at her employer's place, and I didn't want to disturb them." Ethan cleared his throat. "Or get her in trouble if she's taken off somewhere today without giving them proper notice. I mean, I know she had to have been at work this week, because no one called me looking for her, and I'm her emergency contact. But all the same, I'll drive by tomorrow morning and see what's what."

"And I'll text her a couple of times tonight. If I get any response, I'll let you know."

"Thanks. Sorry to bother you on a Friday night," Ethan said.

"No problem. I'm just sitting at home with the cats, since my husband is at a final dress rehearsal for his new production."

"Oh right, that opens tomorrow night. I got a ticket. And fortunately, while I'm working all day, I'm off tomorrow night," Ethan said. "As for tonight—I'm by myself too. Well, except for Cassie. Since my significant other is off working somewhere, just like yours."

"We should set up some 'home alone' dinner dates," I said with a chuckle. "Okay, talk to you soon. I hope you and Cassie have a good evening."

"Same to you and the cats," Ethan said before wishing me goodnight.

After ending that call, I sent another text to Monica, then pocketed my phone and rose to my feet. "Well, guys," I told Loie and Fosse, "I guess I've delayed enough. Time to find out if our family is expanding."

The cats darted in front of me as I climbed the stairs to reach our master suite and, I hoped, the answer to that life-changing question.

Chapter
Twenty-Five

I was sound asleep by the time Richard came home Friday night, yet he was still awake before me on Saturday morning. After a quick shower, I headed downstairs, confident the cats had already been fed since they weren't yowling or dogging my steps.

"Good morning, sleepyhead," Richard called out from the table as I shuffled into the kitchen. "Cats have been foddered and are now on the back porch, coffee's on, and we have blueberry muffins." He held up the basket. "Lydia dropped them off earlier."

"That's good, because I sure didn't feel like making anything." I eyed the coffee maker, knowing I should probably start cutting back on caffeine. I'd have to buy some decaf on my next shopping trip. For now, I'd stick with half a cup.

"Lydia always seems to know when we need something," Richard said, taking a bite out of a muffin.

"She probably figured you'd appreciate it, what with the premiere of the *Folklore Suite* tonight." I sat down across from Richard, cradling my half-empty mug between my hands. "Speaking of which, how did the dress rehearsal go?"

"Terrible," Richard said cheerfully. He grinned when I cast him a concerned look. "But that's okay. Bad dress rehearsal, good performance. It's one of those theater traditions."

I reached for a muffin. "I'm sure it wasn't actually terrible."

"No, just chaotic." Richard shrugged. "Things went wrong, but we were able to fix them last night, so everything should go off smoothly tonight. Besides, I don't expect perfection when working with kids. And that's okay."

A piece of muffin poised halfway between my plate and my mouth, I was on the brink of saying something about having a child of his own when my cell phone dinged. Since that sound indicated it was a text instead of a call, I ate the bite of muffin before sliding the phone from the pocket of my loose cotton slacks.

"Anyway, Karla is feeling confident about everything, so I suppose I should too," Richard said as I read the text.

"Of course you should," I said absently, my thoughts distracted by the message I'd just received. "Sorry," I added, looking up, "but Ethan's sister finally contacted me. Remember, I told you that she's been incommunicado for a bit, and Ethan's been worried."

"Oh, right. What does she have to say?"

"She needs a favor." I sent back a short text before setting my phone down on the table. "Apparently her car broke down, and she needs someone to pick her up and drive her back to her apartment."

272

Richard rose to his feet. "Why'd she call you?"

"I'm not sure, but I'd bet it's because we've been in communication recently. And Ethan is working at the fire station today. You know he can't get away when he's on call."

"So you're going to rescue her?" Richard, pouring more coffee into his mug, glanced at me over his shoulder.

"I told her I would. I mean, there's plenty of time before I have to get ready for the show."

"Where is she?" Richard asked as he crossed back to the table. "I could come with you, if you want."

"Oh no, you should just stay here and rest. You have the performance tonight, after all."

"Yeah, and taking a little drive this morning will help keep my mind off that." Richard set down his mug. "I am anxious, if you must know. I realize I've had innumerable opening nights for my choreographic works, as well as when I've been a performer. But I always get nervous. It's just a hazard of the trade."

"Well, it is a bit of a drive. Monica said she's at Blue Haven Farm, which is on the other side of Smithsburg."

"The Lance place? What's she doing there?"

"I really don't know," I said, although I had a pretty good idea. But I didn't want to add to Richard's anxiety by talking about how I may have inspired Monica to confront Oliver Lance over her firing. I was concerned that the encounter might lead to an argument but didn't think it would escalate into anything too serious. Or at least I hoped not. At any rate, it seemed like a good idea to get Monica away from the farm as soon as possible.

"I still don't mind accompanying you. For one thing, it gives us a chance to spend a little time together, something that's been in short supply these past few weeks."

I studied his face as I finished off my muffin. I didn't want to inconvenience him, but honestly, I knew I'd feel better if he accompanied me. Not that I expected any trouble, but now that I had more to consider than just my own safety . . . "That's a good point. We'll just have to make sure we're back early enough to allow you time to relax and warm up or whatever else you need to do."

"Shouldn't take that long," Richard said before polishing off his coffee. "And maybe we can stop on the way back and grab a bottle of champagne for our own private party after the performance tonight. I know the actual reception is tomorrow, but I'm probably going to want to celebrate tonight as well. I'll invite Karla to stop by and share a glass. That's all I want this evening—just a toast or two between the three of us."

I didn't dismiss this idea despite knowing I couldn't—or, rather, *shouldn't*—be drinking any alcohol. But I could explain that later. I'd just nurse my own glass of champagne until Karla left. *Then you'll be celebrating more than just the premiere,* I thought, hiding my smile behind my hand.

With his confession of nerves and anxiety, I'd decided to wait until after tonight's performance to give Richard our good news, mainly because I was a little worried that it would be too distracting if I said anything before the show. "Sounds good," I said. "We even have cheese and crackers and some fruit, if you guys are hungry. Which you will be, I bet."

"Probably," Richard said with a smile. "Okay then, let's go and rescue Ethan's sister. After all, it's only fair, since he did rescue you."

"True enough. I'll just go brush my teeth and throw on some shoes, and we can drive over to Blue Haven and be back before lunch."

"Long before, I hope." Richard circled around the table to plant a kiss on the top of my head. "I'm sure I haven't said it enough, but thanks for putting up with all my absences lately. I know it probably feels like we've been living in different worlds."

"It's fine," I said, grabbing his hand and giving it a squeeze. "I know how important this is to you and Karla. I'm just thrilled to see it all come to fruition."

Richard pulled me to my feet and wrapped his arms around me. "Don't know how I got lucky enough to find you, but I'm certainly thankful for that too." He leaned in to kiss me. "Can't imagine anything better," he added as he released me.

I couldn't smother a mischievous smile.

"Now, what's this cat-who-ate-the-canary expression all about?" Richard asked, looking me up and down. "Have you planned some sort of surprise for me after the show tonight?"

"Could be," I said.

* * *

"Do you have your phone? Because I think I left mine on the table," I asked Richard as I drove through Smithsburg on our way to the Lance farm.

275

"I believe so." Richard patted the pocket of his jeans. "Yep. Although I don't have your friend's number on my phone, so it might not be that helpful."

"I think I remember it. Anyway, she should be waiting for us, and I know her car. We just have to locate a copper-colored compact hybrid. There can't be that many of those parked at the farm."

"I imagine they have trucks or bigger vehicles, like SUVs." Richard stretched out his legs. "We should've taken my car. More leg room."

"Sorry, I didn't think of that." I took the road leading to the Lance farm, which thankfully wasn't as rutted as many of the other routes outside of town. "You haven't been out here before, have you?"

"Didn't have any reason to visit. Glenda and Oliver donated money to the *Folklore Suite*'s production, but they've never hosted any fundraisers, like Kurt did."

"It's quite a place. A little over the top, though. I prefer Highview, to be honest." As I turned into the entrance to Blue Haven Farm, I was surprised to see the metal gates standing open. "That's odd. I was little concerned that we'd have to be buzzed in. Wasn't sure what excuse to give."

"Picking up a stranded friend wouldn't have worked?" Richard asked as I drove through the open gates.

"I guess it would have. It's just"—I cast Richard an embarrassed smile—"I may have ticked off Glenda Lance just a teeny bit when I was here with Aunt Lydia and Zelda last Sunday."

Richard raised his eyebrows. "You didn't mention that when you told me about your afternoon. Of course, I did notice that you didn't say much about the event."

"It wasn't a major thing. I just snooped in their library a little. Oliver Lance escorted me to the library, by the way. It wasn't like I was wandering around their house on my own."

"Not sure that makes it better. You told me Kurt thought you'd be his type."

"Yeah, but he's not mine," I said firmly. Lifting one hand off the steering wheel, I reached over and patted Richard's knee. "My type is right here."

"Good to know." Richard flashed a grin before turning his head to stare out the side window. "It is an impressive spread. Look at those horse barns. I bet there aren't any cobwebs or other typical farm clutter in those."

Shooting a quick look in the direction of the barns, I slammed on the brakes.

"What the heck?" Richard, who'd braced himself by pressing his palms against the dashboard, sat back and flexed his fingers. "Warn a fellow next time."

"The metallic-blue sedan," I said in a hollow voice. "It's there, in that shed."

"Okay, I see there is something with a tarp draped over it, parked in the shed. What of it?"

"Look closer. Where the tarp has slipped off, you can tell it's a large, older model car. A metallic-blue car."

Richard turned to me, questions brimming in his gray eyes. "I see that now. But what's the significance?"

"I think it's the same vehicle I saw in the parking lot behind the theater the day Meredith was killed," I said. "Nate Broyhill spoke to someone in that blue car but told the authorities that it was just a stranger asking for directions."

"Oh." Richard's eyes narrowed. "But if that same vehicle is parked here, it has to belong to the farm."

"So he lied. Someone Nate knew was there with him that day."

Richard and I stared at each other for a second before he pulled out his cell phone. "What's Brad's number?" he asked as I released my pressure on the brake and continued down the driveway. He entered the number as I dictated it, then said, "No answer. I'm going to leave a message to call back."

"Tell him we're at Blue Haven Farm too," I said, slowing down as I approached the main house.

Monica's vehicle wasn't sitting in the circular driveway, but perhaps she'd pulled into the gravel lot off to the side of the house. As I parked the car, I gazed over toward the lot, noticing that one of the garage doors was open.

Sitting in the bay was a small white car, just like the one that had trailed me to Clarion that day. I swore under my breath as I unbuckled my seat belt. Although I couldn't be absolutely certain that it was the same vehicle, the coincidence raised my anxiety level several degrees.

But I didn't want to mention it to Richard. No use making him nervous as well. "I don't see Monica's car," I said. "I think we should check at the house and see if she's still here."

"Is that wise?" Richard asked, as he joined me outside of the car. "If the Lance family or someone on their staff is mixed up in Meredith's death—"

"We can't abandon Monica here," I interjected.

"If she is still here, or ever was," Richard said grimly.

"Don't you think we'd better find out, one way or the other? She did ask for my help. Besides, you've alerted Brad, so we should be fine." I walked briskly toward the house.

Richard easily outpaced me. Reaching the front porch, he pressed the doorbell right before I joined him. Expecting a maid or housekeeper to answer the bell, I was surprised when we were greeted by Oliver Lance.

"Oh dear," he said, his eyes bright as stars in his flushed face. "I didn't plan on both of you showing up. Still, you'd better come in."

Richard grabbed my hand and pulled me close to his side. "We don't want to be a bother. We're just looking for Monica Payne. She texted Amy that her car had broken down and she needed a ride."

"It's really no bother," Oliver said, lifting his right arm so the light glinted off the gun in his hand.

Chapter
Twenty-Six

R ichard immediately shoved me behind him, which earned
a sardonic smile from Oliver.

"Such a gentleman," he said. "Although I don't think it's the
most effective move. All I have to do is shoot you, and then I
can just as easily shoot Amy."

"No one needs to be harmed." Richard spat out the words
between gritted teeth.

Oliver leveled the gun's muzzle at Richard's chest. "That's
absolutely correct. If you'll just step inside without causing
any problems, we can proceed without gunfire." He motioned
toward the doorway. "Come along."

Richard, still holding my hand, led me into the house.
"I'm not sure what you think you're going to achieve with this,
Oliver. One of your staff is bound to start questioning why
you're herding people around with a revolver."

"I doubt it, since I gave them all the day off. No one is here except me—and you two, of course."

"And Monica?" I asked as Oliver ushered us down the wide central hallway.

"Am I supposed to answer that?" Oliver grabbed my arm, pulling me away from Richard. "Sorry, I don't think I will," he added, pushing me in front of him and pressing the gun muzzle between my back ribs.

Sensing Richard's agitation, I shot him a warning look. "Don't do anything foolish," I mouthed at him before speaking aloud. "Like Richard told you, she texted me. She said her car was busted, and she needed a ride. That's why we're here."

"You're here because I wanted you here," Oliver said. "Well, I only wanted you, Amy, but I guess your white knight just had to tag along."

Pushed by the gun, I stumbled. "Did you send that message then?"

"Stand up. And yes, I did."

I swallowed back a shriek. If Oliver had used Monica's cell phone to text me, that meant she was trapped on the estate somewhere. *Or she's already dead,* I thought with a shiver.

Oliver forced me into a wood-paneled elevator at the end of the hall. "You'd better get in too, if you care about your wife's safety," he told Richard while keeping the revolver leveled at me.

Richard's jaw was so tight his lips were pulled into a grimace. "Hurt her and I swear I'll find a way to kill you." His hand slipped into his pocket as he stepped onto the elevator. *The cell phone, I thought. He's going to try to call 911.*

Unfortunately, Oliver noticed this movement too. "Hand it over," he commanded, pressing the gun against my temple. "No, better yet—throw it on the floor."

Richard, his eyes gleaming with repressed rage, did as he was told.

"Kick it over here." Oliver casually punched a button on the elevator's control panel as the cell phone skidded across the floor and banged against his foot. "I'm afraid I don't want to invite law enforcement to our little party." Waving the gun at me, he added, "I'll need your phone too."

"I don't have one." I pulled my pockets inside out to demonstrate the truth of my words.

The elevator jerked before starting a descent. Keeping his weapon aimed at me, Oliver stomped the sole of his leather riding boot against Richard's phone, cracking the case and shattering the screen into glittering fragments.

Afraid Oliver might mistake my trembling for some aggressive action, I crossed my arms tightly over my chest. I glanced at Richard, noticing that all the color had drained from his face, and his lips were pressed into a line that looked like a gash. I knew he was more worried for my safety than his own, and I felt the same regarding him, although . . . I bit my lower lip. I had to protect myself, no matter what. My safety wasn't just about me—not anymore.

The elevator doors opened onto what looked like a basement corridor. On this level, the flooring was simple concrete, and the walls were white-painted drywall.

Oliver shoved me forward. "Let's go. Down the hall, to that wide door on the left. Move it."

When we reached the door, which stood slightly ajar, Oliver kicked it open with his foot "Step in," he said, shooting a cold stare in Richard's direction. "You first. I'll keep an eye on your lovely wife until you're safely inside."

Richard, his gaze first flitting over the gun pressed to my side, complied with this command. Oliver poked me with the revolver. "Now you."

I staggered into the dimly lit room. *A wine cellar,* I realized. Wooden racks lined three of the walls, their half-moon shelving cradling rows of clear, blue, and green bottles. "Why are you doing this?" I asked as Oliver stepped back into the hallway, the gun still trained on me.

"Do you really expect me to spew out a monologue like some bad movie villain?" Oliver sneered as he gripped the edge of the heavy wooden door. "Sorry, not really in the mood to indulge your curiosity." He slammed the door.

A loud click told me he'd locked us in. "I'm so sorry," I said, stumbling as my knees buckled.

Richard leapt forward, displaying all the strength and grace of his dance training. He wrapped his arms around me to keep me on my feet. "What do you have to feel sorry about? None of this is your fault."

"I suggested we come here, to follow up on Monica's text, even though I knew that Nate and Glenda were suspects in Meredith's murder," I replied, my words slightly muffled by the folds of Richard's loose cotton shirt. "After I'd snooped into the family's business, which probably put a target on my back. And I dragged you along."

"I'm glad you did." Richard, still holding onto my upper arms, stepped back and looked me up and down. "The only thing worse than this would be if you'd been here alone."

"Yes, but"—I wiped the back of my hand under my nose—"you have your premier tonight, and I don't want you to miss that or get injured or . . . anything. I don't want to lose you," I said, a little sob escaping my throat.

"Forget about the show. That isn't important." Richard pulled me back into a close embrace. "Right now I'm focused on making sure nothing bad happens to you. Nothing else matters."

"You matter," I said between sniffles.

"Thanks, sweetheart, but if it's between you and me, I'm going to save you."

"It isn't going to come to that." I lifted my head and looked up into his beloved face. "It just isn't. We're going to find a way out of this with both of us safe. As well as Monica, if she's here." *And still alive,* I thought, as a little hiccup escaped my lips.

"You believe she's actually here?" Richard pulled a tissue from his pocket and wiped the tears from my face.

"She must be. That text came from her cell, and I don't think Oliver Lance is a computer whiz who could spoof numbers or anything like that." I frowned, unable to dismiss the idea that Oliver could've taken Monica's phone and then killed her. *No,* I told myself, *you can't think like that.* "Heck, Monica told me he didn't really even trust computers and kept all his records on paper."

"Which he's probably shredding right about now," Richard said grimly.

"I doubt it. Those are the records for the farm and the entire horse operation. He can't afford to get rid of all of that." I pursed my lips. "Maybe he'll rip a few pages out of the ledgers, but if it's the ones I suspect, he's out of luck. I snapped photos of those."

"You did what?" Richard, who'd started walking up and down, examining the cellar, spun around to face me.

"It was information for Monica," I said. "Not connected to Meredith's murder. Anyway, I didn't think it was at the time."

"But now you're not so sure?" Richard frowned as he gazed around the dimly lit room. "I haven't found another exit yet, which is probably why Oliver locked us in here. A room with only one door." He glanced over at me with a wan smile. "I guess there are worse places. At least we can crack open a few bottles and drink some wine."

I opened my mouth but snapped it shut again before I said anything about my reason to avoid drinking alcohol. This was neither the time nor place to tell Richard that he was going to be a father. *We have to get out of here safely, first,* I thought. *I'm not going to burden him with that extra level of anxiety right now.* "I think we'd better keep our heads clear," I said, earning another smile.

"You're right. It'll require all our wits to figure this out." Richard walked over to the door and fiddled with the latch. "I wonder if we can do anything to this lock. It doesn't appear to be particularly sturdy."

"Don't tell me lock picking is one of your many talents," I said as I crossed the room to join him.

Richard flashed me a grin. "I may have played around with it when I was a kid. Pretending to be a spy and all that. Needless to say, my parents weren't always happy about it. Especially when I broke into the basement storage closet where Dad had stashed all the sports equipment he'd kept from his youth."

"Why'd he keep it locked up?" I asked as I leaned in to peer at the lock mechanism on the door.

Richard's smile faded. "I think it was out of disgust or despair or something like that. He was hoping to pass it down to me, you see."

"But you weren't interested." I remembered the items I'd seen displayed at Jim and Fiona Muir's home. There were no photos of Richard dancing or any awards honoring his dance achievements as a child or teen—just Jim's athletic certificates and trophies.

"I was too busy dancing. Anyway, that's not important right now," Richard said, although his expression told me otherwise. "I don't suppose you have a bobby pin on you?"

"When have I ever worn bobby pins?" As I examined the dusty shelves, a glint of metal caught my eye. "Wait a minute, maybe there's something already here that would work."

I dashed over to the object, hoping to find something useful. "It's a pocketknife," I said, waving it over my head as I trotted back to the door. "Not a sharp one, and certainly not as large as the one that killed Meredith, but maybe it will do the trick."

I handed the knife to Richard, who stared at the rusted blade and broken tip with a frown. "I'll give it a try." As he bent down to work on the lock, he said, "It seems Oliver Lance might be Meredith's killer. Do you have any theories as to why?"

"Not solid ones, but I think it's connected to money somehow. Meredith and Nate were desperate for funds to keep their dance company afloat. Maybe they blackmailed Oliver over something?" I rubbed my temples, trying to ease the tension that was bringing on a headache. "Or perhaps Nate had nothing to do with it, and Meredith was gouging Oliver for money on her own. Glenda did mention something about Meredith being a snoop."

"You think she discovered information that Oliver would kill to cover up?" Richard tapped the hilt of the knife against his palm. "I could see that. Meredith did like to ferret out everyone's secrets. And she certainly loved money. But why would Oliver wait years to murder her?"

"He could've gotten tired of paying her off." I shrugged. "Maybe he went to the theater to have a talk with her about ending their arrangement and just snapped."

Richard leaned in to squint at the lock. "But if he grabbed the knife Conner saw in the vestibule, he was contemplating hurting her ahead of time."

"Perhaps he just wanted to use it to scare her, but things got out of hand." I stepped back as Richard flexed his arms between attempts to release the lock mechanism.

"He was the figure Conner saw, the one dressed in dark clothes and a cap," Richard said.

"And the one Janelle DeFranzo noticed fleeing the area when she drove away. It seems Oliver knew where those emergency exits were located. I guess he must've seen the floorplans related to the theater renovation somewhere."

Richard shot me a glance over his shoulder. "I bet he was given a brochure containing that information when he and Glenda donated money to the theater's restoration fund."

"Oh, right. He easily could've seen the floorplans in the fundraising materials." I sucked in a deep breath when the lock clicked. "Got it?"

"Almost. No, it slipped free again." Richard swore and dropped down on his knees before jamming the knife into the lock one more time.

"I guess it was Oliver in the blue sedan I saw in the parking lot, which means Nate knew he was there. Which also means"—I squeezed my fingers into fists—"Nate knew what was going on."

"Part of it, anyway," Richard conceded. "Although he apparently wanted to handle the situation by talking with Meredith himself. You said the person in the blue car drove off before Nate left the parking lot."

"That's right. Nate was waiting for Meredith to come outside and speak with him, and sent Oliver away—or thought he had." I clasped my clenched hands at my waist. "But I imagine Oliver just drove a few blocks away, to park out of sight. Then he probably sneaked back to the theater from a different direction, entering through the lobby."

"He apparently didn't trust Nate to do what he thought was needed." Richard gave the knife a sharp twist. "Eureka!"

"It's open?" I sprang forward as Richard rose to his feet.

"Yep." Richard flung out one arm but halted the motion before he released his fingers. "I think I'd better keep this," he said, closing the blade and shoving the knife in his pocket.

"It's not much of a weapon."

"Better than nothing." Richard turned to face me. "Now—we should make a plan. We don't know where Oliver is at the moment, but I doubt he's still in the basement. Do you remember much from your tour of the house?"

I shook my head. "I never got a proper tour. But there must be stairs somewhere off the hall outside this room. You can't have an elevator without stairs."

"Yeah, that's code." Richard massaged his jaw with one hand. "Okay, so we find the stairs and try to get to a level where there are exits to the outside."

"Hold on," I said, dashing over to the racks. Running my hands over a row, I searched for a bottle made of thick glass. I pulled the sturdiest one out of the rack and transferred the bottle to my right hand, gripping it by the neck. "Another weapon," I said as I joined Richard at the door.

"Good thinking." Richard leaned down to kiss my temple. "I'm glad I married such a smart woman."

"I'm glad you did too," I said as he cracked open the door.

Richard peered around the edge of the door. "Hall's empty," he whispered. "Let's find those stairs."

"Better keep a grip on that knife," I said as we cautiously stepped into the hall.

Thrusting his hand into his pocket, Richard nodded. "And you'd better stay ready to brain Oliver with that bottle, if necessary."

"Don't worry. At this point, I'd be more than happy to smash it across his smirking face."

We crept along, checking doors. Most were locked, but one at the other end of the hall swung open, revealing a set of stairs. "Let's just hope Oliver is nowhere nearby," Richard said under his breath. He fished the knife out of his pocket and flicked open the rusty blade. "But we should be prepared, just in case."

I tightened my grip on the wine bottle as I followed Richard up the stairs.

Chapter
Twenty-Seven

It took two flights of stairs to reach an upper hallway I recognized from my earlier visit to the house.

"I wonder if Oliver has made a run for it?" I whispered as we surveyed the empty hall.

"And leave all this behind? I doubt it." Richard shoved his short, dark-brown hair away from his forehead, causing it to stand up like a spiky crown.

I pointed toward the other end of the hall. "The library is that way, but there wasn't a landline in there," I told him sotto voce. "Oliver had to go out to take a call."

"Lots of doors and no way of knowing what's behind them," Richard murmured. "Maybe you should make a run for the front door and let me search for a phone."

"I don't think so. First of all, I'm not leaving you. And second—how do we know Oliver isn't outside, waiting to take a shot at us as we exit?"

"Good point." Richard slid his hand along the wall as we crept down the hallway. "I think we can tell by the spacing of the doors how large the rooms are." He carefully cracked open the closest door and peeked inside. "Some sort of guest bedroom. No phone that I can see. I guess they assume everyone has cell phones now."

I studied the layout of the rest of the hallway. "We can ignore the next one, then. There's hardly any space between it and the adjacent door, so it's probably just a closet."

Richard nodded. "Maybe trying to find a phone isn't our best bet. If we can sneak out of the house without encountering Oliver, we can make a run for the car."

"But Monica . . ."

Richard gripped my forearm, forcing me to look up into his concerned face. "If she's here, she's locked away somewhere, and I doubt we can find her without arousing Oliver's attention. Wouldn't it be best to get out and alert the authorities so they can bring in a trained team to rescue her?"

"I suppose," I said with a frown. "I still don't think we should exit through the front door, though. What if Oliver *is* outside? The front of the house is visible from quite a distance."

"There was a garden on the right side, wasn't there? I mean, stage right—it's left if you're facing the front of the house." Richard's knuckles blanched from the grip he had on the knife hilt.

"There was, and it would provide the best cover. Now we just have to find a side exit." I looked up and down the hall, establishing our location in the house. "This is a central corridor, and right now we're looking toward the back of the house, so we need to find an exterior door to our left."

We crept down the hallway, hugging one wall so we could dash through one of the doors if we heard anyone approaching. Toward the back of the house, a half-open door revealed a storage room lined with metal shelves.

"I think that's an exterior door," I said, pointing toward the other side of the room. Sunlight spilled through a round window in a metal door, creating a circular puddle of gold on the dark tiles.

"This must be a storeroom for food and cleaning supplies," Richard said as we quietly maneuvered our way around crates stacked on the floor.

I surveyed the shelves, which were filled with boxes, bottles, and metal tins. "They could survive a nuclear winter, while we barely manage to keep our pantry filled from week to week."

"We don't have staff." Richard closed and pocketed the knife. "I guess it makes sense to have an exterior door in this room. They probably bring this stuff in from some sort of loading dock." He peered through the round window before shoving back the deadbolt on the door. "I don't see anyone in the vicinity, but keep your head down anyway."

"Will do," I said as I followed him out the door.

Richard's guess had been correct—we were standing on a small loading dock. A narrow lane that connected with the dock curved around the side garden. "That must lead to the circular driveway out front," I said, keeping my voice hushed. "But I think we should escape through the garden rather than take the road."

"As you said, better cover," Richard whispered. He grabbed my hand and led me down the loading dock steps and into the lush foliage of the garden.

We cautiously picked our way through the jumble of shrubs, decorative trees, and other plants, brushing aside branches and trailing vines while keeping a lookout for Oliver. *Or Glenda, or Nate,* I thought, not convinced that they were totally innocent. If nothing else, Nate had to have known that his half brother had been in the vicinity of the murder scene, and yet he'd never divulged that fact to the investigators.

And you still can't be sure who engineered the destruction of Aunt Lydia's garden or followed you to Clarion and tried to close the rolling shelves on you. For all you know, they could all be in on it together, I reminded myself, plucking an iridescent beetle off my slacks and tossing it into a clump of irises.

Richard halted at the edge of the garden, holding aside just enough foliage to stare out over the front lawn and driveway. "I don't see anyone," he said in a low voice, "but we still need to move fast to reach the car." He gazed down at me. "Ready?"

Gulping, I nodded.

"I'll go first," Richard said. "If you hear any gunfire, stay put."

"No, we go together," I replied, grabbing his hand. "All for one—"

A smile flitted over Richard's face. "And one for all. Okay, milady, into the breach we go."

We slipped through a small opening formed by the flexible, arching branches of a spirea bush. Pausing for just a moment to gather our wits and take a deep breath, we shared a glance before dashing across a narrow strip of lawn to reach our car.

Richard pulled me down behind the vehicle. "Glad he didn't take the keys along with my phone," he whispered as he pulled his keychain from his pocket.

"Oh no," I said quietly. I motioned toward the back tire. "Looks like Oliver was more thorough than we expected."

The tire was slashed. Examining the area under the chassis, I realized the other back tire was also flat. Richard swore under his breath and settled back on his heels. "What now?" he muttered.

"Back to the house to find a phone?" I shifted my uncomfortable crouched position as a memory surfaced. "Wait—when I was here with Kurt, I noticed a phone on the wall of the main horse barn. Maybe we should try that?"

"Oliver could be in the barn," Richard said.

"And he could be in the house." I struggled to my feet, bending my knees to stay low so I couldn't be seen from the other side of the car. "I think we have to take the chance."

"But that barn is some distance away, and the area is wide open," Richard also rose up until he was standing flat on his feet, but with his knees flexed, keeping his head down.

Looking around, I glimpsed a figure striding from the garage, headed toward the back of the house. "I think we can make it. Looks like Oliver is going back inside."

"Wonder what he was doing," Richard muttered, but he met my questioning gaze with a nod. "You're right, let's try to make it to the barn. Hopefully, Oliver thinks we're still safely stowed away in the wine cellar, and by the time he realizes we aren't—"

"We'll already have called the authorities." I shuffled forward and pressed my palm against Richard's chest. "Please run as fast as possible, even if I fall behind. We have to get to that phone, or neither one of us has a fighting chance."

Richard looked like he wanted to argue, but just pressed his hand to his forehead instead. "Very well. I don't like it, but you're right."

"As always," I said.

"Let's not go completely off the rails," he replied with a fleeting grin. "Ready?"

I bobbed my head and tossed the wine bottle into a flowerbed.

Richard straightened and took off at a fast lope. I followed, running as fast as I could, but still falling behind. Expecting the blast of a gun any second, all I heard was the hoarse screech of crows soaring up from the fields on either side of the road.

The barn at first looked like a toy building in the distance but grew larger as we approached. Of course, Richard reached it first. By the time I joined him, panting and holding my aching sides, he was already dialing numbers on the old phone attached to one of the pillars.

"911," he told me, before turning his attention to the person on the other end of the line.

While he gave them our location and explained the nature of the emergency, I staggered over to a bench set beside a wooden door that had a metal bar fastened with a combination lock. Collapsing onto the bench, I slumped back, banging my head into the slatted wooden wall behind me.

The noise must've disturbed the horses. Rustling and a few nickers filled the barn. Glancing down the central corridor, my gaze was met by several pairs of liquid brown eyes. Their heads poking over the metalwork topping their stall doors, the horses swiveled their large ears in my direction as something banged back.

I sat up and turned to peer through one of the openings between the slats. "Hello, is someone in there?"

"It's me, Monica," said a familiar but strained voice.

"Hold on—we'll get you out," I said, leaping to my feet. I yanked on the lock, which refused to budge. "You wouldn't happen to know the combination, would you?" I asked Monica.

"Not unless it hasn't been changed in four years," she said.

"You never know. Let's give it a try." I attempted to open the lock with the numbers Monica provided, but it didn't budge.

"Help is on the way," Richard said, stepping up behind me. "So what's all this?"

"Monica's locked in there," I said. "Not sure how to get her out."

Richard held up one finger and strode over to the shelves I'd noticed when I'd met Oliver the first time. "Hang on," he called out, earning numerous whinnies from the horses in response. "I think I found something that might work."

He hurried back, clutching something that looked like a small sledge hammer. "I don't know why this was mixed in with the horse grooming stuff, but I'm not going to complain." He took a wide-legged stance in front of the door and ordered Monica to stand back.

"What are you . . ." I managed to squeak out before Richard told me to cover my eyes. He swung the hammer in a wide arc and slammed it—not into the combination lock, but rather against the top of the plate holding the latch hook to the wall.

Wood splintered, flying in all directions, and a large crack appeared in the door jamb as neighing rang through the barn, and metal-shod hooves stirred up the bedding and kicked the partitions separating the stalls. With my hand still shielding my eyes, I stared at the door. The metal plate dangled from a separated strip of wood.

"Remind me not to tick you off when you're holding a hammer," I told Richard, who just grinned and yanked the strip of wood away from the wall, pulling off the plate and freeing the door.

The door swung open, revealing a disheveled Monica. She blinked, her eyes obviously unaccustomed to the light. I surveyed the area behind her, noting the array of saddles, bridles, and other equipment stored in the room.

"Oliver locked you in here?"

She nodded and gestured toward bits of broken glass studding the floor. "And he smashed the lightbulb so I couldn't see well enough to try to find something to break myself out."

"Keeping up his solid streak of jerkiness," I said before giving her a quick hug.

"I probably smell awful." Monica stepped back, combing her tangled loose hair with her fingers.

Richard moved next to us. "I believe you can be forgiven for that, all things considered." He held up the hammer. "I think I'll keep this—at least until the deputies arrive."

"Thanks for coming to my rescue," Monica said, walking over to the closest stall. "But I didn't send that text. Oliver took my phone before he locked me in the tack room."

"Oh, we know," I said. "I guess you came here today to confront him about those dead horses and your firing, right?"

"Yeah, and foolishly called first. Which gave Oliver time to send the staff away so he could 'deal with me without witnesses,' or so he said." As Monica tugged her rumpled T-shirt down over the waistband of her threadbare jeans, Bucephalus poked his head over the stall door and gently nudged her shoulder with his nose. "Then he told me he was going to try to get you to come to the farm too, Amy. I guess he thought he could take care of both of us in some way."

Richard grimaced. "How in the world would he think he could make two women disappear with no consequences?"

"I don't know," Monica said, absently patting Bucephalus while keeping her focus on us. "He didn't tell me anything. But he seemed awfully confident about his ability to get away with whatever he had planned."

"Well, I've already called 911, so there'll be plenty of law enforcement personnel here soon enough. I don't think Oliver is actually going to have a chance to escape."

"Good," Monica said.

Richard's grip on the hammer visibly tightened. "Did he admit to stabbing Meredith Fox?"

I noticed the fire burning in his eyes. *Of course, despite their differences, he was once very close to Meredith, and he also respected her as a brilliant dancer. It's only natural that he'd feel anger over her murder.*

"He didn't confess to anything about that," Monica said, "but I think I can put two and two together and figure out his motive, based on what I found out about the deaths of those two horses four years ago." As she turned and caressed the silken arch of Bucephalus's neck, the horse gazed at her, his dark eyes soft as pansy petals.

Monica looked back at us with an expression as bleak as birch trees in winter. "He had them killed, you know," she said, her voice vibrating with fury. "Murdered them in cold blood, with the help of that snake Winston Duran. For the insurance money."

Chapter Twenty-Eight

"I should've known Oliver was capable of such of thing. He never really saw these guys"—Monica gave Bucephalus's velvety nose a pat—"as living creatures who deserve as much respect and as many rights as we humans have. He always viewed them as property, as investments or tools to achieve his goals. Not that he was cruel, but he only took good care of them the way you'd maintain a valuable car. Not because you really love it, but because it's worth something in dollars."

"No emotional attachment, you mean," I said.

"Going to keep a lookout, for Oliver as well as the authorities," Richard told us as he jogged over to the entrance to the barn.

Monica met my inquiring gaze with a nod. "That's what I always thought. Which makes sense and should've given me a clue. That lack of emotional connection to the horses who were so important to his life and career should've told me that he probably doesn't have much of an emotional attachment to anything—or anyone."

"You're sure he colluded with Dr. Duran to kill the horses and cover it up?"

Monica sighed. "Sadly, yes. I tracked down someone who also used to be employed here. Not in the stables, but in the house. He worked as a personal assistant to Oliver, dealing with business matters. He disappeared without a word one day, which made me wonder if he had a secret reason for leaving."

Maybe he was the one who disabled the security system before the art theft, I thought, deciding not to share this idea with Monica. I didn't know the details about her relationship with this person or where her loyalties might lie. Better to wait and alert the authorities about it later. They could follow up with Monica and her unnamed acquaintance.

"Anyway, I got confirmation from this guy that Oliver had the horses killed so he could collect the insurance on them. Apparently he needed cash, and quickly, because he'd gotten entangled with some less than legal financial operation."

"He owed money to loan sharks?" I asked, casting a quick glance toward Richard. He met my gaze and shook his head.

"That's what I was told. He knew I wouldn't go along with his plan, which is why he carried it out while I was on vacation."

"And kept Dr. Smithy out of it too," I said.

"Right. He made sure no one who'd be likely to expose him knew the truth."

"Meredith must've found out somehow," I muttered.

Monica shot me a sharp gaze. "It's possible, I guess. She was around at the time, and she and Oliver never really got along."

Just as I started to make a comment about Meredith possibly using such knowledge to blackmail Oliver, Richard dashed back to join us.

"Oliver is heading this way, and he's toting a rifle now," he said, his voice breaking on the last words. "No sign of the Sheriff's Department yet. What do we do?"

Monica took an audible breath. "No place to hide in here, and the paddock outside is wide open. Only thing is maybe"— she stared back at Bucephalus—"we head into the stall with Ceph."

"What?" I shared a panicked look with Richard. "Won't we be like ducks in a barrel?"

Monica shook her head. "Ceph's worth a mint. I don't think Oliver would take the chance of hitting him."

"He could easily herd us out and then shoot us." Richard's knuckles blanched as he tightened his grip on the hammer. "You two get inside. I'll stay out here and try to ambush him."

I clutched Richard's other arm. "But he has a rifle. That's different from a handgun. He can fire at you from some distance."

"And he's a great shot," Monica said grimly.

"All right, but I'm keeping this close," Richard said, hefting the hammer.

Monica carefully opened the stall door and stepped inside. Keeping a hold on Bucephalus's halter, she motioned for Richard and me to join her.

I stared at the horse, who loomed over me. He looked massive and dangerous. My mouth went dry. One kick from those hooves, especially in such close quarters, could be deadly.

"Come on," Richard said, pulling me into the stall. I huddled next to him as Monica closed the door.

"Stay away from his hindquarters," she said, keeping her voice low. "Ceph's not vicious, but horses are herd animals and have an innate memory of being prey. They'll strike out at anything they can't see, especially if it comes up behind them."

Still gripping the halter, Monica guided us under the horse's head, and around to his other side. With all three of us standing between Bucephalus and the back of the stall, we waited.

To his credit, Bucephalus remained remarkably calm, simply snorting once or twice as he turned his large head to gaze at us.

"Good boy," I said softly.

Heavy footfalls clumped against the wooden planks in the barn's open corridor. "I know you're in here." Oliver's voice was eerily calm. "You might as well come out. I may spare you if you give yourselves up."

Richard slipped his free arm around my shoulders, pulling me close.

"There's really no way out," Oliver said.

Glancing at Monica, I mouthed, "Need to let him know the authorities are on the way," before I called out, "Not for you anyway. We've called the Sheriff's Department. They should be here any minute. Maybe you'd better leave us and try to flee."

Oliver appeared at the stall door, leveling the rifle at us through the open metalwork. But when he saw Bucephalus, he pulled the gun back. "Very clever, using my horse as a shield."

"Your horse? You don't deserve him," Monica snapped. "Not after what you did."

"Still upset about those two dead beasts?" Oliver tsked. "Such a lot of bother over nothing."

"Nothing?" Monica's strangled cry made Bucephalus snort and paw at his bedding.

"They were my property. I needed the money. It was a necessary evil." Oliver peered in at us. "Sorry it's come to this, Amy. I never wanted to hurt you."

"Really?" I said, taking a gamble. "Is that why you followed me that day and tried to squish me between those shelves?"

"That was just a warning," Oliver said, confirming my suspicion.

"And the vandalism to my aunt's garden, along with the threatening text? Did you do that as well?" I asked as Richard's grip on my shoulder tightened.

"Not personally. I outsourced that." Oliver poked the gun barrel over the top of the stall door. "Now come out. I know Monica thinks Ceph is a proper shield, but trust me, I won't hesitate to shoot him if you three don't get out here."

"So you can kill us?" Monica spat into the straw at her feet. "I don't think so. We'll wait until the authorities arrive."

"I hear sirens, I shoot," Oliver said, his voice sharp and cold as sleet.

Richard released his hold on me and inched closer to Bucephalus's head. "I'll come out. You can use me as a hostage, if you want."

I opened my mouth but snapped it shut again when I realized that Richard was adjusting his hold on the hammer, which he'd kept down by his side, out of sight.

"Not good enough. I want the three of you."

I pressed my palm against Bucephalus's flank, feeling his muscles ripple under my fingers. A new thought filled my mind, unbidden and unwelcome. *If Oliver shoots Ceph, he's likely to react with justifiable wildness—thrashing and kicking and ultimately falling. It might not take a bullet to kill us, and Oliver can just blame it on the horse.*

"We should go," I told Monica and Richard, who gazed from the nervous horse to me as if the same thought had just occurred to them.

"See, I knew you were a smart one, Amy," Oliver said, sliding back the rifle. "You've realized you don't want to be crushed to death by a thousand pounds of horseflesh."

I could tell by Monica's thunderous expression that she'd gladly volunteer to take Oliver out for that comment alone. "Don't harm the horse," I said. "We'll come out." I brushed my fingers over Richard's hand gripping the hammer. "You next, I'll distract," I whispered as I shimmied past him.

Richard's other hand gave my shoulder a swift caress as I ducked under Bucephalus's head.

Oliver threw open the stall door. It clanged, metal hitting wood, raising a chorus of whinnies and snorts from the other horses in the barn. Which in turn unnerved Bucephalus further. He threw up his head, jerking Monica's arm.

Keeping the rifle trained on my chest, Oliver motioned for me to step out of the stall. My mind racing with ideas of how to distract him long enough for Richard to leap forward and attack him with the hammer, I took a few halting steps into the corridor.

Before I could enact any sort of plan, Oliver grabbed my arm and yanked me forward, pulling me close to his side. "Drop it," he ordered as Richard jumped out of the stall, the hammer raised.

Somehow, Oliver had managed to shove the barrel of the rifle up under my chin. I wobbled as the cool metal pressed into my flesh, but Oliver's implacable grip kept me on my feet.

"I said, drop that hammer," Oliver commanded.

Richard, his face white as a sheet of blank paper, complied. He slid away from the door, his back pressed to the wooden slats of the next stall, his desperate gaze fixed on me. "Let her go."

"Very well." Oliver swung the rifle away and shoved me aside. "Line up there with your loving husband."

I stumbled over to Richard, who grabbed my hand when I huddled next to him, leaning back against the rough wooden planks of the adjacent stall for support. Oliver lifted the rifle and aimed it at us as the faint whine of sirens wafted through the air.

Something clicked. *He's cocking the rifle.* I closed my eyes and squeezed Richard's hand. *Wish I could've told you about the baby,* I thought, sending up a prayer as I waited for the crack of the bullet.

But instead of a gunshot, other sounds filled the barn—the tattoo drumbeat of hooves and a piercing scream. My eyes flew open in time to see Bucephalus, who Monica must've released, standing on his hind legs and slamming his front hooves into Oliver's arm. The rifle flew across the barn as Oliver crumpled to the floor, still screaming.

Bucephalus pranced over Oliver's prone body, just barely missing his limbs with his stomping hooves. When Oliver curled into the fetal position, the horse backed away and stood at some distance, tossing his head and snorting, white rimming his dark eyes.

As the wailing sirens drew closer, the other horses neighed and thrashed about in their stalls. Monica, ignoring Oliver's writhing on the ground, approached Bucephalus, murmuring calming words.

Richard let out a gasping breath before hugging me. As he pulled back, he pointed toward the rifle. "Back in a second. Should grab that."

I held onto him. "Stay here. I don't think Oliver's in any shape to move, much less use a gun. Let the deputies secure it."

"As you wish." Richard leaned in, kissing the hollow of my shoulder and my neck before finding my lips. After a minute, he lifted his head, and we both turned to greet the deputies rushing into the scene.

"Everyone all right?" Brad Tucker asked, as he strode up to us.

"We're fine," I said. "Well, except for the guy on the floor. But he deserves it." I turned to face Brad, Richard's arm still around my waist. "Meet your murderer."

"Well, well." Brad tipped back his hat as he surveyed the scene. "Oliver Lance. Makes sense. We've found out some things from his half brother that allows this to all click into place."

"Like what?" I asked, as paramedics lifted Oliver, protesting between moans, onto a stretcher.

Monica, leading Bucephalus back to his stall, paused and fixed Brad with a stare. "Yeah, like what?"

Brad jumped away from the dappled gray's pawing hooves. "First put that beast up, and then I'll explain."

"Hey now, Ceph is a hero, aren't you, boy?" Monica patted Bucephalus's sleek neck.

"Yes, he certainly is," Richard said fervently.

Monica led the horse into the stall, grabbing his water bucket before exiting and closing the door. "Horses can't have water when they're overheated," she told us, as Brad, Richard, and I stared at her quizzically. "It can make them ill."

"Well, we don't want that." I moved close enough to stroke Bucephalus's nose. He snuffled my hand, dripping a bit of mucus. "Gee thanks," I said without rancor. I wiped my hand on my already filthy pants and turned to Brad. "What did Nate tell you?"

"That he knew Meredith Fox had blackmailed Oliver in the past." Brad's gaze shifted to the ambulance roaring away, with Oliver safely stowed on board. "When we got your call, we rounded him up, along with Glenda Lance. They were having lunch together at the Taylorsford Inn, conveniently enough." Brad grinned. "Which made it my jurisdiction. So I asked him to accompany me out here, and grilled him along the way."

"And he decided to come clean with everything he knew?" Richard asked.

"After we told him that we'd gotten a 911 call from Blue Haven Farm, he did." Brad frowned as one of the deputies bagged the rifle. "Be careful—that's evidence," he called out before turning back to us. "Anyway, Broyhill was aware that his former wife had discovered some dirt on his half brother and used that information to squeeze some money out of him.

Apparently to support the dance company Broyhill and Ms. Fox had established."

"Ah, that fits one of my theories like a glove," I said.

"Nate didn't know the secret Meredith was holding over Oliver?" Monica asked.

"He says not, but of course he's lied to us before, so who knows?" Brad shrugged. "He also claims that it was a short-lived extortion, that Ms. Fox didn't continue to blackmail Oliver once her marriage ended."

"And the dance company failed," Richard said.

"Right. That's his story anyway." Brad looked us up and down. "We're going to need statements from all three of you, of course."

"Yes, but I still don't understand." I pulled free of Richard's arm and stepped forward to look up into Brad's somber face. "If the blackmail stopped a few years back, why would Oliver murder Meredith now?"

Brad offered me a wan smile. "Because, according to Broyhill, Ms. Fox recently had a change of heart. He wasn't sure why, but he claimed she came to him and said she wanted to expose Oliver Lance's fraudulent behavior. Something to do with collecting insurance on horses, I think."

Monica's lips thinned. "I can fill you in about that."

"Good," Brad said, casting her an appreciative look. "But whatever the reason, Ms. Fox was about to expose Mr. Lance. And unfortunately, she trusted her ex-husband a little too much."

"Nate told Oliver about Meredith's plan?" I asked. *Of course,* I thought. *That's why he was so determined to shut down your questions. He was protecting his half brother as well as himself.*

310

"He did. He said he thought it wouldn't be that big a deal and that he could handle it. That's why he was planning to have a talk with Ms. Fox at the theater the day she was killed."

"But Oliver got to her first," Richard said darkly.

I glanced over at him. Nate Broyhill had a good deal of culpability in this case, and I knew Richard would be more than happy to see him answer for it.

"Exactly. We don't have all the details on that yet, of course."

"Maybe once you question Oliver, you'll know more," I said, although I wasn't sure he'd be that forthcoming.

"Now—you three need to give us your statements, so you can be on your way." Brad looked Richard in the eye. "I think you have a performance to prepare for, if you're still up for it."

Richard squared his shoulders. "Of course. I'm not going to let anything derail that."

"Glad to hear it," Brad said with a smile. "Alison and I have tickets, and I know she's really been looking forward to the show. I'd hate for her to be disappointed. Pregnant ladies have to be pampered, you know."

"I haven't experienced that yet," Richard said, sliding his arm over my shoulders. "But I bet that's probably a good philosophy."

I leaned into him, burying my face against his chest to hide my smile.

Chapter
Twenty-Nine

By the time we got home, there were only a few hours left before Richard had to drive to the theater.

"I wish you had more time to rest," I said, examining his drawn face with concern.

"It's fine," he said. "I just need a shower and some time to stretch and warm up and I'll be good to go. And adrenaline will kick in tonight."

"Okay, but you're going to need something to eat too. What can I fix?"

"Nothing." Richard leaned in and kissed my cheek. "You head upstairs and get some rest. I'm going to grab some high-protein stuff we already have in the fridge. I don't need anything too heavy."

I wanted to argue with him, but my body told me I'd better take a nap, or I might not be alert enough to truly enjoy the premiere.

After sleeping for a few hours, I took my own shower and changed into the short-sleeved, full-skirted, burnt-orange dress I'd purchased for the premiere. It was a color that set off my dark brown hair and eyes, and the cut was particularly flattering, even if it did feel a bit tight in the waist.

But I wasn't concerned about that. "Good reason for it," I told my reflection in the mirror as I added a pair of amber earrings and a matching necklace.

"Beautiful," Richard said, stepping up behind me. He was already dressed in his dance rehearsal clothes, ready for a formal warm-up at the theater. He kissed the bare skin of my shoulder, above the scooped neck of the dress. "You look gorgeous, sweetheart."

"Thanks." I turned to give him a hug. "I know everything will go splendidly tonight, but break a leg anyway."

Embracing me tightly for a moment, Richard pressed another kiss against the top of my head. "Of course it will. Everyone involved has given their all to this project. Now what we have to do is trust our muscle memory and simply enjoy the performance, and bring all our hard work to life."

I gave him a final hug before stepping back. "You're heading out?"

"I'd better if I want to get there on time." Richard looked at his watch. "Like, right now." He flashed a smile before heading out the bedroom door. Loie and Fosse, intrigued by all this activity, leapt off the bed and followed him downstairs.

When I finished getting ready, I grabbed my clutch purse and a chocolate-brown wrap and slowly descended the steps, watching for the cats. After everything that had happened earlier, the last thing I needed was to trip and fall.

Weeks before, Aunt Lydia and Hugh had made reservations at an upscale restaurant in Smithsburg and had invited Sunny, Fred, and me to join them for a light supper and drinks before the show. As I climbed into the back seat of the car I shared with my aunt, I was prepared to face the onslaught of questions about the events from earlier in the day.

But Aunt Lydia surprised me by calling a moratorium on any mention of the Meredith Fox murder case or the arrest of Oliver Lance.

"We can talk about that tomorrow," she said, sharing a quick look with Hugh. "Tonight should be all about the show, don't you think?"

"I completely agree." Hugh, looking dapper in a tailored navy suit, white shirt, and striped silk tie, lifted one hand from the steering wheel to pat my aunt's knee.

Of course, Aunt Lydia had dressed up for the occasion as well. When we got out of the car at the restaurant, I expressed my admiration for her sky-blue shantung silk dress and pearls. "You two clean up quite nicely," I told them with a grin.

"You look very lovely yourself," Hugh said, bending forward in the smallest of bows. "And, of course, Miss Fields is the picture of sunshine," he added as Sunny and Fred joined us.

"Flattery will get you a kiss." Sunny followed through on that promise, much to Hugh's embarrassment and Aunt Lydia's amusement.

Sunny, wearing a pale gold silk dress with sapphire-blue jewelry, had swept up her hair in an elegant chignon, while Fred had donned beige slacks with an ivory linen jacket that was the perfect foil for his dark skin. "Glad to see you, Amy," he told me. "It's been a while."

"Too long," I said as we entered the restaurant. "It seems that you, like my husband, are always on the job."

"Sad but true," Fred said.

Sunny, linking her arm with his, made a face. "Too darned true."

When we were seated and the waitress came around for drink orders, Aunt Lydia and Sunny both cut their eyes at me when I claimed that all I wanted was water.

"I want to keep a clear head tonight," I said. "After everything that happened today, I'm afraid any alcohol will send me into dreamland."

"That makes sense," Sunny said, sharing a glance with my aunt. "And don't worry—Lydia has already informed us of the ground rules for tonight." She pointed her spoon at Fred. "No discussing art thefts or murders or anything like that."

"All right," he said, "although I did want to tell Amy something we discovered about the robbery at the Lance farm, if you'll allow it. An update on the people involved."

"I'll allow that," Sunny said airily. "But only that."

Fred grinned before launching into a short recitation of the latest facts on the case. "And along with identifying the professional ring of thieves who carried out the heist, we also found out that it was a former employee who disabled the security system at the farm. Someone who worked for Oliver Lance."

"Monica Payne mentioned something about a former assistant who left soon after the robbery. Was that who it was?" I asked.

"Yes, and we actually got that lead from Ms. Payne." Fred met my inquiring gaze with a smile. "Thanks for suggesting we talk to her, Amy."

After dinner, we headed to the theater. Hugh found a parking space next to Fred's car, which was a stroke of luck as the back lot was already full. "It's sold out tonight," I told the others as we circled around the building to reach the lobby.

"That's wonderful. More money for local dance programs, right?" Aunt Lydia asked.

"And to expand Karla's studio," I said.

As we entered the lobby, we were greeted by a free-standing signboard covered in photos of the various dancers, with a stunning portrait of Richard and Karla front and center. "They want to start a company eventually, with a training program. I think that's Richard's dream for when he retires."

"He'd stop dancing?" Fred asked, his tone tinged with surprise.

I smiled. "Oh no, he'll never do that. He'll keep dancing until he drops. It's just that he wants to stop performing professionally at some point. When he can no longer meet his own high standards, he always says." Examining the crowd, I noticed Janelle DeFranzo and Samantha and waved. "They have kids performing in the production," I told Hugh and Fred, who'd cast me questioning looks.

"And of course, Samantha is a library colleague," Sunny said.

The glittering chandelier overhead dimmed and brightened again, indicating it was time to take our seats. As we strolled down the auditorium aisle, I made a mental note of several friends and acquaintances who were in attendance. I wanted to try to catch some of them at intermission, to thank them for their support. Kurt, who was sitting between Richard and Karla's former dance teacher, Adele Tourneau, and his ninety-four-year-old friend, Mary Gardner, lifted one hand in a silent greeting as I walked past.

After we took our seats closer to the stage, Sunny leaned against my shoulder. "Your parents aren't here?" she asked as the small orchestra in the pit began tuning their instruments.

"Not tonight. They're coming to the matinee tomorrow. Along with Zelda and Walt, Emily Moore, and some other friends. The reception is tomorrow afternoon, so they wanted to wait for that."

"That makes sense." Sunny stared at her program. "And Richard's parents? Don't tell me they aren't going to see the show."

"Fiona has a ticket for tomorrow," I said with a quirk of my lips. "Jim's apparently too busy to bother."

"Why doesn't that surprise me?" Sunny said, then pressed a finger to her lips as the overhead lights dimmed.

Once the production got underway, I forgot all about the day's events, my thoughts subsumed in the beautiful sounds and scenes onstage. Backed by mountain folk music, orchestrated and conducted by local high school arts supervisor Martin Stover, the dance sequences told a series of stories based on the folklore of the Blue Ridge Mountains. Although not literal interpretations in every case, the scenes evoked an atmosphere that perfectly captured the homespun yet magical quality of their source material.

All of the children did well, especially in a piece that reminded me of *A Midsummer Night's Dream*, with fairy sprites flitting about a lush forest. There were a few missteps, but no one froze or ran off the stage, which, according to Karla's comments during a rehearsal I'd seen, was the main concern with younger dancers.

Of course, when Richard and Karla took the stage to perform the *Will o' the Wisp* variation, the entire audience grew hushed and remained that way until the piece ended. The fluidity of the dancers' movements, combined with their strength and precision, transported me beyond the confines of the theater. It was as if I were standing at the edge of a forest pond, watching the mist dance over the water while stars glittered above. When their pas de deux ended, a moment of silence stretched like a withheld breath before the entire audience broke into rhythmic clapping and cheers.

Tamara and Davonte were breathtaking as well, dancing to the famous folk song "Barbara Allen," as were the university dancers, whose scenes interpreted some of the popular "Jack Tales" from Appalachian culture. When the entire company performed the final piece—a pastiche of various folk tunes, including "Wayfaring Stranger," which had been the first song Richard and Karla had danced to after a separation of many years—the audience appeared transfixed. As soon as the last scene ended, everyone jumped to their feet, applauding wildly.

Thrilled that the production had gone so well, I yanked some tissues from my purse to wipe my tears while the performers took their bows. As Karla and Tamara stepped forward, several flower bouquets were tossed over the pit and onto the stage.

I clapped for what seemed like forever before slipping from my seat to head for the dressing rooms. Dodging a loudly chattering herd of sprites, who'd transformed back into excited children, and the exhausted but triumphant university dancers, I finally reached the solo dressing rooms. But before I could look for Richard, another dancer called out my name.

It was Tamara. "You were wonderful," I said, looking up into her heavily made-up face.

"Thanks." Tamara's dark eyes glistened with tears. "I just wanted to let you know . . ." She bit her lip before motioning toward one of the rehearsal rooms. "Can we duck in there? I'd like to talk to you alone for moment."

I nodded and followed her into the studio. "Is this about your connection to Nate Broyhill?"

"Yes, unfortunately. I owe you an apology. I wasn't exactly honest with you or the authorities," Tamara said, pulling a silk-leaf and acorn decorated tiara off her tightly braided hair.

I pressed my clutch purse against my heart. "You and Nate were protecting each other, I think."

"Not because we're romantically involved," Tamara said hastily. "I'm not foolish enough to jump into a relationship with a man like Nate. Not in that way, at any rate." She dangled the tiara from her fingers. "Nate was attempting to start another dance company, and he wanted me as one of the premier dancers. And yes, I knew all about the one that failed when he was married to Meredith, but he claimed that was mostly her fault."

"He would, wouldn't he?"

"Of course, but I was a little too dazzled by the thought of headlining a company to think straight at first," Tamara said with a rueful smile. "At any rate, the day Meredith was killed, I saw Nate in the parking lot, in his SUV."

I raised my eyebrows. "So you did hang around a little longer than Riley and Davonte."

"Which I admitted to, during my questioning. And the two guys left, just as I said, although I was distracted by seeing Nate and wasn't really paying attention to who left first or if they walked away together, or anything like that. That's why my story was a little off on that point." Tamara took a deep breath. "But I wasn't entirely forthcoming, as you know. I never admitted to seeing Nate or talking to him briefly in the parking lot before I headed up the street."

"Did you make plans to meet?" I asked, piecing this part of the puzzle together in my mind.

Tamara nodded. "Nate wanted to reassure me that he wasn't trying to convince Meredith to join the new company, which is what I suspected when I saw him in the parking lot."

"So he wasn't lying when he told me that you two met a few blocks away. And you did sit and talk in his SUV before the deputies found you?"

"That was the truth. Which I didn't admit at first, because"—Tamara's kohl-rimmed eyes narrowed—"I was afraid that Nate had killed her. So I didn't want to say I'd seen him loitering in the parking lot for quite a while, right around the time Meredith died. Not because I was in love with him or anything—just to keep my professional dreams moving forward."

"Meanwhile, he didn't want to lose his star dancer, which he was afraid would happen if you were labeled a prime suspect, so he wanted to clear your name." I bounced my purse against my thigh. "But he couldn't come right out and accuse the person he actually thought was the murderer, because it was his brother. So he made sure to mention seeing Conner and Janelle DeFranzo, who were innocent but happened to be in the area at the right—or maybe wrong—time, just to drive the investigation in another direction."

Tamara sighed. "I know the whole thing became a real tangle, and I'm sorry I contributed to that. I just wanted you to know the truth."

"Thanks. I appreciate that." I looked her over, noting the slump in her fine-boned shoulders. "Are you still hoping to work with Nate? Because he might have some legal issues to deal with first."

"No, that's all over, at least as far as I'm concerned. Besides"—Tamara's expression brightened—"Richard asked Davonte and me if we'd consider dancing the leads in *Return* for a traveling production of a couple of his choreographic works. He said he was too busy to dance the lead, and of course, with Meredith gone . . ."

"I'm sure you two would be wonderful in that," I said, feeling a sense of relief. A production crisscrossing the United States at this particular time was great, but only if Richard didn't have to travel the entire route. I was sure he'd agree when he heard our news, but it was nice that he'd already made that decision. "Well, I'm sure you want to change and get out of that makeup, and I want to find Richard, so I'll say goodbye. And thank you," I added with a warm smile. "It does help to have more of the pieces to the puzzle."

"No problem." Tamara wished me a good evening as we left the studio.

I finally found Richard's dressing room, but it was so packed with people that I simply waved at him over the shoulders of several of the university dancers and a few of the children and their parents. "Meet me in the lobby," he called out as Karla's hand landed on my upper arm.

She'd already changed out of her costume and removed all of her makeup. "Hey, would you give Rich a message for me?" she asked, motioning toward the people separating us from him. "I'm not going to fight this crowd."

"Sure. You were magnificent, by the way. Everyone thought so. And the choreography . . ." I pressed my fingers to my lips and pulled them away. "Chef's kiss."

A rosy glow flushed Karla's cheeks. "Thanks—I think it went well. It's quite a relief, honestly. Anyway, I just wanted to tell Rich that I'm going to head straight home. He invited me over to your house for champagne and all that, but I'm not up to it. And I honestly think he needs to just enjoy some peace and quiet too."

"We'll miss you, but I have to agree," I said. "After what he went through earlier today, I have a suspicion that he's going to collapse as soon as we get home."

"Exactly." Karla leaned in and gave me a peck on the cheek. "Take care of him like I know you always do."

"I will," I promised her.

I made my way to the lobby, where I told Aunt Lydia, Hugh, Sunny, and Fred goodbye, before chatting briefly with

Kurt, Adele, and Mary Gardner. By the time Richard appeared, everyone had left, which he didn't seem to mind. "I'll do more schmoozing at the reception tomorrow," he said as we headed for the car. "Tonight I want quiet and calm."

"Oh, I almost forgot—Karla said she was going straight home, so it's just going to be you and me. I hope that's okay."

"Perfect," Richard said with a broad, if tired, smile.

When we got home, he offered to give the cats their treats so I could run upstairs and change. "My dance togs are comfortable enough," he said, "but I have a feeling that your outfit, while lovely, is a little less so."

I heartily agreed and dashed up to our bedroom to change into a soft and roomy oversized T-shirt before heading back downstairs.

Richard, who was slumped on the sofa, had already placed two flutes of champagne on the coffee table. "I thought we'd better each just have one glass tonight. Any more than that and I might pass out."

"Actually, I don't think I'd better have even one," I said, sitting down next to him. "I hate to waste the champagne, but I do have a good reason to abstain."

Richard studied my face for a moment before sitting bolt upright. "And what might that be?"

"Something that will make you happy, I think," I said, reaching out and taking his hands in mine. "Richard Muir, you're going to be a dad."

His eyes went wide as his grip on my hands tightened. "Seriously?"

"I'm pretty sure," I said. "I mean, I suppose three pregnancy tests could be wrong, but—"

Richard cut me off, pulling me close and fervently kissing me. "This is the best news ever," he said when he finally sat back, still holding onto one of my hands. "Well, it ties with the time when you said you were willing to marry me, anyway."

"Come on, you know I was more than willing," I said, wrinkling my nose at him. "But this is going to change things, you know. More than that did. Probably more than we can even imagine."

"I've never been afraid of change. And I love new adventures," Richard said.

His face, while still bearing traces of the exhaustion I was sure he was feeling, was suffused with happiness. "Me too. As long as we go on them together."

"That's one thing I can always promise," Richard said before kissing me again.

Acknowledgments

M y sincere thanks to all the "usual suspects"—
My agent, Frances Black of Literary Counsel.

My editor at Crooked Lane Books, Faith Black Ross.

The Crooked Lane Books team, especially Madeline Rathle, Dulce Botello, and Rebecca Nelson.

Cover designers C. Griesbach and S. Martucci.

My friends and my family.

My fellow authors, many of whom have become dear friends.

Bookstores and libraries—who not only support my work, but also provide me with so many great books to read.

The bloggers, podcasters, Youtubers, and reviewers who have mentioned, reviewed, and promoted my books.

And, as always, my wonderful readers!